LOST WOMAN

To Cousin May & Leo:

Hope you enjoy your copy of "Lost Woman".

If you are interested, my other books can be ordered at Book stores or at Amazon.com.

Hope to meet with you in person sometime soon.

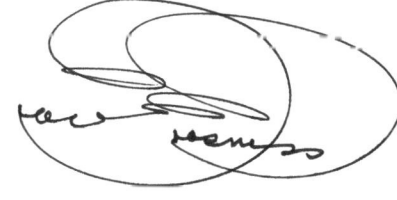

LOST WOMAN

Howard Losness

Authors Choice Press
San Jose New York Lincoln Shanghai

Lost Woman

All Rights Reserved © 2000 by Howard A Losness

No part of this book may be reproduced or transmitted in any form or by any means, graphic, electronic, or mechanical, including photocopying, recording, taping, or by any information storage or retrieval system, without the permission in writing from the publisher.

Authors Choice Press
an imprint of iUniverse.com, Inc.

For information address:
iUniverse.com, Inc.
620 North 48th Street, Suite 201
Lincoln, NE 68504-3467
www.iuniverse.com

ISBN: 0-595-13036-4

Printed in the United States of America

Chapter One

Janet Neilson walked out into the light mist that envelopes the city of Portland most days during the fall season. She started to put up her umbrella, hesitated, then closed it again. Shutting her eyes, she slowly tilted her head back, facing the sky, smiling as she let the soft mist touch her skin. After standing there for several moments enjoying the refreshing feeling of having her face washed with the Oregon mist, Janet clinched her right fist, and punched it into the air, accenting the movement with a loud, "yes!"

Smiling smugly to herself, she began a slow descent of the courthouse steps, towards the parking lot. With the smile still on her face, her now-wet hair hanging limp in tight strands framing her face, Janet pointed her black coded key towards her white BMW. A short, sharp, "beep", and the door latches snapped up. She slipped in, shaking the residual moisture from her hair, wiped her face with a white lace hankie, and slipped in a Barbara Streisand CD to her radio, cranking up the volume as she accompanied Barbara with "Second Hand Rose."

Janet had prepared for this court appearance for the better part of two months, investigating and researching the facts, allowing it to consume her every free moment. Winning the case was, in itself, secondary It was Howard Chase, the defendant's attorney that she was after. There was nothing in the world she wanted more than to beat Chase in court, in front of his peers.

Three years ago, when Janet first started practicing law, the firm of Moller, Christian, and Rice had hired her right out of University of Oregon Law School. At first, as a training-breaking-in period, she was assigned clients whose cases were so simple it was almost an insult for a seasoned attorney to waste his time on the matter, yet the client had to be represented. Then there were the cases where it was obvious that the client either didn't have the money to pay for an attorney or the matter was helplessly undefendable, in which case an attorney's chance of winning was negligible.

Fresh out of law school, her first case had been against Howard Chase. Being the new girl on the block, with an emphasis on girl, both in age and gender, Janet immediately felt intimidated by Howard Chase. In the court room, Chase pranced in front of the jury in his two-inch elevator shoes, reaching the full height of five foot three inches, including his meticulously combed bouffant hairstyle, acting like a bantam rooster patrolling the chicken yard keeping his hens in line. His cloths exuded success. He wore a deep grey silk tie with splashes of maroon hand painted on it. A two carat diamond stick pin had been placed four inches below the windsor knot. It sparkled as he walked back and forth in front of the courtroom. A matching pocket scarf was tucked in his breast pocket for added effect. The suit was a tailored made, Italian model, probably in the eighteen-hundred to two-thousand dollar range. The crease in his pants bore nary a wrinkle. One could see a refection from the windows from his spit-polished black shoes.

He had intimidated and embarrassed Janet with, "Your Honor, her questions are out of line," and, "I object your Honor, there is no relevance to her line of questioning," and, "your Honor, learned counsel has not established adequate groundwork to draw that conclusion," and, finally, "Your Honor, I move for a dismissal. The opposing counsel has not even established grounds to continue this case. This is a blatant waste of the courts time."

Janet had prepared for the case well in advance wanting to make a good impression, not only on the court, but her firm as well. She had studied case histories pertaining to her case, typed and retyped her briefs, trying the case in her mind so thoroughly that when the time came to go to court, she almost felt that she was over prepared.

She had purchased a dark blue, pin-stripped suit at Macy's for the occasion. When her case was announced by the court clerk, she was ready.

In court, she called upon every skill they had taught her in law school, frequently referring to her notes. She made every effort to defend her client and make a good showing of herself, but by the time Chase had finished brow beating and intimidating her, the only thing left resembling a human being was the mere image of a shaking leaf standing alone, there, before the judge, dying to get out of the courtroom, at any cost.

Janet was so deflated that day she didn't even return to the office. After such a humiliating defeat she spent the balance of the day walking Westmoorland Park, gazing blankly into the lake and watched old men lawn bowl, evaluating her future as an attorney. Her thoughts vacillated from feelings that she had definitely chosen the wrong occupation to rage coupled with the drive to retaliate toward Howard Chase. Before she calmed down, she thought of everything from keying his car to slashing his tires. Calm finally prevailed however, and in the final analysis, though obviously frustrated, she decided against flushing four years of college and three years of law school down the drain with such stupidity. She would regroup, compose herself, and go back to work as any mature person would. After all, for every case that goes to trial, someone has to win and someone has to lose. In this case, she concluded, she had simply lost.

But now her time had finally arrived. The gods had been watching over her, training her, preparing her for this moment. The eagle had landed, with both feet, right on the back of the bantam rooster, and justice was about to be served.

Through subtle slips of the lip, she allowed rumors to escape of her impending confrontation. The rumors reached Chase's ears, al planned, but he was so cocksure of an impending victory that he even invited his cronies to the courtroom to watch the slaughter. "Merely a repeat performance," he boasted, promising them drinks and burgers at the Circus Restaurant after the execution and extermination of the "broad from Moller, Christian, and Rice."

Initially the rape case had been referred to Janet's law firm by a friend who, knowing the reputation of the firm's attorneys and their standards, felt she would be given the best representation available. After the initial interview, given the nature of the case, the firm felt the client would be best served if a female attorney tried the case.

After a closed board meeting, it was decided that Janet was the only woman in the firm whose calendar could accommodate the client. The powers-that-be felt it was time to elevate her case load and moved up in the firm. The greatest chip on the scale, however, was that they all knew Janet deserved another crack at Chase. Everyone hated the arrogant little bastard, anyway, and nothing would humiliate him more than to be beaten in court by a woman.

At first, she hadn't been keen on taking on a controversial rape case, but when she heard that the defendant had hired Howard Chase to represent him, the hairs on the nape of her neck bristled and she jumped at the chance to settle an old score.

Janet's client was twenty-two year old Tammy Wilson, a white, middle class woman, married four years. It had all started when Tammy had apparently gone out for an evening on the town after having a fight with her husband, Jerry.

The argument started over the most trivial of matters. Jerry arrived home from work around six thirty, his usual time. Ordinarily, Tammy, dutiful wife that she was, would have had the table tastefully set and dinner waiting, so all Jerry had to do was wash up and sit down to a hot meal that had prepared for him.

On this particular day, however, Tammy had received a call from an old schoolmate who was home from college on winter break. They had gone out for lunch at the Red Lyon Hotel. Lunch eventually led to cocktails in the lounge, where they continued their conversation, talking about school, married life, success, and dreams of days gone by. Before Tammy knew it, time had slipped by, and it was almost six o'clock. Panicked and a little tipsy, she bade her friend good-bye and headed for home, fighting the evening traffic.

By the time Tammy rolled into the driveway of their little two-bedroom West Lynn cottage, it was already a quarter to seven. Jerry's truck was parked in the driveway and Jerry was wearing a rut in the carpet pacing from living room to bedroom to kitchen, talking to himself, working himself into a frenzy. He was home and there was no wife and no dinner! Where the hell was she?

Tammy walked into the house, grinning sheepishly, displaying a happy glow. No sooner had she gleefully begun to tell Jerry about her day, slurring a few words in the process, when he met her nose to nose with a barrage of verbal assaults, most of which went in one ear and out the other with no station identification. Tammy was too drunk to pay attention, but stood her ground, nonetheless, holding onto the cooking island for support. To add insult to injury, she smiled and rolled her eyes throughout the whole lecture.

Frustrated and angry, Jerry issued one last verbal assault before exiting and slamming the door. His parting words were: "Don't wait up for me! I don't known when I'll be home! I may just decide to stay out all night, bitch!"

Admittedly, she had been negligent and was a little tipsy, but she didn't feel she should have deserved such brash treatment from an unsympathetic husband. Still tipsy, giggling and lacking what one might call better judgement, she came to the conclusion that if this was how he was going to act, she'd to do a little steppin' on her own.

She showered, combed her long, jet-black hair into a bun, stacking it on top of her head, accenting her long, Grecian-like neck. She put on her nice, flaming red, low cut blouse, black slacks, a pair of matching black high heel shoes, and that smashing ceramic beaded necklace she had purchased at the local artisans market last summer, topping it off with Sung perfume. Looking at herself in the mirror, she was impressed with how great she looked. "Pretty foxy, even if I do say so myself."

She slipped a pretty fluffy black sweater over her shoulders and drove downtown to the Twenty-One Club. By the time she arrived, the place was jumping with loud rock music and people jammed wall to wall ranging from twenty-one years of age to forty.

There was an empty table near the stage. She sat down and ordered a rum cocktail, then turned her attention to the music and the people. It was unreal, the different types of dress that could be found in one place, she thought. The women's attire ranged from blue jeans with cowboy boots to low cut evening wear with no bra. They danced with wild abandon. The men's dress similarly ranged from blue jeans and opened unbuttoned designer shirts to older men wearing suits and ties.

No sooner had Tammy started sipping her drink when the waitress brought another cocktail. "From the gentleman at the bar," she said, nodding towards a good looking, tall man in a cowboy suit, sitting alone at the bar. He raised his glass with a smile. The man appeared to be in his late twenties, maybe even early thirties, Tammy thought.

The pleasant look on his face coupled with an apparent gentlemanly demeanor disarmed any immediate negativism she may have felt.

Tammy hesitated for a moment, then, smiling, took the drink from the tray, raising it towards the man in like gesture, thanking him. Before she had taken a swallow, he was seated at her table with a cheshire grin on his face. At first Tammy was reluctant to allow him to his sit down, but his charm soon overcame her resistance and, before the first song was finished they were passing time with idle chit-chat.

The band played a slow cowboy tune and he asked her to dance. With her head on his shoulder, she fantasized dancing with her husband, Jerry. The cowboy, picking up her vibrations, thinking she was warming up to him, danced closer. He dance with his leg between hers, pulling her close to him so their bodies seemed to melt into one. Within a few moments, however, Tammy snapped out of her dream-like trance she was in and, in a polite way, asked to sit this one out.

Back at their table, the cowboy ordered another round of drinks. Soon, Tammy was feeling no pain. Nervous and unsteady, she stood up to excuse herself, saying that she had to get home, but found that her legs uncooperative. The cowboy quickly stood up, catching her as she wobbled unbalanced, offering to walk her to the car. "Thanks, but no thanks," she replied, holding up a hand and made her way through the crowd. The cowboy followed her outside.

She dropped her keys trying to open the door and, when she bent down to pick them up, lost her balance again. It was clear she was more than a little inebriated. The cowboy gently put his arm around her waist, and knelt down to retrieve the keys.

"Dropped something," he said with a grin. "I think maybe you need some help, little lady. I'd never forgive myself if I let you drive home in this condition, then read in the newspaper that you ran off the road and hurt yourself or somethin'. Better let me drive you," he said, bending down to look into her eyes.

Against her better judgement, Tammy consented to allow him to drive her "straight home". She would have her friend, June, drive her back to get her car in the morning, before Jerry woke up, if in fact he was even home.

The cowboy turned on some mellow music on the radio, and talked softly to her. After a few moment, Tammy realized the direction he was taking was not the way to her house. She protested, but he said he was taking a different route for a reason that would soon become clear and asked for her to be patient.

The moment of truth arrived when he pulled into the vacant parking lot of the dog race track and turned out his lights.

"What the hell do you think you're doing?'" she protested, as he put his arms around her.

"Just a little affection to top off the evening, darlin'," he said, kissing her and fondling her breasts at the same time.

"Top this off," Tammy said, taking a swipe at his face with an open hand, relieving him of a piece of skin in the process.

"Why, you little bitch," he said, wiping his face, which had started to drip with blood. "I'll teach you some good old southern manners," he said, blocking her arm, which was in the process of striking him again.

Pushing her down and pinning her to the seat of his truck, he held her two hands with his right hand, ripping off the front of her blouse with his free hand, baring her breasts. Tammy kneed him in the groin and hit him in the face with her head while struggling to release her hands.

Aware that he had a tiger by the tail, he hit her hard across the face with his free fist, then back again on the other side with a backhanded motion. Knocked partially unconscious by the blows, Tammy was conscious enough to know that she was being violated, but was too weak to resist.

When the ordeal was over, the cowboy got out of his side of the truck and walked around to Tammy's door where his intent was to pull her out and leave her there in the parking lot. Tammy, however, was alert enough raise her hand and lock the door before he could open it. Swearing, he ran around to the driver's side, but again, Tammy was too quick for him. Unable to move her battered body around quickly, she slammed the door latch down with her right foot. Now the cowboy was locked outside and Tammy was inside.

Looking at the ignition, she spotted the keys still in place. Meantime, the cowboy was bashing his fists on the door window, cursing threats at her, promising bodily harm if she didn't open the door this instant. He had just taken off his boot and was about to bash the heel against the passenger door window when Tammy started the truck and tore out of the parking lot.

Moments later, Tammy squealed into the parking lot of Zim's twenty-four hour market. The truck no sooner came to a stop at the front door, than Tammy scampered out, running into the nearly-vacant store. She had taken no time to assess her physical appearance. The night clerk stared in awe as she ran up to his cash register, shoeless, her torn blouse baring her breasts, which swung from side to side and her jet black hair hanging down looking like a drowned cat.

Tammy quickly relayed her ordeal to the wide-eyed young clerk who, obviously fascinated by the sight before him, had trouble concentrating on her story. When she finished, he pulled his wits together enough to call the police, who arrived within moments.

Chapter Two

☙

Leaning on the jury bar with his left hand, sticking his right thumb in the watch pocket of his vest, Howard Chase studied the front row jurors before he began. "Your Honor, ladies and gentlemen of the jury. It's obvious that, on the night in question, this distraught, unhappy little housewife," he said, raising his outstretched palm toward Tammy with an impish grin on his face, "was out looking for a little excitement. She found it in the form of my client," he said, changing the direction of his palm, now looking at the jury with a deadly serious look, "whom she met at a bar. She accepted drinks from my client, danced with him and after a lovely evening. willingly left with him in his truck! She is obviously of consenting age…twenty-two years old, I believe." He nodded towards Tammy as if expecting an affirmation.

Facing the jury with both hands in the air, he continued. "Now, I don't want to get too graphic here, but it's clear that she wanted my client. He's a good looking dude, you'll all have to admit."

He waited for a moment while the jurors all looked at the cowboy. He continued in a low voice, as if what he was about to say was secretive. "She willingly and knowingly consented to have sexual relations with my client, full well knowing it was a one time deal and her husband would never find out." He bowed towards Tammy Fay with a smile, then, facing the jury, continued. "Unfortunately, after consenting to have sex with my client, she began having pangs of remorse, which I'm sure we can all understand." He made a face that made some of the men smile, knowingly.

He paused for a moment, then looked at Tammy before continuing. "Aware that she might have made a error in judgement, she then attacked him out of self-anger and frustration. Knowing these facts, ladies and gentlemen of the jury, You certainly can't hold my client responsible for this young woman's guilt feelings."

He walked back to his table and before sitting down, said, "You will have no alternative, but to acquit my client of the rape charge with which the plaintiff has leveled against him."

Howard Chase's style hadn't changed one bit since Janet had her unfortunate run in with him several years ago. But this time it was different. This time Janet was not only prepared but was competent. She had been lacking both in her first encounter with Howard Chase, years ago.

"Your Honor, ladies and gentlemen of the jury," Janet started, both hands on the jury rail. She looked each member of the jury in the eye as she spoke. "Not only will we prove that Tammy Wilson was a victim of a premeditated, ugly rape by the defendant, but we will prove that she was kidnapped against her will and driven to a vacant parking lot where she was held captive and brutally beaten. As luck would have it, the defendant made a critical error in thinking that my client, little Tammy Wilson, laying beaten and raped on his truck seat," she said, pointing to Tammy sitting at the plaintiff's table with her head bowed, wiping tears from her eyes with a white handkerchief, "was unconscious when he got out of his side of the truck to go around to Tammy Wilson's side, where we believe, if she hadn't mustered up the strength to lock the doors, she would have been dragged from the vehicle and either left on the parking lot—beaten, raped, semi-nude, and unconscious—or maybe even killed!" She hesitated, looking first at the cowboy, then back to the jury.

Continuing, she said, "This act was accented by the defendant's further attempt to smash the window of his own truck in an effort to get at the now-beaten and half conscious woman."

Hesitating, she looked at the defendant, then back at the jury before continuing, "We will ask you, the jury, to find the defendant, guilty of kidnapping, rape, and assault on Tammy Wilson. When you find him guilty, we intend to ask the court to punish the defendant to the fullest extent of the law."

Finishing her summation, Janet returned to the Plaintiff's table, pausing in front of Chase for a moment to smile before taking her seat.

Suddenly, Howard Chase seemed anything but brimming with confidence. The cowboy's face, now healed from the raking Tammy Wilson had given him with her fingernails on the night in question, was ashen white, glistening from perspiration. And the trial had just begun.

As the trial wore on, Howard Chase continued waging his battle of one-upmanship. Even though he knew the evidence was heavily weighted against his client, he continued projecting the confidence that he had Janet Neilson "by the short and curlies" and was going to teach her a lesson she would never forget. He had said, "When I get through with her, she'll be so humiliated she won't dare show her face in a courtroom again. She'll be reduced to unlawful detainers or forced to hang up her license all together and take up a new occupation, like selling flowers or hot dogs on the street corner," he had laughed.

He tried his usual lines: "Your Honor, learned counsel's questions are out of line," and, "I object, your Honor, there is no relevance to this line of questioning," and, "Your Honor, counsel has not established adequate grounds to continue this trial, I request a dismissal."

Janet was all too familiar with the Rooster's tactics and was not to be deprived of a victory today! That was then and this was now.

When it was her turn to have the defendant on the stand, she found him to have the same arrogance and disdain that his attorney had. "Would you like me to repeat the question, Mr. Mitchell?" she asked the cowboy when he didn't answer an obviously sensitive question.

"No, no, I got it the first time. Dumb broad," he muttered only loud enough for Janet to hear as he glared at her.

As Janet finished summarizing the events leading up to Tammy's rape for the jury, it became quite clear that Janet was quickly closing the door on the cowboy's freedom. Rooster tried one last stab an unnerving his opposing counsel. "Your Honor, this little session in historical ground laying is all very interesting, but not very entertaining. I hardly see the relevance of the matter. My client...."

"Please allow Miss Neilson to continue, Mr. Chase. With your continual interruptions, she hasn't had the opportunity to develop her point," the judge said in a quiet voice. "You've had your turn, now let counsel have hers."

"Yes, your Honor," he said, flipping his pencil in the air, letting it land with a thud on his papers ten feet away.

In the end, the jury found cowboy Mitchell innocent of kidnapping and holding Tammy Wilson against her will, but found him guilty of rape. The courtroom erupted into applause as the verdict was read by the foreman.

Tammy Wilson stood and hugged Janet, tears flowing down her cheeks. The cowboy was led away in handcuffs to be sentenced at a later date. Howard Chase exited the courtroom almost before his briefcase was closed, leaving his cheering section with a smirk on their faces. They didn't care for Chase that much, either, and, quite frankly, even though Chase was a member of their firm, If the truth were known, they were silently rooting for Janet.

Tammy Wilson hugged her attorney one last time as she asked Janet's advice on obtaining a divorce from her husband, who, she says, had disowned her from the day of the rape.

Chapter Three

☙

As Janet approached the freeway on-ramp she turned down the volume as "Second Hand Rose" ended, dialing her office on her car phone.

"Moller, Christian, and Rice," the voice on the other end of the car phone answered."

"Molly, this is Janet Neilson. Put me through to Dave Moore, please."

"David Moore."

"David. Janet here. I just finished...I wiped the floor with the little jerk." She paused, then whispered seductively, "I'm so excited I've got wet pants. I'm not going back to the office. I'm floating on a natural high and hot to trot. What do you say? Feeling frisky?"

"Well! You *must* be feeling good."

"I've never been so high. What do you say, meet me?"

"I don't know, I have this unlawful detainer," he teased.

"Dave!"

"Just kidding. Be there in thirty," Dave said without hesitation. "Usual place?"

"Hilltop." Janet said. "My treat!"

"Well! You *are* in rare form. Can't wait to hear the whole story. I'll bring the champagne."

Janet drove onto the Morrison Bridge, crossed the Willamette River, and headed towards Washington. She and Dave had accidentally discovered this quaint little motel on the outskirts of Vancouver when they had began their tete-a-tete over a year ago. I-5 had since bypassed the Vancouver business district and, unless one had specific business on

Old Highway 101, there was no reason to even be on that road. It was the perfectly safe place to spend an uninterrupted, quiet afternoon.

The relationship with Dave was perfect. There were no emotional ties, no commitments, just hot, passionate sex. It seemed to suit both of their needs.

It was difficult to point to the time or reason in her marriage to Brad had first hit the skids. It started out, like all marriages, full of harmony, blissful love, and happiness but somehow, strange as it may seem, the root of the problem seemed to stem from their difference in occupations.

Brad was a building contractor who was constantly kept busy. Once he located a site to build a house, he spent evenings with the planning commission. His days were filled obtaining building permits, designing and approving plans, finding money to fund the project, then negotiating with subcontractors to do the building, all of which seemed to consume his every waking hour. When he did finally arrive home, it was usually late in the evening. He was always bone tired, too tired to do anything but flop on the couch and catch his breath.

In addition to not spending much time with Janet, a feeling of inferiority began to creep into his consciousness. When he came home she always seemed to be on the telephone with other attorneys discussing important cases, plotting strategies to overcome this obstacle or figuring how to suppress that issue or introduce some point into a case. When she wasn't on the phone she was studying law books, taking notes, or working at her computer late into the night. Her ambition had clearly driven a spike between their relationship and Brad could feel it.

He couldn't remember the last time they had spent a whole day together enjoying each other's company, let alone a day without some degree of animosity arising between them.

It wasn't that there was a feeling of outright war, it was more like two roommates going in different directions, each preoccupied with their own circle of interests with very little interest in the other and very little if any overlapping. There would be the usual grunts of acknowledgement when they shared the bathroom on those rare occasions when they were there at the same time. Brad was usually in bed fast asleep by nine o'clock whereas Janet wouldn't think of going to bed until at least midnight. In short, their sex life was non-existent. Oh, once in a while Brad would want a quickie before going to work. He would nuzzle up to Janet, who was still in dreamland. Usually the whole thing was over before she knew what hit her. Needless to say, the experience was less than satisfying for either one.

Dave Moore had joined the law firm two years ago. From the outset of his employment he seemed to deplore confrontations, which, for an attorney, was highly unusual. As a result, he limited his practice to unlawful detainers, evictions, and the like, the very thing that most attorneys detest but have to do just to get started in the business. Thus, Dave was known as the "Unlawful Detainer King" around the legal circles in Portland. If you had a tenant problem and wanted it handled quickly, with expertise, Dave was your man.

He had graduated from the University of Oregon, middle of his class. He'd joined the Delta Fraternity, otherwise known as the "animal house" as soon as he had been eligible. His big thing was having fun, drinking beer, and chasing skirts. He never seemed to date the same girl twice. The word commitment just wasn't in his vocabulary. He was, in what is known in college vernacular, "a party boy". Have a good time and do only what's necessary to get by.

He was a tall, good looking, well built guy with an easy manner. He could talk to anyone about anything and never leave them feeling that he was anything but a good listener and a "great guy". No one had a bad thing to say about gregarious Dave.

Eventually, he married his college sweetheart, a girl he had met during his senior year while working as a counselor at Sheldon Hall, a freshman dormitory at the University of Oregon. She was the senior counselor at

Stewart Hall. It was a great way to get free room and board and have a little spending money to boot. Now, happily married with kids, Dave still longed for an occasional wild, safe fling in the sack with someone besides his wife, with no strings or attachments, free from the fear of "catching" something.

The periodic passion pit at the Hilltop Motel with Janet was just that—a safe, satisfying, noncommittal relationship for both of them.

* * * * * *

Janet pulled into the parking lot of the Hilltop Motel, parked the BMW in front of unit twelve, and walked to the manager's office. "Hi, Mrs. Alexander," the desk clerk said. "Number twelve for the afternoon?"

"Yes. Thank you, Frank." She paid in cash, took the key, and left. The owner had been used to seeing Mr. and Mrs. Alexander for the past year. They always reserved the same unit. "A chance to get away from the kids and spend some quiet quality time with the hubby," she had told the understanding clerk.

Once inside, she turned the radio to a soft FM station, took off her clothes and hung them in the closet. She walked to the bathroom, and turned on the shower. The water felt good, just standing under there, letting it tingle her skin. She stood there with the hot water beating down on her for a long time, enjoying the solitude.

Finally, she stepped from the shower, drying herself with the large, white terry cloth towel. Standing in front of the mirror, Janet dropped the towel to the floor, studying herself in the mirror.

"You're a lucky man, David Moore," she said, evaluating her body. The mere thought of meeting Dave was already getting her excited. Her nipples were beginning to stand up. She liked her body. No fat. A flat tummy. Firm breasts with nipples that had a pronounced, puffy roundness to them. She drove Dave crazy when she came to the office, braless, wearing a sheer blouse that could just barely be seen through.

She had been lying on the bed only a short while with just a sheet over her when she heard Dave's Jag pull up. In a moment, he was in the room. Without a word, he quickly undressed, went to the foot of the bed, and slowly pulled the sheet from her body, smiling admiringly.

"See anything you like?" Janet asked, lifting her head with a smile.

She slowly surveyed Dave's tanned, muscular body. Her eyes paused midway, admiring that portion of his anatomy that seemed to be expanding before her very eyes.

Without a word, Dave smiled, turning Janet over on her stomach. He began by massaging her feet, first the bottoms, then the toes. Slowly, he worked himself up the calves of her legs, then her thighs. She sighed as his fingers gently dug deep into her flesh.

He paused to kiss each cheek of her posterior as he continued working his way up the small of her back to her shoulders. When he finished massaging her neck, shoulders, and back, he turned her over. He smiled as he noticed the obvious wet spot where she lay. The anticipation was almost unbearable.

Dave began slowly massaging her upper shoulders, then cupping his hands around her breasts, kneading them gently as his fingers, went around, working upward toward the nipples, which by now were straining in anticipation.

He put his lips first on one, then another, cupping each breast in his hand. At first his kisses were soft and teasing, turning into hungry, lustful mouthfuls as Janet's body began to respond. She was quivering in anticipation as she put her hands around his head, pulling his lips down harder on her breasts.

Dave smiled to himself. She was ready. He continued kissing, teasing, as he moved down to her firm stomach, then her inner thighs.

Janet was beside herself. Firmly grabbing a handful of Dave's hair with each hand, she pulled him up to her.

Finally, they made love. It was a lovemaking session like they had never had before. When they were both finally spent, they fell asleep in each other's arms to the sound of the haunting call of a mourning dove outside their window.

Chapter Four

The news of Janet's victory over Howard Chase had spread throughout the firm by the time Janet checked in for work the following day.

"Congratulations," one would say. "Great job," another piped in. Jeff Bridges, one of the attorneys who had joined the firm about the same time Janet did, smiled and said, "Hey, Janet!" giving her a thumbs-up sign.

It wasn't that the case itself had been so all-important or that the victory had been a coup for the firm. Everyone had heard the story of how Howard Chase had decimated Janet on her first court assignment. They felt bad about that one. On top of that, there wasn't a person in the firm that liked Chase. For that matter, there weren't many attorney's or judges that cared much either. Everyone saw him for what he was, an arrogant, pugnacious little fart who had a Napoleonic personality, who would destroy anyone who got in the way.

Standing back and objectively looking at the man, it was painfully obvious that he was over-compensating for his height, or lack of it. The only way he knew how to be superior to his larger counterpart was to beat them intellectually by making himself look superior in the courtroom. Those who had opposing cases with him simply disliked the man. Having a conversation with Chase was tantamount to trying to take a rag away from a pit bull. He constantly brow beat his secretary, younger attorneys on staff or anyone in the firm who opposed him.

Word got out on the street that his associates barely tolerated him. Some even feared him because they knew how ruthless he was. He was striving for a full partnership in his firm and would do anything to achieve the notoriety he felt he desired. He had secretly confided to one of his associates that his ultimate goal was to be the District Attorney for the city of Portland. Everyone would know him then and he would command the respect he deserved.

"Mrs. Neilson, Mr. Christian would like to see you in his office when you have a moment," Molly said with a smile as Janet turned to go into her office.

Robert Christian had been the senior partner of the firm for the past four years. Donald Moller's name appeared at the top of the firm's letterhead however, not just because was he the senior partner, but he had been the founder who had established the firm. Since his death four years ago last Christmas, his name had remained on the firm letterhead by agreement of the remaining partners out of respect for the man and his accomplishments.

"You wanted to see me, Bob", Janet said as she poked her head into Christian's office.

"Yes, come in, Janet, and close the door after you." Motioning to her with his hand, he said, "Have a seat."

Christian's office was appointed with deep, rich cherrywood furnishings with high-back, button-tufted leather chairs and a couch to match. The walls were covered with grass cloth and appointed with early-19th-century oil paintings. There was a bookcase on the wall adjacent to Christian's desk with collector quality leather bound legal books. The floor was built of dark oak planks accented with oriental rugs. The ten-foot sculptured wood ceiling was accented with lighting to pick up the oil paintings, adding to the ambiance of the executive office. The totality of his office lent itself to wealth and power.

"Congratulations on your victory yesterday, Janet," Christian said. "I know you wanted that one bad. You worked hard, did your homework, and it paid off." Pausing for a moment to look at her, letting his words sink in, he continued, "You've come a long way since joining our firm. You've showed maturity in your work and, as a result, you're becoming successful. Like most rookies, when you first joined us, you were impatient, didn't take the necessary time to research a case or think it through thoroughly. Now you take your time, evaluate both sides of the issue, putting yourself in your opponent's chair, trying the case from his point of view as if you were he. By studying and analyzing his strong points as well as the weak points, you've learned to successfully attack opposing issues. It's like a chess game. In order to beat your opponent, you have to put yourself in their shoes, think like they do, and then act accordingly, like solving a mystery after seeing the play…when you have all the pieces."

Janet had never thought about it in those terms, but when you break it down, if you're going to be a successful attorney, that's exactly the path that must be taken. Always give your best, no matter what the sacrifice.

"I've got a new assignment for you, Janet. I think you've proven that you're ready to rise to the next plateau in your career. I want you to join Steve Daniels on the Paragon merger." The Paragon merger dealt primarily with large commercial real estate holdings and was the most prestigious and important case the firm was working on. To work with Steve Daniels was an honor. When it came to major real estate acquisitions, Daniels was considered the elite in the industry. His mind was so sharp, he could anticipate your every move before you thought of having a move, let alone making it. To be on the other side of the table against Daniels was like an amateur playing chess with the Russian chess expert Spasky.

Christian gave Janet a file, already detailed with a summary of the case, a schematic layout of the players, along with what appeared to be a profile of each person to be contacted, along with photos and a financial breakdown of each property and potential disposition of each parcel.

"I want you to assign your current cases to other members of the staff and concentrate all your efforts on this matter. It will mean working late hours and, of course, making personal sacrifices. Do you think that you can handle that?"

That was like asking a sixteen year old if he could handle getting a Corvette for his birthday.

"Yes, sir. You can count on me. I'll do whatever it takes." Janet was so excited, she could barely contain the enthusiasm she felt as she walked back to her office.

Since she had devoted the bulk of her time to working on the Tammy Wilson case against Howard Chase she hadn't taken on any new clients, subsequently, there wasn't much left on her desk that needed disposing of. There was the purchase contract wherein a client wanted to make an offer on a shopping center, and she was to draw up the purchase contract. A new client had been assigned to her to sue the school district because one of the client's children, an arrogant-mouthy, little boy had been slapped by one of the teachers when he kicked her in the leg, refusing to give up a pocket knife he had been flashing around school. Finally, there were a couple of minor matters that could be cleaned up with written documentation to the court, and an appeal needed to be filed for a client who had lost his case in the lower courts.

Janet had begun dictating instructions to her secretary when Dave Moore walked in. He looked behind himself as if he expected to be followed, closed the door, then sat down in the client's chair opposite Janet's desk. "Well, I guess congratulations, congratulations and congratulations are in order," he said curtly, not smiling.

"Have you taken up stuttering? What's with the 'congratulations, congratulations, congratulations' bit?"

"Well, congratulations on your victory over Howard Chase. Congratulations on your excellent choice of a sex partner," he said, cracking a smile, "and congratulations on your new promotion."

"I didn't get a promotion. I'm just been assigned a new case. Done with one, on to another," she said, trying to mask the enthusiasm she obviously felt being assigned to the Paragon case.

"Not when you're assigned to work with Daniels," Dave said. "That's no ordinary case assignment. Most of the guys here would kill to get to work with him. That's the next step to being invited to be a junior partner. From there, you write your own ticket. You're on your way, girl. Pretty soon, you'll be too stuck up for a rendezvous at the Hilltop." He looked a little dismayed.

"Dave, I'll always have time for you, providing I'm not working with Steve, of course," she said, smiling with a wink.

"Maybe Steve will invite you to the Red Lyon," he taunted. "No shabby off the road Hilltop for him."

"I don't think so, Dave. Not my style. Playing hide the weeny with you is one thing. Fooling around with Daniels? No way! I want to go somewhere in this world, not be a plaything for the big boys." She gave Dave's ear a tug as she passed by, her arm full of files.

* * * * * *

"Good Morning, Steve," Janet said as she poked her head into his office.

"Oh, Janet. Good of you to drop in. Have a seat. Give me just a moment while I finish this call and I'll be right with you."

Steve's calendar was always full. He was considered the last word when it came to real estate acquisitions and mergers. He did a limited amount of personal work with special clients, spent a fair amount of time in court, and did some consulting with the staff of the Mariott Hotels, one of the largest hotel chains in the world. He was in his mid-forties, a tall, slender, good-looking man with grey hair beginning to grow around his temples. Janet admired him, not only for his keen mind and sense of fair play, but because he always found time to take care of himself physically. It was amazing, no matter how much time his practice demanded, he always gave exercise a priority. He went to the athletic club at least three times a week to play racquetball or work out in the weight room.

"Well! I understand you'll be joining me on the Paragon Merger. That's great. I don't know, Janet, it seems the more time that goes by, the busier I get. I relish the earlier days when my only concern was whether I was going to have enough clients to get me through the day. Now I'm so busy I seem to be meeting myself coming around the corner. I can sure use your help on this one."

"Mr. Daniels. Your ten o'clock is here," the voice over the intercom said.

"Be with him in a moment," Steve replied. "Tell you what Janet, how about meeting me at the club at one o'clock for a game of racquetball? I have court five reserved and my regular partner can't make it. We can get in a game, then go upstairs for a glass of orange juice and some veggies and I'll fill you in on the deal."

Well! Racquetball with Steve Daniels. The thought of racing around the court banging the ball, working up a sweat, leaving her femininity in the locker room, gave her a rush. Just like one of the guys. "I'll be there," she said, trying to control her enthusiasm. She could certainly hold her own on the field of most sports. Both racquetball and tennis were her favorites. She had been on the girl's varsity racquetball team at Lewis and Clark College her junior and senior year. The demanding schedule she now kept took the bulk of her free time, however, and she hadn't played for a couple years. The change of pace would certainly be welcomed. Working with Daniels was going to be a golden opportunity, she thought. In addition to the fact that there was a lot to be learned by an association with him, it could be an opportunity to get her foot in the door for a promotion. "Sometimes it's not what you know," it's who you know, she thought to herself.

*   *   *   *   *   *

Janet dressed in her dark maroon tights with grey over-clothing and was on the racquetball court by 12:45. She tied her long auburn hair in a pony tail so it swung from side to side as she walked. Being early would give her a chance to loosen up, do some stretching exercises, and hit the ball for a few minutes, she thought. I just need to get back into the feel of the game. It's like riding a bicycle. Once you know how to do it, the skill never leaves you.

Steve was right on time. He wore a Boston Celtics T-shirt and green shorts. As Janet looked at him as he entered the little door to the court, she hadn't realized his upper body was as well developed as it was. She had only seen him dressed in a tailored suit. He looked strong and fit. His legs were solid muscle, rippling as he walked into the court. No one would have guessed he was a razor-sharp lawyer, watching how agilely he moved around the court as they warmed up.

"Ready?" he asked Janet after a few minutes.

"Ready."

"Let's lag to the back wall. The closest one to the wall without hitting it will start serving."

Steve stood an arm-and-racquet's length from the back wall hitting the ball on the front wall. The ball hit six inches from the back wall. Without comment, he bounced the ball to Janet. Janet's ball fell three feet short of his lag. Walking up to the service box in the middle of the court, Steve looked back at Janet. "Ready?"

"We'll soon find out," Janet uttered to herself, but said aloud, "Go for it."

Steve's first serve came hard into Janet's backhand corner for an ace. The next serve was a high lob, again to the backhand court. This time the ball hugged the wall and barely bouncing as it hit the floor. Janet swung at it, but her racquet scrapped the wall as the ball bounced harmlessly back to Steve. The next serve was to Janet's forehand, which she hit back high on the front wall. Steve let it go past him and caught it coming off the back wall, hitting it low and hard. The ball hit the front wall two inches off the floor, bouncing twice before Janet could get a racquet on it. Janet could tell she was in for a long hour.

Steve gave her no mercy. The balls came hard and low. They came high and hugging the walls. Periodically, he would try to hit the ball too low and would hit the floor first, giving Janet a chance to serve. The first game ended with a score of fifteen to two. The second and third games were equally brutal. During the entire time they played, the only conversation either of them had was relative to the game at hand.

When they were finished, Steve took off his racquetball glove, offering his hand to Janet. "Nice game! I'll meet you in the upstairs lounge in twenty minutes," Steve said, hardly sweating at all.

"Right, in twenty minutes," Janet said, wiping the perspiration from her brow.

"That'll give you time to take a quick steamer, shower, and cool off." Steve winked and headed for the men's side of the club, leaving Janet feeling like a million dollar bill—all crumpled up and green.

This had certainly been a gross disappointment for her. She had envisioned herself flying around the room, making great put-away shots, getting praise from Steve and maybe even beating him a game.

"Beating him," she said aloud to herself. "I wasn't even in the same room. He might as well have been practicing with himself for all the challenge I was to him." She really felt like she had let herself down.

When she walked into the lounge, Steve was sitting at the table watching the news on the lounge television, nibbling on a carrot. He had ordered each of the a large, fresh-squeezed orange juice and had already drained half his.

"Well, how do you feel after your workout, Janet?" Steve said with a warm smile.

There was nothing in his voice or facial mannerisms to indicate any facetiousness. "A little pooped and a lot embarrassed. I didn't realize how out of condition I was, nor how much my game had deteriorated from lack of playing."

Steve uttered a modest laugh and said, "I should apologize for being so hard on you, but I wanted to drive home a point. You see, in our business, there can't be any room for any let-up. If your opponent sees the slightest crack in your veneer, he'll concentrate all his energies on that crack and the first thing you know, the small crack has become a major fault. No matter how confident we are in our approach, no matter how strongly we feel that we have won our objective, we must never, ever, let our guard down. Just when we start to rest on our laurels is the time we'll get nailed for lack of concentration.

"The first lesson I have for you today is never, ever, give your opponent a moment to catch his breath. Push him to the wall, and when you have him down, never let up, even for a second. Imagine that your life is at stake and it's your skills against his.

"On the racquetball court, even though I could have lightened up and still defeated you easily, I wouldn't have done either myself nor you justice in giving a half-hearted effort." After pausing, he asked, "Any questions?" He was looking at her, as if he could see right through her outer skin and into her brain. She could feel his strength and vitality. His energy field was so intense she could almost feel it. Never before had she experience this type of inner strength and power. It frightened her, yet seemed to give her strength. It was almost like a quiet religious experience.

"No, sir," Janet said, "just be patient with me. It might take a short time to get the feel of the case, but you can depend on my availability to give you one hundred percent." Janet wanted to project a feeling of confidence. Actually, she was so scared she felt she would pee her pants at any moment. She excused herself to regroup in the powder room.

When she returned, she felt more composed and in charge of herself, grateful for the opportunity to evaluate and digest what Steve had just said. She realized that this could be the most important assignment of her career. How she handled herself and the impression she gave Daniels could well determine her future in the firm.

"The Paragon portfolio which you have been given is highly confidential. You are not to let it out of your possession at any time for any reason. Don't leave it at the office when you go home. Don't leave it in an unlocked case when you are not working on it, and don't discuss anything relative to the transaction or any of the contents of the portfolio with anyone except myself. Is that clear?"

"Yes, sir." Janet said quietly, leaning forward, lending an air of secrecy to the conversation.

"The real estate in this portfolio is valued in excess of two billion dollars. There are properties that need to be disposed of because they are not making money. There are others that are not making money simply because they are being operated incorrectly, and, of course, there are those that are highly successful. The portion of this transaction that you are to concern yourself with includes garden apartment complexes, high rise office buildings, hotels, and business enterprises, all of which I've clearly delineated in the portfolio given to you."

He paused for a moment to give Janet time to absorb everything that he had said.

Janet looked at him in anticipation of the next command. She was scared and felt unqualified, but tried to fix a look of confidence and determination on her face. She wasn't going to let Steve know how insecure she really felt. She wanted this assignment too bad to screw it up with timidness.

"Your job is visit each property, analyze the operation of each complex, and determine, by letting each facility stand on its own merits, whether the property should be kept, restructured, or disposed of. Additionally, I want you to make a cash flow analysis of each property. When you have completed this portion of the task, assign a value to each individual property along with your recommendation. How you view each project will determine the fate of that project."

He paused again. "Any questions?"

"No, sir," Janet said with solemn reverence. She was beginning to really appreciate the man who sat on the other side of the table. How in the world could one person command such a knowledge and grasp complex problems so easily?

"Well, just one, come to think of it," she said. "When do you want this report?"

"Two weeks from today, Janet. Typewritten with your analysis and recommendations. Your contact in California, where the majority of the properties are located, will be one Nicholas Francisco. You'll find a profile of him in the file. He owns the San Francisco Real Estate and Investment Company, which has offices in Los Angles, San Francisco, and Palo Alto. Nick's Company has handled all the real estate acquisitions and sales for the Paragon Group for several years. He's made a ton of money in commissions off our firm." Steve paused, as if wanting to be sure Janet was soaking in everything he had said.

"I want to be clear that you are not disclose any information about the Paragon merger to him." Steve paused again, leaning forward in his chair and looking Janet squarely in the eye. "This is a very sensitive issue. If he gets wind of the merger, it could jeopardize the entire transaction. He doesn't know it, but as a result of this merger, Francisco will lose all future commissions from the sale of these properties when the time comes to complete the Paragon merger."

Janet's head nodded slightly, giving Steve the impression she completely understood the importance of what he had just said.

"Now, Nick is an honest, straight arrow-kind of a guy, but these are tough times, and real estate sales haven't been abundant this past year. Word has it that Nick may have to close one or more of his offices, so I don't want his opinions of the Paragon Properties or any of the information he is going to give you relative to their evaluation, be colored by the fear of loosing some commissions. I want him to be as unbiasedly helpful as possible, without trying to knowingly steer you in the wrong direction."

Janet nodded, but wouldn't fully grasp the meaning of Steve's words until later.

"There are a number of documents in this portfolio that will help determine the values you will need to complete your comparative analysis, but don't rely solely on them. I'm going to depend on your personal evaluation for final disposition."

Janet finished her orange juice and walked to the parking lot with Steve. "You can depend upon me," she reassured Daniels again as they departed. "By the way, thanks for the game," she said as they reached her BMW. "Maybe next time I can give you more of a game."

"I'll look forward to it," Steve said as he sat in his powder blue Rolls convertible.

Right then and there, Janet made a solemn promise to herself that she would never again be embarrassed on the racquetball court with Steve Daniels.

Chapter Five

☙

Brad was busy fixing dinner when Janet arrived home from work at eight thirty. "It smells like something burning," she said, wrinkling her nose. "If you can't boil water without burning it, I'll just have to hire someone else to do my cooking," she joked.

Brad looked at her without saying a word. His look said, "You come home at this hour and the first words out of your mouth is criticism?" Ignoring her jovial mood, he went back to cooking.

"You dining in tonight?" he asked sarcastically.

"Brad, I've had a tough day. Come on, don't start in on me, okay?"

"Sorry, didn't know the queen was out of sorts. Lose a case, or did one of your depositions go badly? Maybe your lunch date didn't show," he said, again in a sour tone.

"What seems to be *your* problem, fellah?" she snapped back.

"Me? I have no problem. I just get up at five in the morning, pack my own lunch, go to work, slave all day for a few measly bucks, come home, cook dinner, and wait for you to register your complaints. Why should I have a problem? I realize you have a tough day, sitting behind that big desk of yours, talking on the telephone, having drinks with the fellows at lunch or after work, and so on. You do put in a tough day."

"Oh, come off it, Brad. You're just jealous because I make twice the money you do."

The moment she had uttered the words, she regretted it. Without saying a word, Brad set the pan down, dropped the apron he was wearing on the floor, and walked out of the kitchen. Janet grimaced as a moment later she heard the front door slam.

"Damn, damn, damn! You stupid bitch," she uttered to herself angrily.

The fact that she was an attorney making nearly twice as much money as Brad, with the potential of doubling that amount in the near future, had always been a source of agitation to him, and she knew it. She also knew better than to bring it up in an argument, especially in the form of an "I bring in more than you do" type of statement. It was a sensitive masculine-feminine issue, and she knew it. Brad subscribed to the old-fashioned theory that the male was supposed to be the bread winner—or at least should bring in most of the money. Now Brad's feelings were hurt, and she knew this wouldn't be the end of it.

Arguing with Brad always took the edge of her appetite. She couldn't let Brad's efforts go to waste, so she finishing making the meal, and sat down alone to eat a portion of it. When she had finished, she stacked the dishes in the dishwasher, putting the remainder of the uneaten food in plastic containers in the refrigerator. Before turning off the lights, she surveyed the kitchen, then went to her desk in the family room to begin her routine of nightly homework. Disappointed that she hadn't had a chance to share her promotion with Brad, she wasn't going to let the excitement of her new assignment be diluted by their tiff.

Before she knew it, it was nearly midnight. She stretched, then, remembering her instructions not to leave her work unattended, even at home, she locked her work in the briefcase. She was looking forward to the challenge of the new assignment.

As she went through her usual preparation for bed, her mind was occupied with the distance that she and Brad seemed to have developed between them. "It's true, my work does seem to occupy the majority of my waking hours," she admitted to herself. "I know I should try to spend more quality time with him. It just that it seems my work has become more demanding by the day, and now, with the

LOST WOMAN

Paragon assignment, I'm going to have to spend even more time concentrating on my work." Her chin firmed up. "This is my big chance, and I'm not going to blow it because of a little family squabble."

Ever since she had been a small girl, Janet had harbored this desire to succeed burning within her—to be someone. To make something of herself. Something that she and hr family could be proud of. She often wondered if this drive came from the genes she had inherited from her parents or was it born out of necessity? Maybe her mother or father were very bright, ambitious, and successful. Maybe her father was a successful lawyer somewhere. Maybe even a judge or a politician. She would never know the answer to these questions.

Her thoughts drifted back to when she had just turned fifteen. She had just completed the last catechism class at church, when her mother had taken her outside for a mother-daughter talk. A talk that would alter her life forever.

It was a warm, sunny, Indian summer day. Janet and her father had just returned from the nearby school where they had been playing their usual Sunday tennis game. She was pleasingly pooped, but happy. The two of them often verbally jousted with one another before and during each match, threatening one another with annihilation. The good natured bantering added to the excitement of the competition. Today, Janet had been the winner.

"Let's sit down and have a glass of lemonade, Janet," her mother had said as she and her father entered the back yard. She was still giving her father the business for losing when she sat next to her mother, wiping her brow with a white terry cloth towel.

Diverting her attention from her father, she looked into her mother's troubled eyes. For a moment, her mother simply sat there, her eyes downcast, as if trying to formulate the words that she must tell her daughter. Finally, she began speaking in an unfamiliar, serious tone.

"Janet. I want you to know that we're really proud of you, honey. Everything about you makes me thank the Lord every day of my life. You do well in school, almost a straight "A" student. You keep busy with school activities, and now that you've finished your catechism training, you're entering into the threshold of womanhood." She squeezed her daughter's hand again and smiled a trouble look at Janet.

Janet sensed a feeling of uneasiness, sending a chill down her spine in anticipation of something unpleasant. Instinctively, she began nervously twisting the hair on the side of her face with her free hand, a trait she had developed as a child, from before her earliest memory.

Janet and her mother had always been especially close. There was no secret that she couldn't share with her mother. This was a special relationship that most girls didn't enjoy. Most of her friends either didn't get along with their parents or their mothers argued and nagged them all of the time. Janet and her mother seemed to share a special feeling between them, almost like best friends. They liked to go shopping together, go for walks in the evening after dinner, and occasionally just the two of them would go to a movie.

Even though she and her father enjoyed a special relationship, he seemed genuinely concerned about her apparent lack of interest in the opposite sex. "Why don't you get yourself a boyfriend?" her father would ask from time to time. "It's not healthy for a girl your age to stay home and study all the time."

"That's okay," her mother would say, looking at Janet's father. "There's no hurry. You have your whole life to have boy friends. Enjoy yourself. Stay just like you are as long as you can. This is a special time in your life. Enjoy it as long as you can."

"I go out for sports and I'm on the school yearbook committee, Daddy, you know that," she would say in her defense. "I just don't have the urge to go out with guys. Frankly, there isn't anyone in my class that even interests me."

She didn't want to tell her father that she longed to date and have fun, but, while the other girls were getting nice round breasts and hips that swung when they walked, she was still straight as a stick. No hips, no bust. She had tried to wear padded bras but, somehow, after a while, that seemed so stupid, especially when she showered with the rest of the girls after P.E. Sometimes, out of the corner of her eye, she would catch a couple of the girls whispering to each other while looking in her direction, then they'd giggle. She knew what they were giggling about. She had heard them call her "Janet the walking toothpick" behind her back. "Not much there to hold onto in the back seat", they would giggle. "Not unless you're a drum player", another chimed in. They would look at Janet and giggle again.

Janet was the type of person that, once someone made fun of her, that burned their bridge. No matter what the occasion, no matter who the girl, Janet would have nothing to do with them from that point on. That would be the last time she associated with them. Subsequently, her repertoire of girlfriends began to dwindle down to a precious few.

It was during this time-frame that Janet began to grow closer to her mother. It could be said that, during this portion of her life, the time spent with her was actually the best of times for both of them. Janet genuinely felt that her mother was her best friend.

Today, she saw a growing tension in her mother's face. She could feel the pressure as she held Janet's hands. The pained expression in her eyes told her that something weighed heavily on her mother's mind. For the first time, Janet sensed the vulnerability of her mother's age. When you grow old with a person and see them every day, time and age seem to pass unnoticed, but today Janet studied the lines on her face. The silver that had come to dominate the jet-black head of hair she'd once had, and, most of all, her face and hands showed the wear of time. Janet was saddened by this sudden illumination that seemed to have eluded her over the years.

She loved her mother with all her being. Suddenly becoming aware of this vulnerability saddened her. The last time Janet could remember her mother talking to Janet like this was when her grandmother had died after suffering for an extended period of time. A brain tumor, they had called it. Such a horrible label with equally horrible results. Her grandmother had been in such pain that even lying in bed had been unbearable. They had given her morphine to ease her discomfort, but in the end, she had died a slow, painful death. Her face had been gaunt from lack of food, and her body had dried up to nothing more than a bag of skin and bones. When death finally came, it had been welcomed by both patient and relatives. Her death had take a terrible toll on Janet's mother. Janet hadn't realized how close they were, nor what a void her passing would leave in her mother's life. Only now did she begin to understand the depths of those feelings.

"I have something I've wanted to tell you for the longest time," her mother began with slow and deliberate words. "It seems the longer I waited, the worse it became." Her words were labored. "I need to talk to you about your childhood—when you were born." She took a deep breath as if drawing in courage and energy for the words that would follow. "I've held this inside me since you first came to us, waiting for the right moment to tell you. Although it never seemed to be the appropriate time, now it seems that the time has come."

She took a deep breath, paused again, then looked straight into Janet's eyes. "You were born in Saint Joseph's Hospital in Pendelton on a beautiful Autumn day," she said with a soft, loving, smile. Looking up at the trees, she continued, "I remember the leaves were turning from green to vivid yellows and burnt orange." Looking back into Janet's eyes, she continued. "We, your father and I, were living here in Gladstone. We had been trying to have a child of our own for several years, but the doctor said I was unable to carry a baby full term and would, in all probability, lose any child I tried to have." She paused for a moment, looking down into her lap.

Janet sat, quietly looking into her mother's eyes, trying to grasp what it was she was trying to tell her. Her mother's eyes were moist and her hands were trembling. Determined, she continued with an uncertain voice.

"We had been looking for a child to adopt for over a year. We even hired an attorney to keep in touch with all the places a baby might become available. One night, he called us at home, telling us that there was a baby girl at Saint Joseph's Hospital in Pendelton, that was available and, if we moved very quickly, might be able to adopt.

We drove to Pendelton the next morning with our attorney. He took us straight to the hospital's administration office. There, we were met by the chief hospital administrator for a brief evaluation. I guess they wanted to see if we would qualify as parents." She smiled thinly, patting Janet on the hand.

Janet's hand tightened, a reflex action of uncertainty.

"They asked a lot of questions regarding our background: why we wanted a child, why we didn't have children of our own, how much money we made, and so on. Finally, after what seemed an eternity, they handed a packet of consent papers to our attorney for us to sign. We went to the courthouse, where a judge interviewed us. He apparently knew our attorney from law school, which, I learned later, was a great help. The judge finally executed the legal documents giving us temporary custody of the child. Custody of you, Janet," she said lovingly, squeezing Janet's hands. Her eyes were moist. "We were then sent back to the hospital where, for the first time, we saw you."

Tears were streaming down her mother's cheeks now. It was impossible to determine if the expression on her face was one of pain or joy.

"There you were, lying in the nursery, sleeping, as if you didn't have a care in the world. How were you to know that your mother had just abandoned you? How were you to know that you didn't have a soul in the world who cared about you? You were so beautiful....So innocent....So tiny."

There was a pause as she stopped for a moment to wipe her eyes with a lace hankie. "Sorry", she said, holding it over her mouth for a moment, sobbing silently.

After a few moments, she recovered her composure and continued. "Just the thought of you lying there, so small and helpless, brings tears to my eyes every time I think about it. We wanted you, Janet. We wanted to have you for the rest of our lives. We wanted to take care of you, to nurture you, to love you as if you were our own." Her mother wiped her eyes again, took a deep breath, and looked at her daughter, who, up to this point, had sat motionless, showing no expression on her face, although her mind was whirling with confusing thoughts.

Her mother continued. "Apparently, the person who had you, your mother, was very young at the time." The words began to tumble out rapidly now. There was no stopping. The sooner she got it out, the sooner it would be over.

"She came from a small town, where to have a child out of wedlock would have ruined her life. She and her parents didn't want to have her go through that, so she told the hospital she didn't even want to see the newborn baby. She simply wanted to put it up for adoption."

Suddenly, Janet jerked, as if hit by an electrical shot. "Are you telling me," she said in a soft voice, "that I'm adopted? That I'm not really your daughter?" Her voice was crescendoing now with each unanswered question. "All these years you have kept this secret from me and never told me... that I'm adopted?" She stood up facing her mother.

Suddenly, Janet covered her face with her hands and began to weep uncontrollably. Tears rolled between her fingers and down her sleeve. She continued to cry for what seemed an eternity.

Her mother sat quietly, looking at Janet, half wishing she could take back the words that hurt so much and lock them in her heart, never to utter them again. At the same time, she was relieved that, after carrying the burden around in her heart all these years, she had finally gotten the secret out.

When Janet finally composed herself, she asked her mother if she knew her biological mother. What she was like? Why didn't her mother want her when she was born? What were the conditions that caused her mother to give her up? Did she have other sisters or brothers? What was her father like? The questions came faster than her mother could attempt to answer until, finally, Janet seemed to have spent herself.

Her mother sat quietly with Janet, her head and shoulders drooped like a balloon half full of air. She felt as if a huge weight was tied to them.

With one arm around Janet's shoulders and the other holding her hand, her mother finally said, "Honey, I don't know anything about your real mother or your father. All the hospital would tell me is that you were born healthy. I did ask about your parents, but the staff at the hospital as well as our own attorney said it was against the law for the hospital to give out information about them. In a case like this, they said, it was best that they remain anonymous. Their advice was to take you into our lives and raise you like our own. That's what we have done, honey. Raise you as if you were our very own daughter. We love you very much."

Janet's mother put both arms around her and hugged her so hard Janet thought her ribs would break. Somehow, she didn't feel like hugging back.

After that day, Janet wasn't the same person. Although her mother forbid smoking in her house, Janet began to smoke, as if in open defiance to her mothers house rule, taking no apparent concern for her mother's delicate raspatory condition. Not only did she smoke cigarettes, but from time to time her mother would find a small plastic bag with contents that had the appearance of cut alfalfa. She couldn't figure out why this strange substance found itself into Janet's room, but assumed it was part of a high school project. She took no special note to the sweet odor that emanated from her room most evenings.

Janet often showed up to the dinner table with blood-shot eyes, talking with slurred speech. There were times she wouldn't show up at home for dinner at all, not even giving her parents the courtesy of a telephone call. Her mom and dad would look at one another other and just shrug their shoulders. They rationalized that she was working hard at schoolwork or staying out late with friends. It never occurred to them that she might be on drugs and was stoned half the time.

Her grades fell from A's with a sprinkling of B's to D's with a sprinkling of C's. Janet seemed to have lost that spark of life that had previously driven her to excellence and perfection.

She fell in with a group of misfits who wore dark and often dirty clothes and stayed out at all hours of the night, showing no respect for the laws of either their parent's house, the school, nor the community. In short, Janet made a one-hundred-eighty degree turn in her lifestyle.

Janet and her mother began to grow apart. A subtle resentment beginning forming between them. Her mother couldn't understand Janet's attitude, nor why she had suddenly turned her back on the one person that loved her more than anything in the world. The once-close relationship she had also shared with her father seemed to have come to a conclusion as well. Finally, Janet made no attempt to hide the deep resentment she harbored towards her parents. She was unable to deal with the real feelings towards them. She only knew that she resented them, especially her mother.

When Janet finally graduated from high school, she applied to several colleges, but was turned down by all of them. She soon found out that a college education was for the ambitious and studious, not a playground for the n'er-do-well.

Resigned to mediocrity, she got a job as a typist in a local legal office, where she was exposed to men and women successful in their field. She saw how they lived, how they dressed, the places they went, the type of friends they had, the cars and houses they owned, and how they lived full, productive lives. In time it became painfully obvious that their lifestyle was dramatically different from hers. Through their ambition and efforts they had made a name for themselves. The more she thought about it, the more she resolved that the time had come to straighten out and fly right. The old flame that used to kindle within her soul was beginning to ignite itself once again.

It was time.

She applied to Lewis and Clark College in Portland, an exclusive Protestant school, Oregon's counterpart to Stanford in California. Several attorneys in the office had graduated from Lewis and Clark before going on to law school, and offered to write letters of recommendation to the administration office for her. It was on the strength of those letters that Janet was accepted into the college as a freshman at the age of twenty-one.

The campus of Lewis and Clark was once the Meyer estate of the Fred-Meyer clothing store chain. It was said that the administrative office, a beautiful English two-story brick house, built on a hill overlooking Mount Hood, had been imported brick-by-brick from England, along with the horse path and carriage house, which was now the biology and zoology lab.

The campus overlooked a large two-foot deep reflection pool, the source of many freshman-sophomore confrontations wherein the object was to see if the class president could be thrown in the pool, cloths, books and all. Of course, each president was well guarded by its classmates, and each friendly confrontation resulted in half of the male participants getting a through dunking, while the girls squealed with delight.

The entire campus overlooked Mount Hood, which, on a clear day, stood majestically, crystal-clear, as a king sitting on his throne, overlooking his domain.

Although, on beautiful spring days, couples could be seen walking hand in hand, winding themselves through the splendor of the campus, one dared not venture outside if they had studies on their minds, for the beauty of the campus would capture their souls and mesmerize their hearts.

In order to enjoy the full flavor of the campus and college life, Janet had decided to live in on campus, in a girl's dormitory. Because of her age, she was assigned to and spent her first two years of college in Akin Hall, where most of the upperclassmen or older students lived. The studies were very hard. On top of that, Janet had to retain her job as a secretary to pay for her tuition, room, and board. Her mother offered to assist her financially, but Janet had refused. She was determined to stand on her own two feet.

She didn't date those first two years of college. She worked hard at her studies until one or two in the morning, then got up at seven A.M. to attend classes, after which she drove downtown to do typing or filing at the law firm until six or seven o'clock in the evening. She then drove home and hit the books until one or two in the morning. Throughout the school year, this ritual didn't change, with the exception of the summer months, where she worked full time at the law firm, saving money for the next school year.

Tragedy struck in the middle of Janet's sophomore year. She got word that her father had suddenly died. Although her parents lived less than an hour's drive from school, Janet hadn't seem them for over a year.

Dreading going to the funeral, she arrived a short time after the service had begun. A large group of friends and relatives had gathered at the church to pay their last respects. Not wanting to create a scene or stir up any unwanted emotions that could be invoked by her entrance into her mother's life after such a long absence, Janet took a seat in the pew at the rear of the church. She felt alone and very sad sitting there by herself. She could see her mother sitting in front, her head bowed, obviously in pain.

Janet rose from her seat and quietly walked down the center aisle to where her mother sat. With her hand, Janet motioned to the person sitting next to her to move over. As Janet sat down, she put her arm around her mother. Looking up, her mother, eyes full of tears, took Janet's hand in hers. Without saying a word, she bent her head over, laying it on Janet's shoulder. Janet now became the mother, and her mother the child.

She was so absorbed by the grief that her mother felt that she momentarily lost her perspective of the loss of her father. At the cemetery, seeing the deep-bronze-colored casket suspended above the freshly-dug earth suddenly made her heart ache as if a hat pin had been driven into it. For the first time, tears flowed freely, washing away all the pain that had accumulated over these past years. She would miss her father, but she still had a mother.

After the ceremony, Janet and her mother remained behind long after everyone had left, holding hands, feeling no need for words. The morning mist enveloped them as they sat on the steel chairs provided by the funeral home. Two lost souls, each filled with her own emotions and thoughts, each feeling her loss in her own way, yet sharing the common sorrow they obviously felt.

"I'm so sorry, Mother," Janet finally said, tears filling her eyes. "I've been such a fool. How can you ever forgive me?" She didn't know if the tears she shed were tears of sadness for her departed father or tears of happiness for finally having found the love she felt for her mother again. All emotions suddenly seemed to meld into one.

"Hush, baby," her mother said. "It's all right. It's all over with now. All that counts is that you are here again. I've missed you so much. You can't imagine how much it means to have you here, to have you back again. We've lost your father. Let's not lose one another ever again."

They hugged, patting each other on the back, tears running down their cheeks. They were both sobbing uncontrollably. It was a necessary cleansing process for both of them, washing away the sadness of losing a husband and a father and cleansing their souls of the bitterness that had passed between them these past few years. They pledged, from this point on, that the bond between them would be stronger than ever, mother and daughter, reunited again.

Arm in arm, they walked out of the cemetery, into a new life.

Chapter Six

It was during her senior year at Lewis and Clark that Janet met Brad. He was a handsome, rugged-looking man that came from a stable eastern Oregon wheat farming family. They had met on a blind date that had been set up by Janet's roommate. On the first date, Janet didn't care for her date. He seemed to be such an air-head, always joking. He didn't seem to take anything seriously. When Janet tried to discuss foreign crisis with him, he just laughed and said the best way to handle dictators was to isolate them by cutting off their economy. "Take Cuba, for example," he laughed. "Eliminate his export of illegal cigars and you've eliminate his income."

His philosophy on political matters was, "We hire professional Bozos to go to Washington and take care of our affairs", "My one vote doesn't make a hill of beans difference", and, "I have my own problems to worry about. Who's got time to worry about everyone else?"

Janet's major in college was political science. She was always up on current affairs and took her political life seriously. She was the president of the political science Current Affairs club, read two newspapers daily, and attended as many political meetings as time allowed. It was clear to Janet, however, that Brad wasn't concerned with international affairs and could care less about the problems that faced her generation. Their first date ended on a very cool note. Brad walked Janet to the door of her dormitory at ten o'clock along with everyone else living in Akin Hall that had taken one of the girls out that night. Unless a girl had special permission to stay out late, even if she was a dorm counselor, as Janet was, the doors were locked by ten P.M.

Brad politely shook Janet's hand and said, "Thanks for a nice evening. Perhaps we can do it again."

She nodded without emotion and walked into the dorm without saying another word.

Three weeks passed before Brad called Janet again. After a short conversation, he asked, "How would you like to go to the library and study tonight? We can get a cup of coffee and a piece of pecan pie at Mel's afterwards."

She had been bored stiff from studying that evening and jumped at the chance to get out of the dorm.

Brad picked her up at six o'clock in his black '54 Mercury, a vintage car that he had completely restored himself. It was in showroom condition. She could smell the fresh wax paste as he opened the door. "Do you mind studying in the stacks?" he asked. "I like it there because it's a lot quieter and there are few distractions." The stacks were a favorite place for many students to study. They were rows upon rows of stacked books—hence the name stacks. At the end of each row there were two or three study chairs that had been placed there for students who were doing research. The only time you saw another person was when someone wandered by, looking for a book or a place to study.

They studied until the library closed at nine sharp. Departing students walked out of the library into the still of the evening, talking in quiet voices, as if not wanting to disturb the tranquility of the night. Brad and Janet began walking towards the dormitory, when a light mist begun to fall. It felt cool on their faces, yet the night air was somewhat balmy. It was so delightful that they decided to walk around the campus, enjoying the evening air.

After a half-hour of walking, they came to a bench under an elm tree that sat in the park across the street from the campus. The bench was sheltered and dry. A light post on the corner shone through the tree, casting light shadows on the pair as they sat talking in quiet tones.

Brad looked at Janet with the filtered light falling softly on her face, admiring her small upturned nose. Her eyes were the warmest brown eyes he had ever seen. Her hair was combed back in a pageboy with soft brown bangs gently sweeping across her forehead.

Gently taking her face in his hands, he slowly pulled Janet toward him and kissed her lightly. At that moment, Brad fell helplessly in love.

They sat in silence for several minutes, looking into each others eyes. A bell sounded in the distance and the realized that it was time to get back in time for curfew. Janet rested her head on his shoulder as they walked arm in arm back to her dormitory. Neither uttered a word. The warmth of their embrace and the look in their eyes was all the communication that they needed.

The next evening, after dinner, Brad called Janet on her private line. "I was thinking of going to the library to do a little research. Think I could sweet-talk you into accompanying me? I'll even buy you a cup of coffee afterwards."

Since their last date, Brad was all she could think of. She couldn't keep her eyes off the clock, which seemed to move at a snail's pace. At six on the nose, the bell over her study desk rang, indicating that someone was in the lobby asking for her. Her heart was like a drum roll as she rushed to see Brad. She made a vein attempt at casualness, trying to mask the enthusiasm she felt.

"Oh, hi." She said, acting as if she hadn't expected to see him.

Brad greeted her with a warm smile as she came through the lobby.

"I'll be just a moment. I have to get my coat and books." In a flash, she was down the hall and back again, smiling eagerly, unable to restrain herself.

Although they studied until eight thirty, neither was able to concentrate on the mass of words in front of them. At eight-thirty they decided to adjourn to Mel's for coffee and a piece of pecan pie. They sat and talked until almost ten o'clock. "Oh my gosh! Look at the time. We'll never get you back in time for curfew," Brad said, looking embarrassed.

"That's all right. I signed out for twelve o'clock," Janet said softly, looking a little sheepish.

As they drove up Palatine Hill to the college, Brad said, "We have over an hour until you have to be in. Want to sit in the car and talk for a while?" He pulled into the vacant parking lot overlooking the football field, turned off the lights, and turned the radio down as "Stand By Me" was playing on the oldie station. He studied Janet's face through the soft light of a half-moon.

The magic from the previous night hadn't worn off. He was still in love. Without a word, he put his arm around Janet and kissed her. The first kiss was soft and light, with their lips just barely touching each other. That was followed by a slightly more passionate kiss, which was followed by a lip-smashing, teeth-touching, kiss, lasting for what seemed to be an eternity.

Brad's hand drifted to Janet's neck, caressing it for a moment. Sensing no resistance, he slipped it down her shoulder until he was cupping her small breast. His lips followed the same pattern his hand had just traveled. Within moments, their bodies were entwined in and around each other in such passion a casual observer might have thought it was the last moment they would ever see each other on this earth.

An hour fleeted by in a moment. As they realized the time, Janet quickly dressed as Brad wiped the steam from the windows. Not a word was spoken as Brad drove the Mercury towards Janet's dorm. He had his arm around her shoulders and her head was lying on his shoulder. They arrived at the front of Janet's dorm with one minute to spare. Brad walked her to the door and held her in his arms one last time, kissing her.

"Call you soon," he said.

"Soon," Janet responded warmly.

From that night until the end of the school year, Brad and Janet spent every evening together, first studying, then sometimes going out for a coke or coffee, but more often than not, cutting straight for the football field's parking lot, where they made mad passionate love, restricted only by the confines of Brad's front seat, until time came when he had to return her back to the dormitory. He was so impressed with her vivaciousness that he nicknamed her "Pash", short for passionate.

Janet was the only woman that Brad had ever known with whom he had had such a warm, passionate relationship. For that matter, she was the only woman that he had ever fallen so deeply in love. He knew from the moment that he had kissed her that he wanted to spend he rest of his life with her. Two weeks before graduation they were married in a quiet ceremony in the college chapel by the college minister.

This was the best of times for Janet. She was happy and at peace with herself. Brad was everything she had ever wanted in a man, with the possible exception of his political orientation. Even that was a blessing in disguise, because there was no arguing about politics. The only section of the newspaper Brad wanted to read was the sports page and comic section. He had no time to worry about the affairs of some country halfway across the globe.

After college, Brad went to work for a construction company to more or less learn the building trade from the ground up while Janet continued her education at law school. Brad immediately began earning a good income. It became no burden to pay for Janet's books and tuition with his salary.

Law school has a tendency to demand a great deal of time from the student. It's not uncommon to find many of the second year law students forming study groups, dividing up assignments to maximize their time and talents for the benefit of the group. Janet was in one of these groups. The majority of her time was spent going to class, after which she grabbed a sandwich, then headed for her study group, then back to individual study time again. By the time she arrived home in the evening, she was so tired, if something hadn't already been prepared to eat, she would simply drop on her bed, dead tired, and be asleep before the water bed stopped rippling. Many was the time Brad had to take her shoes off and pull a comforter over her, kissing gently her on the cheek before retiring himself.

After a year-and-a-half of this routine, it was no surprise that Brad and Janet appeared to be drifting apart. Not only were they beginning to operate on different intellectual levels, but their emotional needs began to change.

Brad loved Janet and would do anything for her. He tried to be patient and understand when she worked long, hard hours studying. But then, he worked long and hard hours too, yet he seemed to find time for her. Why couldn't she find time for him?

Brad's work was physical in nature, leaving him tired and hungry at the end of the day and in need of a little emotional support. Every time he tried to get close to Janet, she seemed to have one excuse after another for not wanting nor having the time for intimacy.

The more Janet studied and the more she learned, the more she desired intellectual stimulation rather than emotional involvement. Striving for excellence in everything she did left no tolerance for the mundane, the non-achiever, the average person. Brad's lack of interest in intellectual jousting and his apparent disinterest in advancing himself intellectually, was taking its toll on their relationship.

The first crack in the dam had been formed and the structure was weakening. The typical American marriage was in the making.

Chapter Seven

☙

Brad was already on his second cup of coffee and had just finished the sports section when Janet walked into the kitchen. He looked up, but made no acknowledgement to her presence as she poured a glass of orange juice.

She took a few sips, dreading telling Brad that she was going to have to be out of town for the next few days. After several moments of silence, she blurted, "I'm going to have to fly to San Francisco on an assignment for the firm today," she said flatly.

She paused, expecting a response. When none was forthcoming, she continued. "I tried to tell you last night but you took out of here like a scalded cat. Anyway, I'm flying out of Portland on Alaskan Air Lines at ten-fifteen this morning. I'll probably be in San Francisco for three or four days." Pausing for a moment, to let her words sink in, she continued, "Then I'll be on to Los Angles, where I'll be another two or three days, depending upon how cooperative my contacts are and how fast I can get my work done, so…" she paused again, assessing his mood, "you'll have the house to yourself. I'll be home for a day before going on to Denver, to get a change of cloths and," pausing again, "just so you don't forget what I look like," she said mockingly, baiting Brad. "Not that you care," she uttered under her breath. "I'm on a strict time schedule, so there's no time to let grass grow under my feet. I'll be busy from the time I get up until my head hits the pillow."

Brad was quiet for a while, sipping his coffee, pretending to read the comic section of the morning paper. "This is getting to be a habit," he finally said, folding the paper, slapping it on the table for effect. "Your coming and going with complete disregard for anyone but yourself. Lest you forgot, you do have a husband. Don't you think it's about time you start acting like a wife with responsibilities and not a world traveler? I mean, I know it's great to be a successful attorney and all, and I'm proud of you for that, but it seems your always putting you're work before everything."

Janet knew when he said "everything" he meant himself.

Choosing to ignore his meaning, she dug in. "That's the price of success, honey. You ought to try it!" Janet said with a note of sarcasm. As soon as she had said the words, she bit her lip, wishing she could have them back. This is getting to be a nasty habit, she thought to herself.

"Listen, I know it's tough to fend for yourself when I'm gone," she said with a softer voice, "but this is a career opportunity. If I do everything right, this could be the break I've been waiting for." She could tell by the firm set of Brad's jaw that he wasn't interested in her excuses.

"Tell you what, Janet, when you return home from your world travels and finish making a name for yourself, I think we should sit down and have a heart to heart talk about where this marriage is going. From where I'm sitting, it appears to heading straight for a brick wall at ninety miles an hour, and unless something is done about it, and I mean soon, there won't be anything left to salvage. Either you're committed to make it work, or you're not. Think about it!" With that, Brad turned on his heels and left the house, slamming the front door so hard the dishes rattled.

Janet could hear his Toyota truck peeling rubber as he backed out of the driveway. Suddenly, there was a loud crash. She looked out the front window. Crushed under the back tires of Brad's truck were the two fully-loaded aluminum garbage cans which had been set out the night before. Garbage was strewn everywhere.

Brad kicked the garbage cans from under his tire like a place-kicker punting an extra point, swearing at the top of his lungs. He laid a strip of rubber, taking two thousand miles of rubber off his tires in the process, leaving garbage strewn all over the driveway, lawn, and the street in front of their house.

Janet couldn't help but smile as she closed the curtains. "Stupid male machoism," she said to herself. "I'm not cleaning up his mess."

* * * * * *

The first city on Janet's itinerary was San Francisco. There were two large garden apartment complexes, a hotel, and two office buildings to be visited, analyzed, and evaluated.

The flight to the Bay area was uneventful. She was grateful for the time to again study the projects she had to visit, making notes of items to check and an itinerary of how to budget her time. Janet was nervous as a school girl taking an entrance exam, but anxious to begin the task. This assignment could open the doors to success and prestige she was looking for. She had to succeed.

Putting her notes away, Janet's mind went back to the altercation with Brad. She regretted leaving him with such a sour tone. Despite the fact that she had chosen the legal profession as a line of work which, just by the nature of the business, was confrontation in nature, she hated discord in her personal life. One way or another, she had to get her marriage back on track. This constant bickering just wasn't going to cut it.

As the plane circled the Golden Gate Bridge, she pushed the altercation with Brad out of her mind, leaving it clear for the assignment ahead. Janet looked out the window, admiring the beauty of the city. She could see Sausalito, Alcatraz, Coit Tower, the Pyramid building, and of course, the Golden Gate Bridge, all set like jewels on the crown of San Francisco Bay.

"San Francisco! I wonder if it's as mysterious and beautiful as everyone says. It certainly looks intriguing from here," she said to herself.

She had called Nick Francisco from Portland prior to her departure, telling him the time of her arrival, asking him to meet her at the airport passenger loading area. She remembered Steve's words about Francisco: "Knowledgeable and highly honest. A straight arrow," he had said. "You won't find many professional men of his standards these days. Not in this market. Everyone is out to make a buck at anyone's expense. You can depend upon Nick Francisco."

Janet was waiting on the curb dressed in comfortable black cotton pants with a top to match, offset by a white polka dot scarf around her neck. Her hand made leather suitcase and matching briefcase wee sitting by her side. Expecting a Mercedes or BMW to pull up, she was surprised when a red Toyota stopped in front of her. The driver rolled down the passenger-side window and asked, "Janet Neilson?"

"Yes! Mr. Francisco?" she said, bending down to look into the window.

Nick Francisco came around to Janet, hand extended. "It's great of you to meet me like this," she said with a big smile. "I really appreciate your taking the time out of what must be a busy schedule."

"Think nothing of it. Hope you didn't have to wait too long," Nick said. "I hate it when people make me wait. I make it a point of being on time."

"How did you spot me so soon?" She asked.

"Mr. Daniels said to look for a tall, good lookin' brunette with a hungry look. When I saw you I figured, that must be her." He laughed. "To be honest, you looked like you were looking for someone, so I took a chance."

"I guess I was looking for a typical San Francisco broker's car—a Cad, Jag, SL 450, or a Beamer," she said, somewhat sheepishly. "You kind of snuck up on me with that Toyota." She smiled. "A conservative, successful businessman. I like that. Shows you know the value of a dollar and how to keep it."

"I've never been one for spending the greater part of my net worth on a hunk of metal whose only function is to get from one spot to another. Mercedes, Jags, and Beamers are just too expensive. I'd rather put my money in an investment that goes up in value, not on an expensive toy whose value goes down the minute you drive it off the lot, plus it demands constant maintenance to boot. As for Cadillacs, only 'house-mouse' brokers drive them around these parts."

"House-mouse brokers," Janet repeated with a hearty laugh. "What's a house-mouse"?

"That's what we can an agent who just sells houses. A house-mouse." Nick joined Janet in laughter. She had this vision of a little mouse in a coat and tie scurrying from house to house with a little briefcase, trying to make a deal.

Nick wasn't at all what she had pictured him. Her mental vision of him had been a tall, slender man in his fifties, greying hair, glasses, and somewhat stuffy. Nick wasn't anything like that at all. He stood five-foot-ten, with a full head of black hair, greying at the temples. He was obviously in good physical condition, as witnessed by the way he fit snugly into his tailored herringbone sports jacket. The veins on his hands and neck stood out, indicating a strong heartbeat. He was easy to talk to and had an obvious sense of humor, laughing generously at anything the least bit humorous. She liked him at once.

"Here's the Stanford Hotel," he said, pulling into its circular driveway. "Want to freshen up before proceeding to the first property?"

"No, let me just register and drop my things off and I'll be ready for action."

"How long do you expect to stay in the Bay Area?" Nick asked.

"My guess would be three or four days," she said, stepping out of the car. "Be back in a flash—keep the motor running, Clyde." She smiled as she turned to go into the hotel.

*   *   *   *   *   *

That first day Janet found Nick Francisco to be a great help in evaluating her assignment. He provided comparable rents as well as recent sales of similar projects, which aided her immensely. The time they had together passed quickly, mostly as a result of Nick's easy manner and sense of humor. What could have been a laborious chore turned out to be an enjoyable breeze. By the end of the first day, Janet felt as if she had known Nick Francisco all her life. "I'm curious, Nicholas. You have a New York accent, yet here you are in sunny California. Are you a misplaced refugee from the Big Apple?" she inquired with a smile.

"Boy, you don't know how true that is." Nick chuckled. "Actually, I was a lawyer once. A damn good one too, if I do say so myself. I specialized in personal injury and real estate transactions. Some combination, huh?"

"So, what made a successful attorney leave a thriving business and the big city? I always heard that once you lived in New York, everything else was just hamburger. You have the best entertainment, theater, sports, parties, fashion, etc. There you are, in the melting pot of the world."

"Right and wrong. Living in the city of New York is like living on the fast track all the time. That city never sleeps. Unlike the western part of the country, in New York, one's circle of friends are often limited to one's family and work force. Own a car in New York city and you may never find a place to park it. A person can live a lifetime in a thirty story condo and never get to know his neighbors, let alone everyone in the building. Did you know that you can actually live in that city and never go out of doors?" he asked with a smile.

Janet shook her head in wide-eyed amazement.

"That's right. By taking a subway from building to building, one could live, shop, and work and become an indoor hermit, never letting a ray of sun touch one's face. Great for the complexion, but not too good for the disposition." Nick smiled. "If you try to be friendly with a stranger in New York, or even give a friendly smile to a cashier, they think you're either a masher or out on a pass from the funny farm. Here, of course, you get to know everyone on your block, and if you live in a relatively small town, eventually you'll get to know everyone and everyone knows you."

"Is that why you left? It sounds like city life became too hectic for you and you wanted a little more intimacy. Buy why did you change jobs?" she added without waiting for an answer. "I would think someone as bright as you obviously are, and successful as you are at your trade, after spending all that time in law school and all, nothing would deter you from your calling." Suddenly, she blinked. Good grief. He's going to think I'm a drill sergeant or something, she thought to herself.

"I don't know," Nick responded with a frown. "I guess it was a number of things. I was always taught that ethics, honesty, and reputation were among the most important assets a business man could possess. If you weren't able wake up in the morning, look yourself in the mirror, and like the guy looking back at you, there was something dramatically wrong with your lifestyle." Nick heaved a sigh.

Janet sensed that she was treading in sensitive waters. "I'm sorry, I didn't mean to pry," she said knitting her brow as she looked at Nick. She touched his hand, saying, "It must have been very hard for you to leave, what with your family, a successful business practice, and all. Whatever the reason, I admire you for it. You must have had a very bad experience to have left such an impression on you," Janet said sympathetically.

Nick seemed relieved to be talking about it. It was as if it was something he had wanted to get off his chest for a long time. "Until you've been in a situation that really tests your mettle, your honesty, and morality, you really don't know how you'll respond until you've been put to the test." He paused for a moment, and took a deep breath.

With a vacant look in his eyes, as if looking into the past, he continued, "While I was an attorney in New York, I had this particular client who, after working with him for an extended period of time, I discovered was tied in with some sort of organized crime. Eventually, I unearthed the extent of his underground connections, but by that time, he had been a client for so long it was too late to back out."

"I don't understand what you mean, you found out but couldn't back out. It seems that...."

Nick, who suddenly seemed wound up, interrupted her. "To give you an example, this guy, my client, bought and sold real estate for a living. What else he did, I have no idea, and to be perfectly frank, didn't want to know. He would make an offer to buy an office building, for example. He would do his own negotiations.

When he was ready to close the deal. He would always come to my office carrying a briefcase full of money. My role was to read the legal documents and count the money. In short, I was his personal escrow officer and attorney all rolled into one!

"I should have taken the clue when, curiously, both the buyer and seller brought their own bodyguards to these meetings. I mean, these guys were big and ugly, just like in the movies. They used to scare the shit out of me, standing around like zombies. Their eyes were blank like mummys. I guess they weren't suppose to see anything. Can you imagine anything so ridiculous They always carried guns in their shoulder holsters. These guys would stand behind their bosses with their coats open, exposing their weapons to each other. Kind of a one-upmanship, you know what I mean, a I see your gun, see mine, kind of mentality."

Nick paused to shake his head as if in disbelief. "Large amounts of cash changed hands in these meetings. Sometimes a million dollars or more! This client of mine had this scam. He would buy or sell a property, but only report a small amount of the money from the sale to the Internal Revenue, walking off with a suitcase full of unreported, tax-free money. Like, he'd sell a building for a million dollars cash, but only report a quarter of that amount to the I R S, thereby not only reporting a loss from the sale, but now he has three quarters of a million dollars of tax-free money." Nick waved his hands in the air as if performing a magic act.

After breathing a deep sigh, he continued. "The other guy, he doesn't care. He got his tax-free money from someone else doing the same thing. Then, when he gets around to buying a building, he'll use the money from some drug deal—all cash, of course—and report a modified sales price. The ball never stops rolling, and the stupid Internal Revenue Agent who audits him every year, never catches on, because most of the money went to overseas banks.

"It was like a game to them. Beat the government and keep all the dough for themselves. Of course, I got paid a handsome fee to read documents, count the money, pass it from buyer to the seller, and, of course, keep my mouth shut. Every body wins. Tax-free dough." Nick paused.

"Except...." Janet said, waiting for the next shoe to fall.

"Yes, except." Nick's eyes looked down. "There was this one deal. My client, and I use the word loosely," Nick said, with a snarl, "came into my office this particular day with the usual suitcase full of money, and bought a shopping center. The usual procedure took place. My guy paid the seller a large amount of cash, signed the papers, and left. The whole transaction probably took fifteen to twenty minutes. The only conversation that took place was each party confirming that everything was in order.

"Six months later, my 'client' stormed into the office with his bodyguard, slammed the door, put one of his hands on my desk, and shook the other one in my face, saying, 'I lost money on that shopping center deal, Francisco. After I bought the deal, the tenants began moving out.

You were my mouthpiece. If you had done your job, I wouldn't be in this pickle!'"

"Naturally, I was torn between being in a state of shock and feeling stupefied by the acquisition. Gaining what was left of my composure, I responded: `Mr. Franco, I don't know what you're talking about. You already had the deal made when you....'"

"Grabbing me by my tie, he raised me out of my chair and put his greasy face next to mine, saying I owed him five hundred G's, and if I wanted to see the light of day, I better have the dough by Friday.

"I tell you, Janet, I was scared stiff. I had no idea what was going on or what to do or say. I think for a while there my mind lapsed into a comatose state."

"What did you do?" Janet asked, wide-eyed.

"I regained my composure long enough to say, `Just a damn minute Franco, what the hell are you talking about? I had nothing to do with your deal. All I did was sit here at my desk, count your goddamn money, and watch you bastards try cheating each other!'"

Nick looked at Janet and shrugged his shoulders. "Sorry about my French."

Janet waved her hand, dismissing the need for an apology.

"Then this thug reached for my tie again. I leaned back in my chair, just out of his reach, and sat there looking at him. Thinking back on the situation, I probably looked scared as a skunk with a hound dog after his ass and mad as a bag lady who just had her stuff stolen."

Nick paused, looking in space. "At any rate, he just nodded to his gorilla, who immediately took charge of the situation. This was beginning to look like a wrestling tag team at Madison Garden, and I was it.

"This guy looked like Mr. Clean, shaven head and all. He didn't even bother coming across the desk for me. He grabbed my desk and threw it aside like a Frisbee. All my stuff scattered around the room. I had visions of my body following the stuff. I backed up to the wall, trying to

Lost Woman

escape his grasp, but he had me by the lapels of my jacket. He lifted me off the ground, and uttered his first words. "Da boss wants his dough. Ya got it, pal? He wants it *now*!"

"With that, he slammed me against the wall so hard I thought my back was broken. Kicking the chair with his foot, he slammed me in it like hamburger in a tortilla." Looking at Janet, he said, "I don't mind saying, I was scared. So scared, I thought I would shit my pants."

"Then what happened?" she asked breathlessly.

"Now, 'da boss' leans across the desk and grabs my goddamn necktie again. That asshole had a fetish for neckties. 'You got twenty-four hours to get the dough, Francisco, or your ass is fish bait!' he said. 'Twenty-four hours. Got it?'"

"This being Wednesday, I could see I was in a lot of trouble. 'Where am I going to get that kind of money? I have only a few thousand in the bank,' I said, 'All my money is tied up in that shopping center deal I'm developing.'"

"I could see that I was really getting his attention. 'Frankenstein' Franco backed up and motioned to the gorilla with his head. The next thing I knew, I was making like a ping pong ball again, bouncing from wall to wall. The gorilla definitely made it clear that Franco meant business. They left and he said they would be back the next day. I have to tell you, Janet, I have never, ever, been so scared in all my life. I had this vision of myself wearing cement shoes and becoming fish bait."

"What did you do?" Janet asked, her eyes wide open. She could feel Nick's frustration. Even the veins in his neck were standing out as beads of perspiration formed on his forehead.

"After taking stock of my redecorated office, which now looked like mid-Civil War, I went home to tell my wife, Shirley, what had happened. At first, she thought it was a joke and I was pulling her leg. It didn't take long for her to realize that the shaking in my body and my sweaty palms wasn't from the evening air. Once she finally realized the graveness of the situation, she went into a sort of shock. All of a sudden, our lives were about to come apart at the seams. I mean, there I was, fifty-five years old. I had worked hard, scraping and saving our money and investing it for the future, and now all of a sudden, I was faced with the prospect of getting my head knocked off by a brainless gorilla."

Nick took a deep breath before continuing. "We talked about it for a couple hours, then decided to call a few influential friends in an effort to try to find out what kind of trouble I was really in here. After a few telephone calls, it became evident that this guy had been responsible for several broken arms and legs and even a possible missing person or two in his career as a thug. Through it all, the one piece of advice that stood out was, 'Don't mess with him unless you got muscle.'"

"Oh God, Nick. That must have been awful." Janet squeezed his hand. "What did you do?"

"I did the only thing I could do. The next day, there was Franco waiting for me in the parking lot with his gorilla."

"Well," he said, "where's my dough?"

"I said, 'Let's go up to my office, where we can settle this matter in a businessman-like manner.' Once we were there, I took out a colored rendering and a set of plans of the shopping center I was building for Shirley and myself.

"I told him, 'This land cost me over six hundred thousand dollars, and I have three hundred thousand dollars in construction costs to date. At this stage of construction, the project is worth well over a million dollars. Here's what I'll do,' I said. 'I'll give you a note against my shopping center for the five hundred thousand dollars you say you lost money on your. In exchange, I'll take over your project for you, releasing you of any liability.' The next thing I knew, I was a piece of decoration on the wall, playing the ping pong role all over again. The gorilla was doing his thing. I swear, Janet, I thought the guy was going to kill me."

"Couldn't you call the police or something?" she asked.

"Sure, I could call the police. There were no records to prove anything. I could even press charges, but it would be my word against his. Even if the police arrested him, he would be out on bail before I drove away from the police station. Then I *would* be fish bait.

"No, I had to handle this the best way I knew. I got myself into this mess by dealing with scum. Now I had to get myself out, hopefully in one piece.

"When the gorilla got tired of bouncing me around, Franco took his turn. He grabbed my goddamn tie again," Nick explained through clinched teeth, "and pulled me so close to his face that his nose touched mine. With that rancid cigar breath of his, he said, 'Sign over the whole center and consider yourself a lucky man, Francisco.'"

"You didn't," Janet exclaimed in a shocked voice.

"Lock, stock, and legal license," Nick responded.

"Oh, Nick! How can such things happen in this day and age? This is the nineties, not the thirties."

"I'm afraid it happens more often than you care to know, kid…. a lot more. It's a tough world out there, and you have to save your ass any way you can."

Nick was silent for a long time after that. Janet felt as if she had just heard a private confession, meant only for the ears of the holy. She felt guilty having heard it, but grateful to Nick for sharing it with her. She certainly had seen a side of Nick Francisco that few knew even existed. She couldn't help but wonder what sort of man he really was, underneath those tailored clothes and well-conditioned body. After hearing the dissertation on his financial ruin, she couldn't help but deduce that he must have a disciplined mind, maybe even with a larcenous bent to it, considering his past. This is one man not to cross! A cold shiver ran down her spine as she really looked at his hardened face for the first time.

"I guess that's when you moved out west?" she said in a quiet voice.

"I left New York as fast as my Italian ass could move from the office to the condo and out of town without passing Go. Me and my wife were history. We didn't even take our furniture. Just packed whatever duds we had that fit in the car and left. Adios, Big Apple. We didn't even leave a forwarding address," Nick said as he waved his hand like a plane taking off. "H i s t o r y," he said slowly with emphasis.

"If you could do it over again, Nick, what would you change?"

"I think the first thing I would have done was get myself a gun and shoot the son-of-a-bitch," Nick said between clinched teeth. "But, you live and learn. I made a stupid mistake and I paid for it. It doesn't pay to be greedy," he said with a smile. "I can attest to that."

"How did you happen to get into real estate?" she asked, changing the topic.

"That whole New York mess soured me on the legal profession. Shirley was a great help. Her background is in psychotherapy. I think I was her personal patient for several months following our move to California. I wouldn't have made it without her love and understanding. With her professional training she was able to land a job at San Francisco General Hospital, but even with her working, our bank account began to dwindle to the point where we could see the bottom coming up to meet us quickly. One evening, after one of our many long discussions about our situation, I picked up the Chronicle. There, on the front page of the real estate section, was an article about the successful real estate men in San Francisco. There was a picture of each man, the company he worked for, how much money he had made the previous year, where they lived, and their respective lifestyles. Right then and there, I decided to join their ranks and go into commercial real estate."

"It must have been difficult to make the transition from lawyer to real estate sales," Janet said sympathetically.

"No, not really. You'd be surprised how interrelated the two fields are. To be a successful real estate salesman, you have to be energetic, ambitious, and creative. And above all, you have to have the killer instinct. Believe me, after my New York experience, I qualify for all of the above."

There was a note of determination in Nick's voice that told her that Nick Francisco would stop at nothing to succeed. For the second time in their conversation, Janet felt ill at ease next to this man.

"I understand some of your offices have fallen on tough times and you might be forced to cut back." Janet reiterated the earlier confidential conversation she'd had with Danielson. As soon as she had said the words, she realized she was not only way out of line, but was again stepping on sensitive toes.

Before she could apologize for her lack of tact, Nick offered, sharply, "Times are tough, but the tough will survive. Nothing and no one will ever keep me down again, and you can take that to the bank!"

Nick and Janet sat silently, each locked in their own thoughts as Nick drove toward Fisherman's Wharf. Even though it was a week day, the traffic was heavy. The evening lights from the city were beautiful and seemed to soften the tension in the car. Soon, Nick said, "How about a bite to eat? What you say? You like fish?" Nick pulled into Tarrintino's parking lot on the waterfront. "This place always has the freshest catch of the day."

They sat by a window overlooking the bay. The fleet of fishing boats were moored for the evening with sea gulls going from one boat's deck to another looking for scraps of fish. The moon rippled on the water, creating a Garcia-like painting for the diners' delight.

Before the waiter took their order, Janet excused herself to wash her hands and powder her nose. "Watch my stuff?" she asked as she set her briefcase on the chair next to Nick.

"Sure, you go right ahead. I'll hold down the fort."

What a complicated man, she thought as she washed her hands. God, the webs we weave for ourselves.

Janet had been in the ladies' room for approximately fifteen minutes, washing her hands, fixing her face and hair, when all of a sudden a cold shiver went through her spine. "Shit! The briefcase. Steve said to *never* let it out of my sight!"

Chapter Eight

Janet returned to their table. Nick was gone! Her briefcase was gone! Frantically, her eyes searched the room. Neither Nick nor her briefcase was anywhere in sight. Slowly, Janet sank in her chair. She felt as if the weight of the entire world had just been set upon her shoulders. She could actually see her career flying out the window, across the bay, and out of sight.

"Stupid, stupid, stupid," she said, hitting herself on the forehead with the palm of her hand.

The waiter came to the table, menu in one hand and a white cloth draped over his other arm. "Would madam like to order something to drink?" he asked in a thick Italian accent.

Janet didn't even look up. She just waved her hand, dismissing the waiter. What was she going to do? What was she going to tell Daniels? She had utterly failed the first major important assignment of her career. If there was ever a low point in her life, this definitely exceed anything she could remember ever having experienced. Her stomach felt as if she had swallowed a golf ball.

"Did you order yet?"

A voice sent from heaven!

"Nick!" She looked up at him. He stood before her, holding her briefcase, smiling down at her. She tried to mask her feelings which vacillated from rage for putting her through the thought that she had lost her briefcase, not to mention her career, to ecstasy in seeing the briefcase safe and sound in his hands.

"When I returned, I didn't see you. Thought you might have run off with a tall lanky blond or something," Janet said, composing herself, trying to appear calm, taking the episode light hearted.

"I thought I would hit the sand box while you were in the powder room. Kill two birds with one stone, you know. Oh, here's your briefcase," he said, holding it out to her. "I didn't want to leave it at the table. Might be full of money or something," he chuckled.

Janet thought she detected a hint of sinisterness in his voice, but dismissed it once she had her hands on the briefcase. "I appreciate your thoughtfulness," she said, smiling gratefully. That's the last time this baby gets out of my sight, she thought to herself, smiling as they sat down again.

"You can't be too careful in this town," Nick said, looking around the room as if everyone was under suspicion. When the waiter returned, Janet, at the waiter's suggestion, ordered the catch of the day, fresh grilled salmon. Nick had his favorite, clam fettucini. Nick asked Janet what her favorite wine was and ordered a bottle of White Zinfandel. The dinner was excellent, as Nick had stated it would be.

"Well, you've had a full day, young lady," he said after they finished a serving of cherries jubilee. "I suppose you're ready for a good nights rest."

Janet nodded. "I am tired, but I have a lot of paperwork to do before I retire." She rubbed her neck. "I could use some exercise, though. After riding around in the car all day I feel like my body is tied up in knots. All this brain work leaves me tense," she said, shaking her head as if trying to shake out the cobwebs.

"Want me to drop you off at a 24 Hour Nautilus or something?" Nick offered. "I have a membership—you could be my guest. They have weight rooms, machines, saunas, the whole works."

"No, thanks anyway. I brought my jogging duds along. After I finish my paperwork, I think just I'll go for a run around Golden Gate Park, then take a nice hot bath. That should relax me. I'll be good as gold for tomorrow."

"Wish I had your energy," Nick said. "Well, listen, I'll pick you up at eight A.M. sharp. We'll have breakfast and discuss the plans of the day."

"Sounds great!"

Nick dropped her off at the Stanford Hotel

"Thanks again, Nick. I really appreciate your help today," she said as she got out of the car. "Couldn't have done it without you. Good night,"

If there was a single aspect about being an attorney that Janet hated, it was the paperwork. "Thank God for memo machines," she mused. "Without a tape recorder, I'd be back in the Stone Age."

She had kept detailed notes of their conversations, along with figures she had calculated pertaining to each building that they had visited that day. Organizing them into the categories Danielson wanted wasn't too time consuming.

As she went through the process of organizing her thoughts, she couldn't help recalling how interested Francisco was in her work. She noticed that he had watched her every computation, even corrected her once or twice. He even offered suggestions from time to time as she wrote down her thoughts on the property being viewed.

Janet wasn't used to this cloak and dagger game, having to watch every word she said to Francisco. After the previous slip of the lip, letting Nick know that she knew he was in financial trouble, made her realize that her mind wasn't as disciplined as it should be if she was going to succeed at this assignment. After all, the reality of the situation was that she, indirectly, was taking money out of Nick's pockets. The facilities they were visiting and analyzing were properties Nick thought he was going to obtain listings on to sell. That would amount to a significant commission for his firm. Little did he know, this was not going to happen.

Janet suddenly felt like Benedict Arnold, betraying a friend. It wasn't a good feeling. Her mind flashed back to the abandoned briefcase at Fisherman's Wharf. That eerie feeling that something wasn't right sent shivers down her back, but she fluffed her hair with her finger tips and continued with her work.

Finally, she was finished. Her mind was saturated, and her body tense. She felt like a tightly strung violin. "Sure could use Dave Moore about now," she mused aloud. "One of his deep body massages would be great."

Janet slipped into her jogging outfit, complete with orange florescent wrist, leg, and head bands. It was dark outside, but the streets were brightly lit and busy with commuters going home, people going for walks, and other joggers out for their evening exercise.

The evening was cold and crisp as a light mist from the ocean filled the air. Janet took a deep breath. "Damn, that air feels good." She did her stretching exercises in the courtyard before started off in a slow jog towards Golden Gate Park.

It felt great, jogging in the evening air. She found the crisp, cool air cleared her mind, accelerating her thinking, as if it were on a fast track. The feeling was exhilarating.

Janet had been following a couple fellow joggers, until they turned away toward a residential district. Calculating that she had been running for about thirty minutes, she figured she would take the next right turn, run through the park, and follow the street back towards her origination. Although having never been in the park before, she had consulted the San Francisco street map before leaving. She visualized the streets in her mind, following the route through the middle of the park towards the other side and back on a busy boulevard.

She could feel the ocean breeze blowing strong and cooler as she turned the corner following the path through the park. Three men wearing dark sweat shirts and blue jeans riding dirt bikes passed her, looking over their shoulders, nodding a greeting as they rode by.

Suddenly, Janet began to feel a bit uneasy. The street lights were spaced further apart now and, since she had departed from the heavily trafficked street, she had a sense of being alone in the park.

Picking up the pace a bit, she felt her heart pound, not necessarily from jogging, but from anxiety. Of what, she had no idea, just fear of the unknown. Passing a park bench, she thought she heard a soft voice whisper, "Janet."

She slowed the pace to a walk, looking around, jogging backwards. There was no one.

"Over here," a soft voice with a southern accent demanded.

Janet turned towards the park, looking for the voice. At that exact moment, a figure stepped out from behind a large tree that was next to the bench. Then another appeared out of no where. It was then that she recognized the men who were on their bikes that had passed her previously.

The first figure quickly stepped forward, frightening Janet. The next thing she knew, without warning, she was hit squarely on the nose by one of the men wearing a leather glove.

Now, there were three of them. She struggled with all her might as they dragged her off the dimly-lit path, into the bushes. She tried to scream, but one of them had her by the throat, his other hand around her mouth.

Her powerful legs caught one of the men in the groin, sending him to the ground reeling with pain. Just then, one of the men hit her hard in the stomach, then in the kidneys. Another hit her full in the face.

She fought back with all her strength, but there were too many and they were to strong for her. She dimly remembered having her clothes violently torn from her body. Hands were grabbing, pulling, probing her private parts. She tried to scream, but there was no voice. The blows continued to her face and body until she lost consciousness.

The last thought she had was that she would die in a city where no one knew her. No one would miss her, and perhaps no one would ever find her.

Chapter Nine

When Janet awoke she felt no pain. It appeared that she was on a balcony overlooking a group of people gathered around this table. They were feverishly working over someone. Large, silver lights illuminated the pure white room. The people were dressed in white smocks with masks over their faces. They wore rubber gloves and worked silently, seemingly oblivious to Janet's presence.

Not wanting to bother them, yet nervous about where she was, she asked as loud as she could, "Excuse me. Could you please tell me where I am?"

No one paid any attention to her. She didn't even hear herself speak. Even though she had spoken as loud as she could, no words came out of her mouth. She had only thoughts. Panicked, Janet began to move among the people. She found that it was not necessary to walk, she just sort of…floated.

She looked at the person lying on the table. The person lying there seemed to be in very bad condition, as if she had been in an auto accident or something. The face was swollen and and was black and blue with lacerations. The medical team seemed to be concentrating on the body, however. A large incision had been made down the center of the chest, exposing the person's internal organs. Two doctors were clamping and suturing. The anesthetist had all his facilities focused on the person's vital signs.

At first, she didn't recognize the figure lying on the table, then the realization set in. It was Janet! "I'm there," she said. "I'm there... yet I'm here," she repeated to herself softly.

She looked at the television screens on the wall monitoring her life support system. The white lines on the green monitor spiked erratically. She lay on the table with her body looking like an open book. She could see her heart, her lungs, her intestines.

Looking at herself that way, lying helplessly on the table, all open and exposed, she was amazed at how calm she was, watching all those people working on her. "I'm going to die," she said to herself. "Maybe I"m already dead!"

There was no feeling of panic, no remorse, no hatred. She was calmer and more at peace with herself than she had ever been before. Her thoughts went to her husband, Brad. Her mother and father. Her work. Her whole life seemed to be reflected in her mind's eye, like a life-size, multi-faceted television screen, not flashing by as she had heard people say. The images were present all at once, like dozens of three-dimensional television pictures.

There was no remorse, no regrets, no feeling of wasted moments or misused time. Janet basked in a feeling of love and tranquility that seemed to surround her. It was if she could feel the colors she saw. It was as if she could feel her past accomplishments. She could view her total life unemotionally, without feeling. The only feeling she experienced was the warm glow of love. The feeling of love seemed to be beyond anything she had ever felt before. Total forgiveness, unconditional acceptance.

Suddenly, she felt a sharp pain in her chest. Then everything became a blur. Tranquility was replaced with panic and fear. She seemed to be falling. Falling from a great height at incredible speed.

She screamed.

She fell faster.

Multi-colored streaks of light went by as if the world were on fast forward and she was in slow motion.

*   *   *   *   *   *

"Hello, miss," a voice said from afar. "Can you hear me?"

Janet tried to open her eyes. She had great difficulty, as if her lids were secured with weights. She could see a white blur through what she imagined must be tiny slits in her eyes. She blinked and tried to open the eyes again, but all she could do was open them a tiny amount. The weights of her eyelids would not let them open any more.

"Hi," a soft feminine voice said. "I'm Doctor Talman, Carol Talman. You've been in an accident," she said slowly, as if speaking to a child. "You're in San Francisco General Hospital. Can you understand me?"

Janet tried to speak, but only a slight squeak sounded. She tried to swallow. It was too difficult. She was beginning to be aware of an intense pain. The pain enveloped her entire body like a thousand little knives cutting her apart. She tried to cry, but even that was too painful. She felt like a prisoner in her own body!

"If you can hear me, squeeze my hand," the voice said.

Janet felt the soft warm touch of a woman's hand, gently squeezing her hand. She could feel the warm healing powers radiating from the doctor's hand to her own. Janet gently squeezed back.

She felt The Doctor's hand on her forehead, gently caressing her brow. "You're going to be all right honey. You hang on in there. I am going to take care of you. Just rest and don't worry about a thing. I'll be right here by your side."

Janet slipped back into the black security of unconsciousness. She dreamt of babbling brooks running through a mountain meadow where deer and birds lived in harmony. There was a soft, cool breeze in the air. The world was simple and uncomplicated. She didn't want to leave.

When she woke up, she had no conception of how long she had been asleep. The only thing that she was immediately aware of was the intense pain radiating throughout her body…pain that was so intense it seemed unbearable. She tried to scream, but the only sound she could make was muffled gurgles originating somewhere deep in her throat, and even that hurt. She struggled to move her arms, but was unable to do so. They were tied to the sides of the bed!

She didn't know how long she cried, or even if she cried at all. She lapsed back into unconsciousness and the pain subsided.

* * * * * *

"How are we feeling today, honey?"

It was the voice of an angel. She remembered that warm radiant touch. Janet tried to open her eyes. After blinking a few times, she began to focus on the figure in front of her. The figure was a tall, very pleasant looking woman with a large smile. Her light brown wavy hair hung loose around her shoulders, matching her soft brown eyes.

Holding her hand, the doctor said, "Hi. I'm Dr. Talman, Carol Talman. How are we today?"

Janet opened her eyes as much as she could. The image of Dr. Talman slowly came into focus. Janet tried to smile, but her lips felt like two leather shoe tongues rubbing against sand.

Understanding, Dr. Talman put a moist cloth to her lips. The feeling was heavenly. Janet blinked her eyes in thankful acknowledgement. She tried to speak, but still there was no sound. She looked deep into Dr. Talman's eyes, trying to find the reason she was there.

Her eyes slowly focused on the back wall behind the doctor. There were no pictures, no curtains in the windows—just a television screen with green wavy lines running through the monitor. She strained to turn her head. At the side of the bed were more television screens, some with wavy lines running through them; others had moving irregular spike lines. Next to her bed were several bottles of fluid, hanging upside down with tubes running from the bottom of the bottles to her bed.

Understanding her fear and confusion, still holding her hand, Dr. Talman repeated the words she had spoken earlier. She said slowly, "You've been in an accident. The police found you and brought you to the emergency room. Do you have any recollection of what happened to you?"

Panic seized her senses. "Hospital! Police brought me here! What happened to me! Why am I here?" she thought to herself. Her eyes showed a mixture of horror and fear.

Carol Talman had seen this look many times before. It was not uncommon for a patient to go into shock upon learning that they had been in a severe accident or that something had happened to them which had resulted in their being admitted to the emergency room of a strange hospital. Usually, the injured party has no immediate recollection of the cause of their being there.

"Do you remember anything at all?" Dr. Talman asked Janet again. "Can you tell me what happened?"

Janet slowly shook her head. What was she doing here? Why was she here? She wanted to go home. Tears began rolling down her cheeks as Dr. Talman gently blotted them away with a tissue.

"Can you tell me your name?" Dr. Talman asked again.

Janet looked up at the woman in horror. My name! They don't even know who I am. She was in a panic now. Struggling to get loose, she found that her hands were still tied to the side of the bed with gauze bandages.

"We had to be sure that you didn't take the intravenous tubes out of your arms while you were sleeping," Doctor Talman said. "Here, let me undo them for you."

Janet was grateful to be let loose. She tried to move her arms, but found that any movement was extremely painful.

"You've come through quite an ordeal," Dr Talman said. "You've had internal bleeding, bruised internal organs, a collapsed lung, and a brain concussion." She paused for a moment, still holding her hand. "You obviously have a strong will to live," she said admiringly. "That, coupled with your being in good physical condition, saved your life. You're lucky to be here, "she said, patting Janet on the arm. "You get some rest now. I'll be back in a little while. The pain medicine I have prescribed will keep your discomfort to a minimum. You need lots of rest and sleep. We'll talk later."

Janet closed her eyes, welcoming the sleep that soon overcame her.

She had no idea how much time had elapsed, but was awakened by someone changing the sheets on her bed…while she was in it! First they changed one side of the bed, then carefully picked her up and put her on the side they had just changed and did the other half. The pain of being lifted from one side of the bed to the other was excruciating. She found that she could make audible sounds as she protested what she felt was harsh treatment. The orderlies had heard such protests many times a day, however, and more or less ignored her.

"Sorry, honey. This will only take a moment," the large black lady in a white uniform said.

The ordeal left her exhausted. Then Dr. Talman entered the room. "How are we doing?" she inquired in a cheerful voice.

Janet looked at her and smiled thinly. "Better," she said through swollen lips. It sounded like she had a mouth full of marbles.

"We need to talk, honey, if you're up to it," Dr. Talman said.

Janet slowly nodded.

LOST WOMAN

"Can you tell us your name?"

She paused for a moment, as if thinking. "Janet. Janet Neilson," she said, looking up at Dr. Talman.

"Good. Now, Janet, can you tell us where you live? Is there anyone we need to call that might be worried about you? You've been here for a week now, and if you have family, a husband, or mother and father that we should notify, tell me and I'll take care of it."

Again Janet paused. She closed her eyes. "A week! I have been in the hospital a week! What will the office think? What will Brad think?" She gave the Doctor names and telephone numbers of Brad, her mother, and the office.

"Now, Janet, can you remember what happened to you before you were brought to the hospital?"

Janet paused, searching her mind for an answer. She shook her head. She didn't remember anything at all.

"What's the last thing you remember?"

"Getting off an airplane in San Francisco." Pausing, she said, "That's all I remember. What happened to me?" She looked up with tears welling up in her eyes.

"We don't know for sure. You were found unconscious, nude, badly beaten, and bleeding in Golden Gate Park. Your clothes were found in the bushes but there was no identification in them. You were found by a couple of joggers in the park who called the police. An ambulance brought you here. Do you remember any of that?"

Janet shook her head and closed her eyes, tears rolling down her face. "I'm scared. Am I going to die?"

"Not as long as you have me by your side, honey," Carol said, squeezing her hand. "Now, you get some rest. We'll talk again later."

"Doctor," Janet said as the doctor opened the door to leave. "Was I…" she choked back her tears, "Was I raped?"

"You're exhausted and your body has been through a tremendous ordeal. I don't think we should talk anymore just now. I know there are a lot of unanswered questions, both for you and for me, but for now let's get some rest, and we'll hit it again tomorrow. What you do say? Okay?" she said, stroking Janet's forehead with her hand.

Janet smiled up at the doctor, nodding her head, saying, "Thanks for everything." Exhausted, she fell into a deep sleep with a few moments.

The next few days were filled with dietetic technicians trying to get her system back on solid food, physical therapists working her muscles, nurses taking blood samples, while others took periodic electrocardiograms. It was difficult for her to get a decent period of rest without one interruption or another.

One day Janet Dr. Talman was in the room by herself. "There's a small matter that's been bothering me ever since I became conscious. I need to know… I have to have the answer."

"I'm all yours, my dear, ask away," she said with a smile, knowing the question that was to follow.

"Do you remember, when I first woke up and you asked me if I remembered anything? When I said I didn't, you told me I was found beaten and…well I asked you if I was raped at the time, but we never got to finish the conversation. Would you tell me…when I came here and you examined me…was I? I mean, was I raped?"

Dr. Talman closed the door and walked to the side of Janet's bed. Caressing her hand with her thumb while holding it tightly. She said, "Yes, Janet, you were raped. It seems that who ever beat you wasn't satisfied with just giving you physical punishment. For one reason or another, they apparently wanted to add insult to injury by raping you, too. According to the semen extracted from you, the indication is there was more than one person was involved."

"Oh! Oh my God." She sobbed uncontrollably.

Dr. Talman bent over and put her head next to Janet's, holding her tightly. "That's Okay, honey. Let it out. Go ahead and cry. It's all right."

Janet sobbed uncontrollably for a few minutes, then, as suddenly as she had started, she stopped. Wiping the tears from her eyes with the back of her hand, she said aloud, "What if I get pregnant? What will Brad think? Oh God, what will Brad say when he finds out?" she said, looking up at Dr. Talman as if expecting an answer.

"You'll work it out, Janet. Whatever comes in the future, you will work it out. As to your getting pregnant, it's hospital policy to administer a drug that would prevent such an occurrence, especially in cases of rape when the patient is unable to give an immediate response themselves. There's always an outside chance of a pregnancy, however, but that's so remote that it isn't worth worrying about at this point, so don't think about that now. As for your husband," she said, looking Janet in the eyes, "it all depends upon how strong your marriage was before this happened. I've seem marriages get unbelievably strong in the face adversity, and others just fall apart at the seams from lack of inner strength. Now, you get some sleep, young lady," she said with a smile as she dried Janet's tears.

Janet looked up into those warm brown eyes of Dr. Talman and smiled back. "Oh, Dr. Talman?… does my husband have to know about… you know…about the rape?" she asked hesitatingly.

"No, Janet, I'll leave that up to you to deal with as you see fit."

"Thank you. I really appreciate your kindness. Good night." Janet drifted off into a fitful sleep.

A few days later, she was visited by Detective Larry Logan of the San Francisco police department. "Mrs. Neilson. Do you mind if I ask you some questions?"

Detective Logan was a rugged-looking, six-foot-four-inch, blond-haired Scandinavian with a bushy blond mustache. "Are you up to a few questions?" he repeated.

"I think so."

"I understand you don't remember what happened to you the night they brought you in here, is that correct?"

"Yes, sir."

"You have no recollection at all?"

"Detective, aside from what I've been told by Dr. Talman there and others, I don't have a clue as to what happened to me. I wish I did, but maybe it's for the best. Sorry."

"That's to be expected. If your memory ever comes back, you be sure to give me a call, you hear?"

"Right."

"Now, with the help of your office and Mr. Danielson, your boss, we were able to trace your arrival to San Francisco, when you checked into the Stanford Hotel but... everything after that seems to be a blank. Do you remember checking in at the Stanford Hotel—Room 226?" He looked at the notebook he carried in his pocket.

After pausing, Janet said, "Yes, now that you mention it, I do remember that. I remember being picked up at the airport by a Mr. Nicholas Francisco. He checked me into the hotel, then we went to work."

"Did you check out of the hotel, Miss Neilson?"

"I don't think so...I can't remember."

"Did you leave your belongings at the hotel prior to going on to work with Mr. Francisco?"

"Why, yes. I checked in, left my suitcase in my room before proceeding on with Mr. Francisco. Why do you ask?"

"Well, when the clerk let us in your room, there wasn't any evidence to show that you had ever been there. There wasn't a single item in the room that belonged to you."

"Nothing?" Janet said, wide-eyed.

"Not even a bobbie pin."

"Well...what happened to my clothes? My briefcase? My briefcase! Oh my God. Danielson's going to kill me. The stuff in my briefcase was highly confidential. The whole Paragon deal could be in jeopardy." Janet was beginning to show definite signs of stress.

"I think you had better leave now, detective," Dr. Talman said. "Janet needs her rest. She's still weak from the operation and her system is just beginning to cope with the ordeal."

"No...no, I'll be all right," Janet insisted, holding up her hand. "I'm sorry. I just got a little carried away. Please stay. Tell me what happened to my briefcase and all. I need to know. It's very important."

"I'm sorry, I don't know. I thought maybe you could tell me. Was there some special significance about the briefcase that would shed some light on the reason you were attacked?"

Janet hesitated for a moment, as if trying to decide if she should say anything. "I was sent here, to San Francisco, on an important assignment from my office in Portland. The documents in my briefcase were confidential relative to an important transaction my firm was handling. If they fell into the wrong hands, it could be disastrous. It could endanger the whole project."

"I'll send over a stenographer tomorrow, when you're stronger, and you can relay, in as much detail as you can recall, the contents of your briefcase. If you feel it was so sensitive, there may be a clue there as to the motive for your attack. Your purse and all your identification are also missing, along with the rest of your goods. If you can remember the contents of your purse or wallet, it would be helpful. There might be something there that would give us a clue as to where to start looking for your assailants."

"I always take my fanny pack with me when I jog," she said, "just in case I need identification or something."

"Fanny pack?"

"Yeah. You know. That belt that people wear when they go out and don't want to carry their personal items in a handbag."

"Did you have any valuables with you the night of your attack?"

"Not much. A few dollars in cash. The only other things of value were my watch and wedding ring which I never leave." She quickly looked at her finger for her wedding band. It was still there. Throughout this whole ordeal, she had never thought to look to see if she still had it on. Her watch was missing, however.

"Any credit cards?"

"The usual. A Shell card, Visa, Versatile card, several identification cards. That's about all. Oh, I did have my check book, from Oregon National Bank."

"Did you have any money in the account?"

"A few thousand dollars."

"Well, we'll start with those items and take it from there. If you could remember any of the names, telephone numbers, and addresses of who to contact for additional information about your credit cards or bank account numbers, it would be of great help."

Standing up, detective Logan said, "Well, that's about it for now. I guess I'll be on my way," he said, setting the clipboard on the stand next to her bed.

As Detective Logan was about to leave, he paused, turned around, and said, "By the way, whatever happened to this Mr. Francisco?"

"I don't know. I suppose when I didn't show up the next day, he probably thought I had left town."

"Has he been in contact with the hospital?" he asked Dr. Talman.

"To my knowledge, except those names I gave you previously, no one has made any inquiry about her."

"Strange," Logan said, shutting the door behind him.

Two weeks after Janet was admitted to the hospital, bruised, battered, and unconscious, she was fit enough to be dismissed. She was still in pain, showing some physical tell-tale signs of her ordeal, such as deep circles under her eyes and a noticeable limp as she walked, but glad to be leaving. Carol Talman was at the check out desk to greet her. Janet looked into her deep brown eyes and gave her a big, long hug, kissing her on the cheek.

"Thanks a lot for everything. I couldn't have made it without you." Her eyes were moist as she squeezed Carol Talman's hand.

Janet hugged Carol one last time and turned to Brad, who had been with her at the hospital since being notified by Detective Larry Logan.

"Let's go, pal," Brad said. "I'm going to take care of you from now on."

"I like that," she said, slipping her arm around his waist as he put his arm around her. Looking back over her shoulder, Dr. Talman waved and gave Janet a wink. Janet sighed, knowing her secret was safe. Now maybe she could get her life back in order. "Sometimes it takes a tragedy to bring people together," she thought to herself, laying her head on Brad's shoulder.

Chapter Ten

This was their first night home together since Janet's ordeal. Brad was attentive, but Janet seemed to sense an underlying emotional issue. There appeared to be a sense of detachment, maybe even a resentment that she couldn't put her finger on. *I wonder if somehow he got wind of the rape,* she wondered, but after thinking it through more thoroughly, concluded that probably wasn't the case. *Maybe he's just overcompensating for my injuries and wants to let me rest and recuperate. Yes, that's it,* she concluded.

Despite strong objections from Brad, Janet insisted on going to work the next morning. The reaction of everyone in the office was almost too overwhelming for her. The moment she walked through the office door, everyone stopped what they were doing. All eyes were upon her. Having never been the center of attention before, she felt as if she were standing naked in the entryway.

Suddenly, she was conscious of being thin and pale from the ordeal and lengthy stay at the hospital. Some of the office girls came up and hugged her with a smile. Others had tears in their eyes and were unable to speak. They all knew what she had gone through…at least a part of it. No one knew she had been raped, and she wanted to keep it that way. She knew from her experience practicing law that a rape victim was often looked upon, not necessarily as the victim, but often as either a willing participant who later changed her mind or one who "deserved it" as a result of some overt action. In any case, the end result was usually viewed as 'spoiled goods' in most people's eyes.

The men's reactions to Janet were quite different, however. Some came up and hugged her, holding her for a very long time, as if giving her a message that they were there to protect her. Others looked down, unwilling to meet her eyes, as if they shared part of the guilt simply by being a male. Others just nodded, with wiry smiles conveying distant and detached condolences, as if saying, "I feel sorry for you, but I don't want to get involved."

Steve Danielson came out of his office. Seeing Janet, he paused for a moment, then said, "What the hell are you doing here, Neilson? I strictly ordered you to take the rest of the month off and recuperate. I don't want to see your face around here—period." Having said that, he came up to her and hugged her, holding her for a long time, like some of the others. When he finally let go, he turned his head, wiping a tear from his eye. "Damn cold."

Janet grabbed him and hugged him back, unable to hold back her tears any longer. They both stood there, hugging each other for a long time, letting the emotion of the moment run between themselves, tears rolling down their cheeks. When they finally let go of one another, the whole office, who by now had surrounded them unnoticed, broke out in applause.

"Come into my office, sport," Steve said, after wiping his eyes with a handkerchief and blowing his nose. "Let's have a little chat."

Shutting the door behind him, he asked, "What really happened out there in San Francisco, Janet? Tell me the straight scoop. None of this bullshit about… you don't remember anything. I want to know what really happened. Start at the very beginning, from the time you got off the airplane at San Francisco International until you left the hospital, and don't leave out a single detail".

Janet relayed the entire chain of events as calmly and clearly as she could, as if filling out a police report. When she had finished, she concluded, "I don't have the faintest idea who attacked me, who stole all my things or... who raped me, or, for that matter, why. The more I think about it, the angrier I get. I would do anything to find those bastards, Steve, anything."

Steve sat back in his chair, hands clasped, forefingers pointing at his lips. He sat for five minutes or more, staring into space, thinking. Janet knew his razor-sharp mind was working at lightning speed and was confident he would come up with an answer. She sat quietly, letting him think, grateful for his interest.

"Tell me, Janet. You said the only time your briefcase was out of your sight was when you went to the bathroom at the restaurant at Fisherman's Wharf and when you went jogging?"

Sheepishly, Janet nodded and softly said, "Yes." She still felt guilty about the ordeal at Fisherman's Wharf. She knew she had let Steve down.

Picking up on her feelings, Steve said, "Don't blame yourself, kid. This could have happened to anyone. If anything, I blame myself for sending you down there alone. I should have known better, and I'm sorry." He patted Janet on her bowed head. "It's okey. It's not your fault."

"Do you know who did this to me...to us?" she asked.

"No, not yet, but I have a few ideas that I need time to develop. Tell you what, I want you to go home and get lots of rest. Don't worry," he said, holding up his hand as she started to protest. "I'll have your case load taken care of. You just go home and rest."

As Janet closed his door, she turned to meet Dave Moore, who was standing in the hall waiting for her. "How you doing, baby?" he said softly, taking her chin in his hand, looking her in the eye. "You know, I love you. It breaks me up to see you hurt like this. I'm here for you if you need me, okay?" He gently wrapped his arms around her, stroking her hair, kissing her on the forehead.

Janet kissed him lightly on the lips, "Thanks, Dave. I love you, too."

* * * * * *

The house was cold and empty when she got home. "Kind of like my life right now," Janet said. She was disappointed that Brad hadn't taken a little extra time off work to be with her. She could have used the moral and emotional support along with a little tender loving care.

Sitting home alone, she started thinking about the argument they'd had before she had gone to San Francisco. "Maybe he's still angry about my leaving," she said aloud to herself. Remembering his attitude and the comments he had made during his unpleasant departing scene the night before her fateful trip got her angry all over again. By the time Brad returned home at seven o'clock that evening, she had worked herself into a powder keg waiting for a spark.

She had just stepped out of a warm bath, trying to calm her nerves, when Brad walked into their bedroom. "How are you doin' there, kid? How's it feel to be on disability in the land of leisure?" he said in a sort of off-handed manner. "Feelin' better now that you've taken a nice warm bath after a long day's rest? When you get rested up, maybe you'll have time to catch up on little wifey household duties like cooking dinner for the breadwinner for a change."

The words were innocent enough, but she read something in the tone of his voice that hinted at nonchalant sarcasm with a little resentment mixed in for good measure. Dropping her robe from around her shoulders, she stood totally nude in front of Brad. Her body was marked with deep red scars still prominent from the operation she had had in San Francisco. Her bones stuck through her thin skin from lack of real food and exercise. She looked like a refugee from the German death camps.

Putting his hands to his eyes, Brad turned his head. "My God, woman, put your robe back on! Don't you have any decency!"

"Look at me, Brad. Now ask me how I feel 'kid'." The repressed rage she had felt earlier kicked in, spurred by Brad's words. "Look where they cut me open, Brad. Look at what they did to me." Brad averted his eyes, turning his head away from her. "*Look at me!*" she demanded.

Janet was full of anger and resentment. Anger because Brad appeared to have no compassion or pity for her. Resentment because he was in one piece, safe and sound, and she was marked for life. He was denying her pain and the horrible experience she had suffered. He simply wanted to sweep the experience under the rug and forget it, but Janet wasn't going to let him off that easily.

"I didn't tell you this before, Brad, but now I feel you have a right to know."

Brad turned his head as Janet put her robe on again. "What do you have to tell me that I don't already know?" he demanded with disgust.

"When I went to San Francisco, I wasn't just beaten and left for dead, Brad. Something else happened to me. Something I didn't want anyone else to know, ever, not even you! But now, seeing how broken up you are about the whole thing, I believe you deserve to know the truth."

Brad looked at her without comment.

"I was raped, Brad. The people who attacked and beat me…also raped me. Not just once, but repeatedly."

Janet was amazed at how calm she felt all of the sudden. It was as if a huge weight had been lifted from her shoulders. She could talk about it in a sort of a detached manner, as if she were talking about some other person, not herself.

"Raped?" Brad said in disbelief. "Raped!" the corners of his mouth turned down in disgust. "Why didn't you tell me this before? Why didn't you tell me those filthy pigs had you? I suppose next, you're going to tell me that you enjoy it," he snarled, putting his face close to hers.

Janet slapped him with all the strength she could muster. "You son-of-a-bitch!" She tried to hit him again, but he blocked her swing with his forearm. "Get the hell out of here," she screamed. "Get the hell out of my life!"

Brad left, slamming the bedroom door behind him, but not before taking one last long look at her.

Janet went to the door and slammed it again, so hard bottles of perfume fell from the dresser. She was so angry, she picked a bottle of perfume off the floor and, running to the open window, flung it at Brad as he stomped towards his pickup. The bottle missed him by inches.

Brad looked up and gave her the finger as his pickup squealed out of the driveway, brushing against the light pole, leaving a deep scar on the rear quarter-panel of his truck.

* * * * * *

"Mrs. Neilson?" a voice inquired over the telephone.

"Yes."

"This is Detective Larry Logan of the San Francisco police department. I spoke to you while you were here in the hospital."

"Oh, yes, Mr. Logan, what can I do for you?"

"Well, we had a streak of luck this week. An unemployed Mexican worker from Salinas was caught trying to cash one of your checks at a liquor store in San Jose yesterday." He paused, waiting for a response from Janet, who was content to just listen for the moment.

"Mrs. Neilson?"

"I'm here, Detective Logan."

"We interrogated him," the Detective continued. "He claims that he and two of his buddies were hired to find you and beat you up. The guy apparently gave 'em a case of beer and a hundred dollars each."

"Did they say who it was, who hired them or why?"

"No, he said they never saw him before, nor ever again. Apparently he drove up in what we surmise was a rental car, cut a deal with the Mexicans, then drove away, never leaving his car. The guy we caught said the man in the car told them he would be watching to be sure they did the job right. If they didn't, he said he would take care of them the same way they were supposed to have taken care of you. Apparently he was convincing enough to have the thugs do the job, not just take his money and run."

Janet hesitated for a moment. "And did you ask him... did you ask him about the...the rape? Did the man tell them to rape me?"

"At first he denied raping you, but when we told him we had semen samples that could tie him to the rape and he could be facing life in prison if he didn't cooperate, he became a willing witness. Apparently the only instructions given to them were not to kill you, just work you over good. Actually, the word he used was "to discourage you". Apparently, everything was left to their discretion."

"What about the other two?"

"We have an A.P.B.—All Points Bulletin—out for them, but to tell you the truth, it's really hard to catch these migrant Mexican workers. They're always on the move and never have a permanent address. They usually work for cash and never report anything to the authorities. And to tell you the truth, once you've seen thousands of these guys, they all seem to blend together—their clothes, mannerisms, you know. No one ever seems to pay much attention to them. Our chance of catching them is probably less than one in a thousand. To be perfectly honest, I doubt if we'll ever see them again, unless we accidently catch them like this one, making a stupid mistake,"

"Did he have any of my papers on him?"

"Nothing. Just the blank checks. We asked him about the stuff in your room. He said he didn't even know you had a room. I tend to believe him. At this stage, something as trivial as that compared to the possible rape charge he faces would tend to indicate that he has nothing to gain by lying to us. No, whoever removed the contents of your room was someone entirely different than our Mexican friend."

"What now?" Janet inquired somewhat reluctantly.

"I need you to identify this man in order to make the case stick. Once the Legal Aid attorney gets involved, without a positive I.D., we lose him."

"I'm sorry, Detective. I still don't remember a single thing about that night, aside from what I've already told you. He could be standing next to me right now and I wouldn't recognize him. My mind is a total blank when it comes to that night. I really would like to help, but...nothing. Sorry."

"Perhaps if you saw the man, it might trigger something in your mind. Something might come back to you."

"I really don't want to fly to San Francisco, Mr. Logan. I don't want to go through that again. I'm sorry." Janet hung up the telephone.

Shortly after Detective Logan's call, Steve Danielson called. "Janet, Steve here. I just got off the phone with a Detective Logan of the San Francisco Police Department."

"Yeah, he called me earlier," Janet said. "What did he want from you?"

"He just called to tell me that they had a suspect in custody who they think was responsible for your... you know. You should try to go to San Francisco, Janet. Maybe we can get to the bottom of this mess. I want to know what, why, and especially who is responsible for this almost as much as you."

"Sorry, Steve. I have no desire to go back to that city, ever. And even if I did go, I can't remember anything, anyway. So what's the point?"

"Tell you what, if you don't want to go, I understand. Considering all you've been through. Let me have Logan fax up a picture of this dude to look at, anyway, and if it jogs your memory, then we will talk about it. Okay?"

"Okay."

"Good girl. Now tell you what, I've been doing some thinking. How would you like to join me in a little witch hunt of our own? Just you and me. I've hatched a little plan I think will flush our guy out and, at the same time, hang him by his balls until they drop off. You in?"

"You bet your sweet ass I'm in. Be there in an hour."

Chapter Eleven

Mary Lee stood five foot five. She wore her hair in soft frosted curls that framed a face radiant with a "Pepsident smile". She had a figure that no normal man in a sane state of mind could help but admire. When she smiled, the whole room lit up. She had a light bouncy laugh that filled every corner of the room wherever she went. It was near impossible not to get caught up with her easy manner. Many men have gazed upon Mary Lee for several minutes and couldn't begin to tell you the color of her eyes. They could tell you, however, that she had a very well-developed breathing apparatus—chest for the uninformed. 38 DD! And those puppies were firm as freshly- picked cantaloupes and just as large.

Mary Lee wasn't one to flaunt her wares, however. She never wore a low cut sweater or a see-through blouse. The secret of her well-developed frame lay in the imagination of the viewer. Mary Lee's motto was, "It's more sexy to wear a negligee than be nude". More men have mentally undressed and slept with Mary Lee than Carol Doda of San Francisco's North Beach fame.

It was no surprise that Nicholas Francisco nearly bit through his cigar when Mary Lee walked into his Palo Alto office looking for a place to invest the two million dollars that her dear departed had recently left in her care.

She stood a little over five-foot-five-inches. She wore a tailored, pink, pearl-beaded leather suit. The skirt tightly bound her legs, causing her to walk in quick, short steps. A set of perfectly formed pearls hung just above her breasts, accentuating their fullness.

She extended a gloved hand to Nick as she entered his office. "I heard you were an honest and straightforward man, Mr. Francisco," Mary Lee said as she sat down across from Nick, her pink skirt riding high, displaying a pair of tanned, well-developed legs. "I really don't know much about investments or anything. I'm just looking for something to invest my money in and hopefully get a return to live on. I don't need much, you see. The house, the Rolls, and Jag are all paid for. Just me and my two cats, Peaches and Peanut, live alone in that big hilltop house in Los Altos Hills, now that Harry has passed on, God bless his soul." She dabbed at her eyes with a pink lace hankie.

Pausing to look at Nick through soulful eyes, she inquired in a soft voice, "Do you think you could help me, Mr. Francisco? I would be ever so grateful." Mary Lee looked at Nick Francisco as if he were an ice cream cone in the middle of the Sahara Desert. Nick could feel himself melting in the hands of this Venus with arms.

An uncontrollable urge was welling within his shorts. He moved sideways to avoid detection. With a slight flush, he said, "It would be a shame to let a damsel in distress go without my professional assistance." He reached out to stroke her hand. "Investments are my specialty, and helping attractive young ladies is my pleasure."

"I have a feeling this is going to be the beginning of a beautiful relationship," Mary Lee said, stroking Nick's outstretched hands with her fingers.

Nick instantly fell in love beyond his wildest dreams. Mary Lee had walked into his life with a smile that would put most women to shame, a body that wouldn't quit, two million in cash and a free and clear home worth at least another two million. This was too good to be true. Lady luck smiled on Nicholas Francisco today, and good fortune was sitting on his shoulder.

Nick led her to his lush office, where he sat behind a large, glass-topped walnut desk shaped like a half moon, with a telephone on either corner. Massive sculpture pieces sat on marble pedestals at either corner of the room. One was a piece with two men wrestling and the other was a sculpture of an athlete in the process of throwing the hammer. A computer and lazar printer was on the matching walnut credenza behind him. One wall was lined with a matching walnut bookcase filled with legal and real estate books. Numerous plaques, trophies, pictures of himself with various signed photos of people holding golf clubs and framed certificates of achievement adorned the shelves and surrounding walls as well. The heavy, dark-walnut plank floor was tastefully accented with colorful Oriental rugs. A San Francisco FM radio station playing soft music was piped through wall mounted picture speakers. The flashy ambience gave the impression of a showman more than a sophisticated real estate man's office.

Nick spent the next hour gaping at Mary Lee's abundant breasts while taking down information such as the type of investments she might be interested in looking at, what income did she need, her living expenses, lifestyle, and so on. He managed to skillfully slip in a few personal questions intermittently, such as what does she do with her spare time and weekends now that she's alone, what does she see the future holding for her, and how is her social life?

At the end of the interview, Nick had a pretty clear picture of Mary Lee's lifestyle. He also had every inch of her body implanted in his brain's memory bank.

Seeing a golden opportunity in the making, and not being prone to let such a situation pass, Nick wasted no time inviting Mary Lee out to dinner that night to further discuss her financial situation, Away from the telephone and other bothersome distractions. "This way, I can give you my undivided attention."

Mary Lee touched Nick's left hand again, twirling the gold band on his ring finger. "And the little woman?" she inquired with an impish smile and teasing voice.

"Aw, it's okay. She understands that business comes first. Anyway, we don't have much going these days. It gets kind of old after so many years. You know how it is." He wrinkled his nose. "It's gotten to be more of an 'understanding' between us, if you know what I mean," he said softly with a wink.

"Well, I do have to be in the city this Friday to clear up some legal matters with my attorney," she said, putting her finger to her lips as if thinking. "Perhaps you could meet me then, say at the Fairmont? Around eight o'clock in the evening? I usually stay in the city when I'm here late. I just hate driving home in the dark. There are so many crazies around these days. A single girl just isn't safe alone anymore, is she?" she said, lowering her head, fluttering her eyelashes at Nick.

"Oh, you'll be safe with me. Plenty safe. I know how to take care of my women—I mean, I know how to take care of myself if I have to," he quickly corrected himself.

"I like a man who knows how to be a man," Mary Lee said seductively, running her hands up and down Nick's arm, pulling it close to her body.

She had Nick glassy-eyed and purring like a kitten when she finally left his office. Just before closing the door after, she looked over her shoulder with a wink. If there was one thing Mary Lee had learned throughout her thirty-five years as a woman, it was how to play a man like a violin, especially an older married man hungry for a little affection.

Friday, Mary Lee called Nick at his office at four o'clock, reaffirming that she would be staying at the Fairmont Hotel, in the Francisco Suite. She would meet him there instead of in the lobby. "I do detest crowds," she cooed. "And if he would be so kind as to call for her at eight. And don't be late," she teased.

Nick could feel his loins rising to the occasion already. The balance of the day was virtually shot as far a business was concerned. The only thing Nick Francisco had on his mind was Mary Lee, specifically Mary

Lee's body. He was so mesmerized by the thought of seeing her alone that he nearly forgot the reason for the meeting. He scampered through sales brochures and other broker's listings, looking for various real estate investments to demonstrate that he had spent a great deal of time working on her financial problem.

At eight sharp, briefcase in hand, freshly showered and groomed, smelling like a cologne factory, Nick rang the gold bell at the Francisco Suite. A tall, attractive Latin girl dressed in a maids uniform answered the door.

"Yes, may I help you?" she said with a deep, sultry French accent.

"I'm calling for Miss Mary Lee. Nick Francisco."

"Who is it, Marie?"

"A Mr. Nick Francisco, ma'am."

"Oh, yes. Thank you. Please show him in. And that will be all for tonight, Marie. Good night."

Marie, hat and coat in hand, closed the door behind her without comment.

"Nick?"

"Yes."

"Nick. Why don't you make yourself comfortable. Pour yourself a drink if you like. The bar is behind the louvered doors to your left. I'll be out in a moment."

The bar was amply stocked with scotch, Jack Daniels, Wild Turkey, the best of every brand flanked by leaded crystal goblets. "Now this is what I call living!" Nick looked around the room. The carpet was a plush, soft peach. Oak paneling came partway up the wall, accented with a marbleized wall covering that took on the appearance of real marble. The room was lit by soft golden lights emanating from a large crystal chandelier hanging in the middle of a vaulted sculptured ceiling. The furniture was covered with a soft, tufted silk fabric that easily gave way to the hand.

"Quality. Nothing but the best." Nick mused aloud.

"See anything you like?" a soft sultry voice asked.

Nick turned. Standing in the dimly lit doorway was Mary Lee. The light behind her was just bright enough so, from Nick's vantage point, all he could see was the outline of her figure standing sideways in the doorway. Nick's pulse quickened and his hand quivered as he drank in the vision standing before him.

Mary Lee walked into the room wearing a light chiffon evening gown with pink feathers around her neck. The gown was loosely tied around her waist, covering what appeared to be a sheer nightgown. She had on pink glass slippers, pink sheer stockings that glittered as she walked, and a crystal necklace with teardrop earrings to match. Soft music from ceiling speakers completed the scene.

"I took the liberty of ordering dinner to be delivered at my suite, Mr. Francisco. I hope you don't mind," she said in a soft voice. "I do hate to go out in the cold evening air when we could spend our time…more efficiently and…enjoyably right here."

"Mind? No, not at all. Not at all."

Dinner was served on fine Franciscan China by a gentleman dressed in a black tailored suit. His manners were impeccable. He spoke only French to Mary Lee, inquiring about the serving and portions for each person. After he'd served dinner and poured each a glass of full-bodied, red French wine, Mary Lee dismissed him. Nick was very impressed. If this was how the rich lived, he wanted to be a part of it, at any cost.

After dinner and two bottles of wine, most of which was consumed by Nick Francisco, they retired to the sitting room.

"Could I entice you with a little dessert, Mr. Francisco?"

"You've got to be kidding," he said, unbuttoning his vest, sitting back with both arms resting outstretched on top of the couch. "That was the best meal I have ever had, and boy, am I stuffed! I couldn't eat another thing if my life depended upon it."

LOST WOMAN

"No dessert? Not even a little nibble?" She cooed. She sat back, letting the string that held her nightgown together fall loose.

Nick looked at her scantily-covered breasts for what seemed an eternity. Finally catching himself, he looked into her eyes. She leaned forward slightly, pouting her lips, and closed her eyes.

This was it! Nick's heart was beating so hard, he feared he might have a heart attack. He kissed her softly at first, then forced his lips on hers so hard she thought they would break.

Putting the palms of her hands firmly on his chest, gently breaking herself free, she said, "Not here. Let's go where we can be more comfortable."

She led Nick to a huge circular bed perched upon a two-tier pedestal with a canopy overhead. Mary Lee slowly, gently, seductively, took off his shoes, jacket, vest, and pants. When he was undressed, she gently laid him on the bed where the silk comforter had already been pulled back, exposing four king size pillows.

"You like to do things in a grand fashion, don't you?" Nick said, looking into her eyes.

"Everything I do is in a grand fashion," she said, nibbling on Nick's ear.

Nick removed the nightgown from her shoulders, letting it drop to the tier below. Putting his finger under the strap of her nightie, he slipped it from one shoulder, then the other, exposing the greatest pair of firm breasts he had ever laid eyes on. They greatly exceeded his every expectation. He devoured them with his eyes, then his hands, and finally his lips.

Francisco gently laid Mary Lee down on the bed, pulling himself on top of her. She put a finger to his lips and said, "First, a little precaution."

"Aw, you don't have to worry about me." Nick said. "I'm a married family man, clean as pure-driven snow. Besides, I never wear those things. It's…it's like taking a shower with my boots on. Takes all the fun away."

"You don't mind indulging me a little, now do you? After all, it's for both of our benefits." She tickled his chin with her finger. "Come on now, you want me to enjoy myself, too, don't you? No worries, no fears…no regrets." Putting her nose next to his, she said with a smile, "Okay?"

"Okay. Just this once. Anything to please you," he said with a smile. In reality, Nick was so obsessed with having Mary Lee, he would have hung from the chandelier by his toes if she had asked him to do so.

When they were through making love, Nick fell into a deep sleep. The wine, food, and lovemaking was all his system, and brain for that matter, could handle for one evening.

He was awakened the next morning by a knock on the door. "Maid service. Hello. Anyone here? Maid service."

Nick stuck his head through the partially opened bedroom door. "Can you come back in an hour? I'm just getting up," he said, looking around the suite for Mary Lee. "Oh, by the way, do you know the whereabouts of Miss Lee? She doesn't seem to be here just now. I guess she left before I woke up," he said sheepishly, looking at the bewildered maid.

"Miss Lee, sir? Sorry, all I know is that the room is rented at one o'clock to another party. Check out time was eleven. Please hurry. I need to get in here and prepare the suite for the next guest."

"What time is it?" he said, looking at his watch. "Twelve! Holy smoke. I've got to get out of here! I'm supposed to meet my wife in half an hour. You say you don't know if Miss Lee checked out?"

"Sorry, sir. I don't show a Miss Lee on my ledger. Perhaps you can check at the front desk."

"Never mind. I'll be out of here in ten minutes."

Putting on his pants with one hand and holding the telephone with the other, he dialed his home. "Shirley? Shirley, you'll never guess who I ran into last night," he said with a nervous laugh. "Remember my old roommate from college? Roger Wilde? Well, he just dropped in the office unannounced yesterday and, well, we had a few beers, started talking about old times, when all of a sudden, I couldn't believe where the time went…Shirley? Hello, Shirley."

"Damn, she hung up on me!"

Chapter Twelve

"Mr. Francisco? This is Janet. Janet Neilson. Remember me?"

"Janet! Why…I'm surprised to hear from you. The last time you were here…you disappeared all at once. I didn't know what to think, and then later, I heard about your misfortune. I don't know what to say. So unfortunate," he said nervously. "I really feel badly about what happened. Then I heard you were all right. You are okay aren't you?"

"Oh, yes. Yes, I'm just fine, thank you. A bit of an unfortunate turn of events, to be sure. No need to feel badly, though. It certainly wasn't your fault…was it? Actually, I blame myself as well as anyone. Stupid of me to go jogging alone at night that way. Well, no real damage done. Just a few bruises is all. I'm young and healthy. Onward and upward, so they say," she said with a lighthearted tone.

"Then you weren't hurt that bad? I mean, you're all right? No real damage?" His voice sounded concerned.

"No. Not really. I'm fine. Just fine. Say, Nick, the reason for my call is Mr. Danielson has asked me to complete another assignment for him. Real estate again. Right up your alley, of course. He speaks so highly of you. Thinks you're the best thing since buttered popcorn when it comes to real estate."

"Well, that's nice of him to say. I always do my best for the firm. We go back a long way, you know. We've made a lot of money together. No sense breaking the daisy chain now, is there?" he said with a light laugh.

"No, I suppose not. Say, Nick, I was wondering if I might impose on you to pick me up at the San Francisco Airport again. I'm flying in on the early flight with Air Cal tomorrow. Danielson's got me looking at a hotel that a client might want to buy. Could be a chance for you to pick up a nice fee. What's your share of a ten million dollar deal? Three percent or so? That works out to a little over a quarter of a million dollars. Could buy a few rounds of golf. You may even consider getting yourself one of those high end cars you keep talking about you don't like."

"Sounds great to me. Who knows, that could be the deal that changes my life." He laughed.

"I'm sure it will, Nick. I'm sure it will. See you tomorrow, then," she said as she hung up the phone.

Danielson winked at Janet. "You're nasty. Remind me to never get on the wrong side of you."

"Yeah, just you wait until I get you on the racquetball court. I'm going to get my sweet revenge then." She smiled.

* * * * * *

Francisco was waiting for Janet at the arrival gate. "Hi there. Good to see you again," he said in his usual easy manner. "Have a good flight?"

"Uneventful. As long as the plane goes up on time and down at the appointed spot with no surprises in between, I'm happy."

"Luggage? Did you bring any luggage?"

"No, just my briefcase and this overnight bag. No jogging outfit this time."

"Well, where should we go first? I assume you're staying overnight. Want to freshen up first or just get right to work?"

"Tell you what, Nick. I could use a little freshening up, if you don't mind. Why don't you drop me off at the Stanford Hotel. I'll be just a few minutes, and then we'll be off to work."

"The Stanford Hotel? I'm surprised you still want to stay there, considering your last experience and all."

"Oh, think nothing of it. It's kind of like riding a horse. You know, once you fall off, if you don't get right back on, you may never ride again. I figure that was a fluke accident, my being there in the park at night, alone and all. Kind of stupid, when you think back on it with a clear head."

"Sure you wouldn't like to check in somewhere else? How about letting me take you to the Mark Hopkins or the Fairmont? I'll even treat," he said with a nervous laugh. "You can't beat that, now can you?"

"No thanks, Nick. The Stanford will do. Besides, I already have reservations. Paid by the firm and all. Wouldn't want to waste their money, now would we?"

Nick pulled in front of the office and waited for Janet to return. "Okay. All checked in. Room 226. Right around the corner."

Nick looked disturbed. "Isn't that the same room you were in the last time you were here?"

"Why yes, I guess it is. I'm impressed that you remember, Nick." She smiled as she tugged at his coat sleeve. "Like I said, when you fall off the horse, better get right back on again. Would you be a dear and help me with my overnight case?"

"Sure. Sure thing. Happy to oblige," he said stiffly.

Opening the door, she said, "Well, here we are." Motioning with her hand, she said, "Come on in for a moment. I won't be but a minute."

"No. I'll just wait in the car, if you don't mind."

"Aw, come on in. I won't bite. Besides, I have something to show you. You won't want to miss this. I promise," she said with an impish smile.

"Well, if you insist. I guess it can't hurt, now can it?" He said somewhat nervously.

"Be with you in just a moment, Nick. Make yourself comfortable," Janet said from the bathroom.

A moment later, Janet came out of the bathroom, wearing only a bra and panties. She walked over to where Nick was seated at the round gaming table. The scars from her operation were still highly visible, standing out in bright red welts, as if outlined by a felt marking pen.

"What! What is this? What are you doing?" Nick asked, raising out of the chair, backing up to the wall, half startled and half angry.

"I thought you might like to see the results of your handiwork, up close, kind of a like a private showing, you know," she said walking up to him with a firm look on her face.

"I don't know what you're talking about. I'm getting out of here. This is disgusting." The corners of his mouth turned down displaying anger and disgust.

"It's all right Nick. There's no one here. Just you and me. You see, I finally figured it out. You were dying to find out why I was here on the Paragon assignment. You've made a lot of money on those people. When you thought there might be a deal in the making that could make you rich, or conversely, ace you out of a fee, especially considering the financial bind you're in, curiosity got the better of you and you just had to know.

"That's when you took my briefcase when I went to the powder room at Tarantino's."

"You're out of your mind, woman. Crazy. You've lost it, and now you're grabbing at straws."

"When you opened my briefcase," Janet continued without losing a beat, "your worst nightmare was confirmed. You knew the Paragon deal had a time clock ticking, and if you could interrupt that clock by, say, delaying my work, the deal would fall through and you would be back in business." Janet smiled, walking in front of Nick.

"Well, Nick, it might have worked, except the cops picked up one of your henchmen trying to cash one of the checks taken from the fanny pack that I was carrying that night. And guess what? He I.D.'d you. Put his finger right on your picture."

"You little bitch. You're bluffing. If what you say is true, why haven't the cops arrested me? Why am I still running loose?" he said nervously, looking around.

"Real simple, Nick. It's a matter of pride. The Paragon group can't afford any adverse publicity, or their stock would plunge, and everyone in the company would be hurt. So, you see, you lucked out and fell between the cracks of the floor, just like a bug. The big foot of the law missed you, Nick, but I didn't."

"If you are so fuckin' smart, how come you got the balls to come back and face me!"

"I just had to see your face one more time. I couldn't believe I was taken in by such a sleazeball. Too bad the goons from New York didn't finish the job on you when they had the chance."

"You skinny little slut." Nick swung his fist hard, hitting Janet firmly on the cheekbone below her eye. Blood trickled from a cut.

"I'm going to finish what those greaseballs started. I should have had them kill you instead of just mess you up a little."

Nick pulled out a pearl handled switch blade and started for Janet. She tipped a chair over to block his path, screamed, and ran for the bathroom door, locking it behind her. Nick kicked at the door, but the solid oak door would not give.

Just then, Danielson rushed through the front door, holding a .38 caliber pistol with both hands, aiming it at Francisco's head.

"You're through, Francisco. I'm glad I finally found out what a slimeball you really are. You can bet your bottom dollar I'll do my best to have your license revoked and you carried out of the state on a rail, tarred and feathered."

"Big talk. The dummy there already spilled the beans. You can't touch me without shaking up the Paragon group. The skinny one there can thank her lucky stars you showed up before I made fish bait out of her. Next time, I won't be so generous. I might even take a poke at her skinny ass myself. I always did like a stray piece of ass." He laughed and slammed the door behind him.

"Stage one completed with perfection," Danielson said as Janet emerged from the bathroom in a robe. "Ready for act two?"

"Watch, and you shall see," Janet said, dabbing the blood from her cheek with the bed sheet.

"Are you going to be all right? I had every intention of getting in here before anything happened to you."

"Hey, I couldn't be better. You better get out of here before someone sees you."

Danielson quickly left the room, taking one last look at Janet. It was the first time he had seen her marked body. He gnashed his teeth as his eyes revealed the pain she must have felt.

Janet picked up the phone and dialed 911.

"Police Emergency."

"My name is Janet Neilson. I'm in room 226 of the Stanford Hotel. I've just been beaten and raped. Could you please send someone over right away?"

"Do you need an ambulance? Are you badly injured?"

"I think I'm okay. I'm beaten up a little and probably should see a doctor, but I don't think anything is broken. Please send someone over as soon as possible. I'm scared, and he might come back."

"Someone will be there shortly. Is there anyone else with you at this time?"

"No."

"Stay in your room and keep the door locked. An officer will be there shortly. Don't open the door for anyone else. Do you understand?"

"Yes."

Janet went into the bathroom and opened the overnight case containing a plastic box full of ice. She lifted a glass vial from the ice, took a syringe, and inserted the nearly-frozen milky substance between her legs.

After washing the glass container with soap and water, and pouring the ice down the toilet, she put everything back into her overnight case, then locked it. After that, she returned to the bedroom and started to cry.

Within minutes, she heard the sound of a siren. Moments later, she admitted two uniformed officers from the San Francisco police department. After composing herself, Janet relayed the course of events to them. Nick Francisco had picked her up at the airport at ten forty-five, as previously arranged. He had driven her to the Stanford Hotel, where she had previously booked lodging. She had asked Francisco to wait in the car, but he had insisted on carrying her luggage into her room. Once inside, he had locked the door and forced himself on her. She had resisted, but his strength had overpowered her. In the process of forcing her against her will, he had hit her on the face, drawing blood. There was blood on the sheets and her clothes.

Janet's eye was beginning to discolor at this point. One of the officers got out a cold pack from the first aid kit in the squad car and applied it to Janet's face.

She continued, "After he hit me, he forced me on the bed and began tearing off my clothes. He was too big and strong for me to resist. Besides, he had this pearl-handled switch blade knife. He held it to my throat. He said if I didn't cooperate he would kill me this time." Janet was crying uncontrollably now.

The officer handed her a damp towel from the bathroom to put on her face. "What did he mean when he said he would kill you *this time*, Miss Neilson?"

Janet looked at the officer. "I'm here on business from out of town. I was beaten and raped while visiting here in San Francisco a few months ago. They never caught the man or men, but apparently Mr. Francisco was involved, because he told me that this time he would finish the job?"

"What do you mean, 'finish the job.'"

"He was going to kill me after raping me." Janet sobbed.

The officer comforted Janet's sobbing by giving her a fresh damp towel to put on her face. After a few moments, she seemed to calm down, and the officer continued. "Now, this man in the room. What seemed to scare him away?"

"I was able to get his hand off my mouth for a second and I screamed. Someone outside must have heard me, because there was pounding on the door. Francisco must have panicked. He knocked the guy down going out of the door."

"What happened to the man outside?"

"I don't know. I guess he got spooked and split. All I know is, whoever he was, he saved my life."

Just then, detective Larry Logan came into the room. "I'll take it from here," he said to the officer in charge. "Mrs. Neilson? What in the world are you doing here? Seems like you have an propensity for getting into trouble in my city. What in the world have they done to you this time?"

Janet quickly relayed the story to Detective Logan, who looked angry. "Are you telling me this is the same Francisco character that disappeared when you were hit in Golden Gate park last time you were here?"

"I'm afraid so. I didn't make the connection until it was too late. I don't know how I could have been such a fool."

"Well, don't blame yourself. There's no way you could have known he was involved before." Just then, an ambulance drove up and two attendants came to the door.

"I don't want to go to the hospital. I'm all right."

"It's for your own good," Logan said. "Don't worry, it's just a routine procedure. In the case of rape, we always have the victim checked out at the hospital. We have to take precautions, for your own sake. At the same time, they'll take seamen samples and stuff. You know."

Janet nodded.

"Before you go, do you know where this Francisco character went, by any chance?"

"To his office, home, hell I don't know." Janet said.

"Don't worry. We'll have him in custody before the day is over. You just take care of yourself. I will have a few more questions and will ask you to sign a complaint, but they can wait until you're dismissed from the hospital."

* * * * * *

At the hospital, it was a stroke of luck that Carol Talman was on duty. "Well, what have we here?" she said, looking at Janet. "Don't tell me. Not again!"

"Hi, doc. Thought it was time for a reunion."

"What have you gotten yourself into this time?"

Janet again relayed the same story to Dr. Talman. "I can't believe my ears. You do seem to have an attraction for this sort of thing don't you. Well, we'll try to complete the necessary tests as quickly as possible. We'll be as easy on you as we can. You have definitely gotten your money's worth from this hospital."

When the tests were completed, it was verified that Janet was in fact raped. They logged the blood type for future purposes, took sperm samples and completed her examination. The report stated that she had no broken bones and, aside from a bloody nose, bruised eye, and an unfortunate experience, was physically sound and able to return home.

Doctor Talman asked if she wanted to have her husband called to pick her up.

"I would appreciate it if we could keep this just between us girls, if you don't mind, Doctor Talman," Janet said, making a face.

"I'm like a clam," she said, running a finger across her lips. "Whatever you want, you got. You may have a hard time explaining that cut and black eye," she said with a smile.

"You haven't heard of running into a door?"

"Oh, by the way, you may want to talk to detective Logan before you leave, just to be sure that nothing escapes from his office and accidentally finds its way to Brad's ears."

"Good idea. Thanks. As soon as I leave, I'll try to get in touch with him."

"No need for that. He's waiting in the outer room."

"That surprises me." Janet said, somewhat uneasy.

She dressed slowly, her mind buzzing, replaying the past events, wondering what it was that detective Logan could want so soon. She had been brought to the hospital only a few hours ago. A cold shiver ran down her spine, although the hospital was anything but cold.

Detective Logan was sitting in the waiting room, apparently making a written report as Janet walked up to him.

"Busy at work, as always, detective?"

"Good news," he said, standing and extending his hand to Janet with a smile. "We picked up Francisco almost immediately. He didn't give us any trouble at all. Came peaceably until we advised him that he was being arrested for assault, rape, and possible attempted murder."

"What did he say to that charge?" Janet asked quickly.

"Said that he didn't touch you. Claims he picked you up at the airport, just like you said, but when the two of you reached the hotel he says you had a disagreement about some business dealings and he just left. He said when he last saw you, you were somewhat hysterical, blaming him for some deal gone bad."

"Doesn't surprise me. That creep will say anything to save his bacon. Well, I guess the proof will be in the pudding, so to speak," Janet said. "As soon as the tests are completed and the DNA matched with

Francisco, I assume then you'll have definite proof that he attacked and raped me."

"I understand the tests will be completed tomorrow. Then we'll have a lot more answers than questions. I trust you'll be staying in town?"

"I've had enough excitement from San Francisco, thank you. I'm booked on Alaskan Airlines to Portland later this afternoon. You don't mind me leaving, do you?"

"Let's complete our paperwork, and I'll give you a call tomorrow and let you know what we've got."

By six fifty-five, Janet and Danielson were sitting side by side in the first class section of Alaskan Airlines, anxiously awaiting take-off. Once in the air, they breathed a sigh of relief, looked at one another, and gave each other a "high-five"

The next day, Janet and Steve Danielson were sitting in Steve's office when the receptionist rang.

"Yes."

"A Detective Logan for Janet Neilson, sir."

"Put him through to my office." Steve put him on the speaker phone.

"Detective Logan? Janet Neilson here. What have we got?"

"We have a very unhappy man, I'd have to say. The blood DNA matches Francisco's blood perfectly. This, coupled with your written complaint and testimony, will send Mr. Francisco away for a long, long time."

"Good work, detective. I appreciate your calling. Bye now."

Steve buzzed his secretary on the intercom. "June, would you please send Mary Lee two dozen red roses to her flat on Russian Hill, along with a card saying "Thanks for a job well done, and sign my name". Oh, and June...enclose a check for ten thousand dollars. Designate it...`research'."

Chapter Thirteen

☯

Christmas in the Northwest is an especially beautiful time of the year. Mother nature thoughtfully decorates the landscaping with a deep dusting of snow, periodically accenting the landscaping with a silver thaw. In the evening, the children play under street lights, running with their mouths open, trying to catch the falling snowflakes on their tongues. They make runways for their sleds, weaving through the trees, onto the street. They start at a slight knoll, then pick up speed, and end up racing down a cul-de-sac, hands and feet flying, ending up in a snow bank, laughing and rolling in the snow. The child who is lucky enough to spend a winter in the suburbs remember that time for the rest of their life. It occupies a special moment in their hearts.

After spending a hard day playing in the snow, parents have no trouble putting the little ones to bed, where they sleep fitfully, dreaming of the hours past, playing in the snow, making snow men, and looking forward to the next day.

Morning often brings a silver thaw, encasing wires, bare limbs, branches, shrubs and trees in a clear frozen segment of time. Kids break off two-foot icicles from the eves of their houses and lick the frozen delicacies.

Parents, on the other hand, view mother nature's handiwork in one of two ways. Those who are fortunate, cut loose the kid in themselves and join their younger counterparts, enjoying those rare winter days. They tire much easier, of course, fall farther and harder, and don't last as long before they retire to the fireplace with red noses and hot toddies, warming their cold hands and feet. They may be sore and even hurting a little, but they're living and getting the most out of life.

The majority of adults, however, face mother nature's challenge with a release of fury and ill-gotten vocabulary, fit for a seasoned seaman. Woe be unto he who stalls his car driving up an incline, causing everyone behind them to do likewise.

Driving in the icy, snowy roads requires a skill equal to Rommel's desert survival training. The first rule for the unfortunate traveler is, once your car gets going, don't stop under any conditions, because once you do you'll never get it going again.

One could make a lifetime study, and probably a make fortune in the process, of positioning oneself at an intersection during the icy season, filming cars as they attempt to come to a stop once the traffic light changes. Slamming on one's brakes causes the vehicle to automatically turn into a sled, sliding in slow motion, quietly, into the intersection, into the oncoming traffic.

The occupant of the sliding car usually stomps on the brakes so hard circulation ceases to flow to their feet. Likewise, their knuckles turn a bright white as they pull back on the steering wheel, trying to pull the car to a halt, eyes wide as saucers, mouth open emitting a silent scream, while the car slowly slides into the side of an oncoming car (whose driver's eyes are wide open, and whose mouth is screaming silent screams, and whose feet's circulation has since ceased to flow from stamping on their brakes). Such as it is on a cold, snowy winter day.

Despite the turmoil of getting out of the suburbs, once the driver finally merges into major traffic patterns, things begin to look up, and the proceeding ordeal is quickly forgotten, unless, of course, his car is sporting a new wrinkle.

The stores of downtown Portland are brightly appointed with Christmas trees and decorations. Santa and his Elves, nativity scenes, children playing in the snow, and toys adorn every window. The corners are occupied with bell ringers for the Salvation Army. Every light pole is decorated with huge colored balls, trim, and holly. Music permeates the air from every store, with shoppers carrying shopping bags full of gifts and cheer.

The air is filled with lighthearted love and affection for mankind. It's that time of year when, if you have a grudge to bear, a bone to pick, a hatchet with someone's name on it, it's time to put all grievances aside and make amends.

So it was with Janet and Brad. Brad brought home a seven- foot, heavily-flocked Christmas tree, setting it in the corner next to the fireplace. With the stereo playing Christmas carols, both Janet and Brad enjoyed decorating the tree. After two hours of lovingly placing each colored ball, each ornament, each symbolic treasure on the tree, Brad turned off the house lights, turned on the tree lights, then they stood back in silence, admiring their work.

One could not help but wonder, at this special peaceful moment, why their lives couldn't be filled with the same affection they now felt for one another instead of constantly trying to be at odds, destroying their marriage.

At this moment, Brad and Janet were the picture of togetherness, basking in the glow of the tree, engulfed in the warmth and love they felt for one other, as the stood there, their arms around each other.

* * * * * *

Mount Hood had always been one of their most favorite places to go in the winter. It was only a forty-five minute drive from their house, and the skiing was excellent. Brad had reserved a room at Timber Lodge earlier in July, assuring them of a place to stay for the holidays. Each year, since before they had been married, they had spent five days of their Christmas vacation skiing on Mount Hood. It had proven to be one of the highlights of the year. Janet had taken ski lessons the past few years and, though she wasn't as accomplished a skier as Brad, for the most part was able to ski on the same runs. Janet preferred to ski from side to side, skiing in the snow moguls, taking her time getting down the hill, enjoying the sport, whereas Brad liked to ski balls-out straight down the mountain.

They took it easy the first day of skiing, exercising precautions. After a year of desk sitting for Janet and working in the field without much physical exercise for Brad, they both wanted to be sure they didn't break or injure anything that would spoil their vacation.

Ski conditions were perfect their first day on the mountain. There wasn't a cloud in the sky. After a few warmup runs, both Brad and Janet took off their ski jackets and spent the afternoon on the slopes in their sweaters. They stopped on one of the plateaus to have their picture taken by a photographer, with the city of Portland showing crystal clear in the distant background. After a day of constant skiing, they were both so tired they hardly had the energy to eat. A hot bath hit the spot and they were off to bed, fast asleep by eight o'clock.

The next morning on the slopes was somewhat tenuous, each feeling their sore muscles. By mid-day, Brad was loose and skiing well. He felt he was ready for the "expert run".

Getting off the chair, he skied to the black diamond run, accompanied by Janet, where a sign designated expert skiing only. They looked down the hill. The path was narrow and steep—the steepest run the mountain had to offer.

Janet decided not to follow Brad, saying she would take the scenic route around the side of the hill, knowing that Brad would brave the uncharted route straight down. Because of the degree of difficulty, there were few skiers to contend with. Those that did ski seemed to be expert skiers, heading straight down the hill, leaving a rooster tail of snow behind them.

Janet started out cautiously, skiing from side to side, while Brad chose to take the more daring route of parallel skiing straight down the hill, picking up momentum as he went. From time to time, he felt as if he was getting out of control, and would lean upward into the hill to slow himself down before continuing on. Janet would eventually catch up with him, as the easier trail crossed the black diamond path. She would be tired and ready for a rest, but by the time she got to the plateau where Brad had been patiently waiting for her to catch up, he would be rested and bored and would take off just about the time she came to a stop next to him. Needless to say, this was a source of irritation.

Towards the end of the day, Brad wanted to make one last run, but Janet's body was aching to the bone. "You go ahead," she said. "I'm dog tired, I'm going to ski down to the lodge. See you there. Be careful!" she said over her shoulder as she skied off.

Brad started down the hill on his last run. There was only one other skier ahead of him. The trees were casting long shadows across the run now, giving the illusion the sun was about to set. He could ski from side to side a little, but by this time of the day the path had turned into a sheet of ice, frozen solid from the sun melting the snow during the heat of the day, then freezing the melted snow into one giant ice cube as the air cooled down.

Brad's weight, coupled with the ice-packed, steep ski run, hurled him down the slope at such a speed that it gave him the uneasy feeling of inability to control himself. He tried to turn his skis uphill to slow himself down, but the skis, chattering on the ice, wouldn't obey. As his speed increased, Brad tried unsuccessfully to maintain control.

As he was forcing his skis parallel with the hill to slow him down the downhill ski caught an ice ridge, vaulting him head over heels in an uncontrollable slide down the steep grade. When he finally came to a stop three quarters of the way down the run, face down in the crusted snow, he knew he was hurt, but was unsure of the extent of his injury. It was difficult to breathe and his ribs hurt like hell, not to mention his face was scraped up from the slide.

One of the skis had detached itself and was racing downhill. Even the spring breaks on the ski skipping on top of the ice didn't stop it until it buried itself in the deep snow on the opposite side of the run, fifty yards downhill. Clutching his side, grimacing and moaning, he slid sideways down the hill towards the ski. By the time he reached it, perspiration was pouring from his forehead. He felt as if his lungs were tied in a knot.

Brad lay on the ice-packed hill, out of breath, weighing the options of his next move. A skier swished past him, heading for the lift that would take him to the top of the hill again. Brad looked up at the chain of moving chairs. They were all empty, save a single skier every twenty chairs or so. He knew that soon the ski patrol would sweep the hill, making sure all skiers were safely off the mountain. He also knew that if they found him, they would order a first-aid skier's stretcher, put him in the basket, loading him on the specially designed chair for such purposes, and take him to the first aid station at the lodge. There determined that was no way he was going to allow a bunch of ski bums strap him on his back and bring him off the mountain with everyone in the lodge looking up at him lying helplessly in the stretcher.

Struggling to put his ski back on, it took two tries to maneuver his boot into the bindings. Bent over, which was the only way he could stand, he slowly went from one side of the ski run to the other, clutching his side to ease the excruciating pain, inching his way downhill in the process, while his skis chattered rebelliously. When he finally neared the bottom, he turned his skis towards the lift, gritted his teeth, and let go. When he reached the bottom of the hill, a lone ski-lift attendant was stamping his feet in place in an attempt to stay warm.

Brad pushed himself up to the chair area with his ski poles, nearly losing his balance in the process. He slipped, and one ski shot straight up in the air. Brad instinctively grabbed the lift attendant by his coat, then, apologized as he righted his ski again and finally sat on the next approaching chair, exhausted.

The ride was painfully slow. Adding discomfort to injury, the wind had started whipping up, stinging his face, lowering the chill factor to well below zero. Brad put his mittens to his face in an attempt to block out the cold, biting wind. After what seemed an eternity, he reached the top of the hill. By this time, his ribs and lungs were in such pain he knew that he had broken a rib, fearing it may have punctured a lung. Setting his pride aside, he skied down to the first aid station.

Once inside, Brad relayed the story of his accident to a young first aid girl who seemed hardly qualified to assess his injuries. Apparently, their job, aside from treating simple cuts and bruises, was to determine if the patient needed further aid and if so, to act accordingly. In Brad's case, it was apparent that he had been injured and needed treatment beyond their medical capability. "Call for an ambulance, Jason," the young attendant said to her blond male counterpart.

"No, I don't need no goddamn ambulance! I'll just drive myself to the hospital," Brad growled. He started to get up, but was unable to even raise himself off the table.

"You stay just where you are," she demanded. "If you do have a punctured lung, you could pass out while you're driving and endanger not only yourself, but everyone else on the road," the female attendant said sternly, with authority. "And I can't allow that."

Resigning himself to their care, Brad stated with a concerned voice, "My wife will be wondering what happened to me. She'll be worried."

"Is she still skiing? If so, we can post the last run with a sign telling her to go to the first aid room."

"No, she's either in the lodge or in our room."

"Don't worry, then. Give us her name and tell me where you're staying and I'll get in touch with her for you."

Brad gave them the necessary information, then he gave her the data needed to fill out the accident report.

Soon, two ambulance attendants came in, a guy and a girl, both in their early twenties. They looked like ski bums themselves. They took his pulse, listened to his heartbeat, checked his respiration, asked questions about allergies, and did he have any injuries they should know about? They asked if he was he dizzy, was he taking any medication, and so on. After they had finished their evaluation, they escorted Brad to the rear of the ambulance, where he sat with the female attendant who strapped him in. She then picked up a two-way radio and called in Brad's name and condition to the hospital.

As the ambulance drove toward Government Camp, there was no siren, no panic, and no apparent interest in Brad outside of monitoring his vital signs from time to time. Everything was impersonal and sterile.

At the hospital Brad was escorted to the admission desk by the two ambulance drivers. The usual barrage of questions ensued, repeating the earlier interview. As he was answering them mechanically, Brad's eyes scanned the waiting room. Everyone in the room had ski clothing on. Some were wearing bandages around their legs, others on their arms, and others seemed to have head injuries. Some were obviously in need of immediate medical attention. Others, it seemed, would eventually just go home and get some rest. Every cubicle in the emergency room was packed with people either being attended to or waiting to be attended to.

After twenty minutes of waiting, the girl from the ambulance said she had to go on another call, wished Brad luck, and left. A moment later his name was called. He was ushered into the x-ray room, where they took four shots of his chest, front, back, and one from each side. Another twenty minutes passed while he waited in the cold cubicle.

"Mr. Neilson? You have a couple of fractured ribs," the doctor said without waiting for Brad's response to his name. "Nothing major, mind you, but we'll wrap you up tight, give you a prescription for some painkillers, and you'll be on your way in no time. You'll have some discomfort for the next ten days to two weeks. Try not to exert yourself, stay calm, and you should be all right." He departed as quickly as he had entered.

A young woman in her early thirties brought in a flesh colored elastic bandage and wrapped Brad's ribs so tight he could hardly breathe. "Need to pull everything back together," she said. "There, how's that? Feel better?"

Brad tried to take a deep breath, but the pain was too great.

"Don't breathe too deeply. Expanding the lungs against the bruised rubs will only make them hurt. Slow, easy breathing does it."

Brad breathed shallowly. "That's the ticket," she said. "Here's a prescription for your medication," she said, handing him a small piece of paper containing the doctors writing. "You can fill it next door or at a drugstore, as you like. Just check out at the counter there," she said, pointing to the desk where the business end of the clinic was transacted. "You're free to go."

Brad signed the papers, paid for the bill with his Visa card, and looked for a telephone. "How do I get out of here?" he asked the nurse at the counter.

"Just dial the number written on the yellow tag there on the telephone. That'll get you a cab."

"Great. They get you down the damn mountain and you have to find your own way back up again," he grumbled as he punched the numbers on the phone.

* * * * * *

The look on Janet's face when Brad walked in was one of both relief and empathy. "Oh Brad, your face!" His face had begun to discolor from the beating it had taken on the ice when he fell. "The first aid station called and said you had a skiing accident," she said running, over to his side, putting her arms around his neck. "They didn't say how bad it was. They just said they had taken you to the hospital emergency room. I've been worried sick to death ever since," she said lightly touching his face with her fingertips. "Ow, I'll bet that hurts."

"Well, you can stop worrying," he said, twisting out of her arms. "I'm safe and sound." His voice had a tone of indignation. He didn't know why he was irritated about Janet's concern over him all of the sudden, but it seemed to set him off. The rest of the night he was moody and spoke only when spoken to, answering in brief, curt sentences. Janet tried to comfort him several, but was rebuked each time. She finally concluded that his pride was hurt as much as his face and ribs, and decided to cut him a wide berth the rest of the evening.

Janet suggested they leave for home the next day, considering Brad's obvious discomfort, but he insisted they stay the remaining time they had paid for. He tried to put on ski clothing, but was unable to even bend over to put on his boots. Brad insisted that Janet not hang around the cabin and spoil her vacation, insisting she enjoy herself skiing.

The next few days, Janet attempted to ski alone on the intermediate slopes, but her heart simply wasn't in it. Without Brad to ski with, even if he did ski ahead of her or without her, it just wasn't the same. It wasn't any fun without him.

In the final analysis, it turned out to be a vacation they both would have rather done without, and it certainly did nothing for their marriage.

Chapter Fourteen

After that vacation Janet looked forward to getting back to the office. She found solace in losing herself in her work. She may have had trouble with her own marriage, but she was good at solving the problems of others. Today was different for some reason. By mid-afternoon she had a case of the jitters, and to the point of irritability. She just couldn't seem to keep her mind on her work. Whenever she turned to a task, her mind wandered. "You would think after a whole week of skiing, I would be raring to go," she said to herself. "I know what I need," she said with an impish smile.

She walked over to Dave Moore's office. The lights were off and there was no sign of Dave. "Molly," she said to the receptionist, "I have some documents for Mr. Moore to sign. Do you know when he'll return?"

"I think he took the afternoon off. He said it was a slow day and he was all caught up. He mentioned something about taking care of some loose ends at his apartment. Would you like to leave him a message?"

"No thanks. I'll catch him some other time. I think I'll run a few errands myself. Punch me out for the rest of the day will you, Molly?"

Janet drove her white BMW up the steep, curvy streets of Palatine Hill, where the snow-covered hills and rooftops looked picturesque as a Swiss painting. Fresh fallen snow always gave the city a softness that seemed to relax the soul, especially in the hills, where the tall, snow-capped pine trees stood majestically.

She had been to Dave's "hideaway" condominium several times during the early days of their "friendship". Dave had acquired the unit from a contractor that he had represented and had done a considerable amount of legal work for. Instead of a fee, he had taken the condo, using it as his place away from home.

With the passage of time, however, they both agreed it was in their mutual best interest not to be seem at the condo together, as he often lent it out discretely to clients or friends who wanted a "safe place" for an afternoon or weekend. No use taking a chance of being seen by a client, an office mate or, worse yet, his wife, they conceded. That was when they had discovered the Hilltop Motel in Vancouver, which had become "their place".

As Janet had suspected, Dave's red Jag was parked in the driveway. Just seeing his car made her pulse quicken in anticipation. Parking in the designated visitor's area, she opened the glove compartment, retrieving the gold key that Dave had made for her when they used to meet here.

Smiling to herself, she let herself in quietly, wanting to surprise him. Hearing water splash in the bathroom, Janet quietly removed her clothes, leaving a trail of shoes, blouse, skirt, bra, and panties from the entrance to the bathroom, where she tiptoed in.

The tub was around the corner, behind a short, five-foot brick-glassed in wall. Her heart thumping in anticipation, she jumped around the wall, hands in the air, totally nude, and squealed, "Surpri…."

Sitting in the tub with Dave, chin-deep in bubbles, was Mary Lee. Her hair was tied on top her head with a yellow ribbon. Her double D's were floating above the water line, partially encased in bubbles. Dave was sitting behind her, supporting a breast in each hand. It's difficult to tell who was the most surprised; Dave, Janet, or Double D.

Surprised and momentarily speechless, seeing Janet standing with outstretched arms, Dave was the first to compose himself, saying with a grin, "Well… what the hell, might as well hop in!"

Janet uttered an unintelligible apology, quickly retreating to the bedroom, gathering her clothing, muttering obscenities as she retreated. Dave and Mary Lee's tantalizing laughter followed her, adding fuel to her anger as she slammed the bedroom door. She didn't know whether she was more mad, insulted, or simply hurt.

While hurriedly dressing, she tried to figure out how to save face, when Dave came walked the bedroom, bathrobe on, dripping wet.

"What the hell you doing, coming here like this!" he challenged. "You know better than that." He glared at Janet, who was now squirming into her panty hose. If there was any indecision about her feelings before this moment, there was none now. She took the gold key from her purse and flung it at Dave's chest, along with the pantyhose.

"Here's your goddamn key. Give it to Miss Big Tits in there. One thing's for sure, you'll never drown with her around."

Dave looked startled at first, then laughed at Janet's dry sense of humor as she slammed the door on her way out. "She'll be back," he said to himself, tossing the gold key in the air, catching it behind his back. He smiled as he returned to the tub and Double-D.

Janet was so irritated for allowing herself to be humiliated in front of Mary Lee and Dave, she banged the steering wheel with her fist. "Now, I suppose the whole damn office will hear about it!" she screamed at the top of her lungs. "On top of that, I'll be the laughingstock of the courthouse." She banged the steering wheel again.

Just then, her car phone chirped. "Neilson!" she barked.

"Janet, this is Molly at the office. I'm so glad I found you. I've been trying everywhere."

"What is it, Molly? This isn't the best time to reach me."

"Sorry. I just thought you should know. Your Mom has been admitted to the hospital. They didn't say why."

A cold shiver ran through Janet's body. Suddenly, the altercation with Dave was but a wisp of wind in comparison to what was racing through her mind. "Hospital? Which hospital?"

"Providence Hospital, here in Portland."

Janet hung up without even a "thanks", and sped towards the hospital. She arrived to find Brad pacing the floor of the waiting room. When he saw Janet, he ran towards her, put his arms around her, holding her tight.

Janet was in no mood to be held or coddled. "What happened?" she said, pulling herself free. "Molly said Mom was here in the hospital. Has there been an accident? Is she sick? What's happened?"

"I don't know. I can't seem to get anything out of anyone except that she's in intensive care and the doctor has given instructions not to be disturbed." He nodded down the hall. "There's Dr. Hofmann now. Maybe *you* can get something out of him. He wouldn't tell me a thing."

"Dr. Hofmann. I'm Janet Neilson. Mrs. Friend's daughter. What's happened to my mother? Why is she here?"

"Come into my office and we can talk," he said, putting his hand behind Janet's back, guiding her.

Dr. Hofmann's office was smaller than she had anticipated, just large enough for his desk and two consultation chairs. The walls were covered with certificates, college degrees, specialty certificates, commendation plaques, and a few pictures of Dr. Hofmann playing golf with other men.

"Your mother came to see me last month about a mole on the side of her neck," he said quietly. "It had been growing rather rapidly and the color bothered me a great deal. I removed the growth and had it sent to the lab for analysis." He paused, looking at Mrs. Friend's medical file on his desk.

"Yes," Janet said impatiently.

"The lab's analysis showed the mole to be malignant. I thought at the time, I had removed all of the contaminated tissue, but apparently we didn't go deep enough into the healthy tissue. Today, when she came to the emergency room, it was obvious that the incision wasn't healing properly, plus there's evidence that the cancer has spread. To compound the matter...." He sighed deeply, "there appearers to be a great deal of drainage, which definitely should not be occurring. As a result of my examination, I admitted her immediately and have began running tests." He paused again.

"And?" Janet demanded impatiently.

"And, although the results aren't final, I'm afraid she has spreading melanoma," he said, with his eyes looking at Janet, then to the file.

"What's to be done now?" she asked in a more subdued tone.

"In view of the extent that the cancer seems to have spread, I'm afraid the next thing is to go back in and try to get it all."

"And what does that mean?" Janet asked fearfully.

"I'm afraid we'll have to perform a degree of radical neck dissection. That means going back into healthy tissue again, beyond the unhealthy tissue area, to ensure we get all the malignant tissue. Even then, I can't guarantee that one hundred percent of the cancer will be curbed. In a relatively short period of time this type of cancer can attack the central nervous system and spread to areas that...."

"That what?" Janet was becoming increasingly agitated.

"That just can't be cured—that's inoperable. Oh, I don't mean to imply that it's not possible to cure the disease, but her chances of recovery are growing slimmer by the day."

"What are the odds of her survival if you do the surgery?"

"If I had to make an estimate, I would say probably fifty percent"

"And if she doesn't have the surgery?"

"My guess is she will live six months to a year."

Janet's mind went into shock. This was the first time in her life that anyone had put a time frame on life and death. The thought of her mother dying six months to a year from now was overwhelming.

She covered her face with her hands and began sobbing uncontrollably. Brad went to put his arms around her, but Janet shrugged them off. She was angry, and didn't want anyone touching her or attempting to shield her from the pain. Her mother, her own mother—dead in six months! It was a concept unable to be grasped.

"If you do this radical surgery, what are her chances?" she pressed, wiping her eyes with the back of her hands.

"With chemotherapy, hospitalization, and proper care, maybe one to three years. A lot depends on her strength. Unfortunately, her age is a negative factor. The fact that the first incision didn't get all of the cancerous tissue and didn't heal is obviously an important consideration as well. I don't know. In retrospect, I might have to say a year."

"A year! One goddamn year? Operate—cut the hell out of her neck and face, keep her on drugs, cooped up in the hospital, and let her live for a year? To hell with that nonsense. Before I let you do that, I'll take her to Palm Springs and let her enjoy the balance of her life lying in the sun drinking pina coladas. At least she would have had some enjoyment."

"Now, Mrs. Neilson, I appreciate your frustration, but...."

"Frustration. I'll tell you about frustration. You cut the fucking mole off her neck, only to leave part of it to fester for a month before you figure out it's spreading, then you want to cut her goddamn head off to be sure you get the rest of it. Then, if that's not enough, you want to drug her up until she doesn't know her ass from fat meat. No! Sorry! Not my Mom. You can bet your sweet ass on that!" Janet stormed out of the room like a football coach behind sixty-to-zero at half time.

*   *   *   *   *   *

"Molly, This is Janet Neilson. Put me through to Daniels, will you?"

"He's in consultation with Chuck Morrison on the Culver land deal, Mrs. Neilson."

"Molly. I don't give a shit if he's in conference with president Clinton and Pope John Paul the second debating the legal size of rubbers! Put me through!"

After a short pause, Daniel's voice came over the phone. "Janet? What's so goddamn important? You know better than to interrupt a conference with a client and another attorney."

"I wouldn't have interrupted if it wasn't gravely important, Steve. I've got a problem, and it just can't wait another minute." She relayed the chain of events leading up to her call. "I need some serious help. I know you have connections and don't believe in all this surgery stuff. My mom is in trouble and I really need your help." Steve could hear her softly sobbing at the other end of the phone.

There was a pause for a moment then Janet wiped her nose and eyes, then apologized to Steve, who was patiently waiting at the other end.

"Tell you what. Go home. Take a hot bath, get some rest and I'll get to work and see what I can dig up. Okay?"

"Okay, but don't be long."

"I understand. I'll be as quick as humanly possible."

*　　*　　*　　*　　*　　*

"Janet, I may have something for you. This friend of mine in Santa Barbara had a brother who had cancer. He heard about a "whole health" clinic in Mexico, where they don't deal in medications or surgery. Their philosophy is treatment of the illness by giving the person proper nutrition in conjunction with working on the "self help theory". According to my friend's brother, he had a form of inoperable brain cancer. The hospital couldn't operate because of its location. Subsequently, the doctors sent him home to die. His eyes were swollen shut, his neck was puffed up like a watermelon, and he was so dizzy he couldn't even stand up. The poor guy was in such pain he was reduced to tears. He just couldn't take it. The day before they took him to this clinic in Mexico, they caught him trying to take his own life."

"When was that?"

"Last year. Once they took him to the clinic and started treatment, the tumor subsided and was gone in six months, the circulation returned to his body and his dizziness disappeared, his face returned to normal, and the son-of-a-bitch was back working eight months later."

"It sounds too good to be true, Steve, but goddamn it, I'm willing to give anything a try. Can you get all the information on the place for me?"

"It's being faxed to me as we speak."

"You are a sweetheart. I'm on my way."

Chapter Fifteen

Janet arrived at Providence Hospital with Brad in tow. She went directly to the admissions office and requested release slips to take her mother home. The head nurse paged Dr. Hofmann from the head nurse's desk. Answering the page from another part of the hospital wing, he instructed the nurse to show Janet to his office.

He was waiting, seated behind his desk when Janet arrived. "I want you to know, by taking her out of here, that you're signing your mother's death warrant," he said sharply. "She's getting the very best medical attention possible. It's very irresponsible for you to take her life in your own hands this way. What makes you think you know what you're doing?" Doctor Hofmann was clearly irritated.

"Doctor, the one thing I do know is that whatever time she has left, it's not going to be spent hooked up to tubes, being fed through her veins, cut apart, disfigured, and then jammed full of drugs until she doesn't know whether she's coming, going, dead, or alive. No thank you, Doctor Hofmann! I'm going to do my level best to find a way to either have her survive this thing or, at the very least, live comfortably during the time that she does have left."

"Well, if you insist on this insane line of reasoning, you must first sign these release forms acknowledging that your mother has cancer and it's against my judgement and hospital policy to take her out of our care, and that you are willing and knowingly demanding her release despite all I have told you about her condition."

"C.Y.O.A. eh, Herr Doktor?"

"Eh, what do you mean?"

"C.Y.O.A. Cover Your Own Ass. Typical medical movement. You forget, Dr. Hofmann, I'm an attorney. You know you're safe only if you operate and take unhealthy tissue as well as a gob of healthy tissue surrounding it. In other words, instead of taking out the lump, you remove the whole friggin' breast. Instead of taking out a mole, remove the neck to be sure you get all. All you doctors subscribe to the same overkill principal. Sure, you don't get sued, but the patient either dies or has so much of her body removed that it really doesn't matter anyway. She might as well be dead. You guys make me sick."

Janet was working herself into a frenzy, pacing the floor, waving her arms in the air. "There was a time when the medical profession was held high on a pedestal, next to gods. Now you're just a bunch of butchers looking for high fees to buy expensive cars, build swimming pools, go to Europe, or buy your girlfriend a condo. You make me sick," she repeated.

"I'm sorry you have such a low opinion of me and my profession, but...."

"Save it, doctor. Just get my mother and let me get on with it. Time is the one precious commodity that I can't afford to lose sitting here jawing with you."

"If you don't want my help and won't take my advice, at least be considerate of your mother's comfort. Take this prescription for Darvon. It'll take the edge off her pain until you get where you're going."

"Thanks. I appreciate that," Janet said sheepishly. "I'm sorry for my outburst. I'm so wired about this whole affair it's got so I don't know if I'm coming or going."

Hofmann gave an understanding nod, handed Janet the prescription, and walked out of the room without further comment.

* * * * * *

Lost Woman

Janet's mother was packed and sitting in the car heading for Mexico with5in an hour of being released from the hospital. Brad stayed behind, by agreement, to take care of the house. He wasn't thrilled with the prospect of playing bachelor again, but Janet left no room for negotiations. She gave Brad orders, or instructions to be more precise, to be carried out in her absence which, in view of her mother's condition, could be a long time. A very long time.

"Where are you taking me, honey?" she asked as they drove off the hospital grounds. She was still pretty drugged up from the morphine the hospital had given her, and wasn't really with the program. She knew Janet had taken her out of the hospital and that they were on their way to a clinic, but beyond that, there had been no time to go into elaborate explanations. She had no sooner asked the question, than her head nodded and she was asleep again.

Hours later, the morphine that had been injected into her system was wearing off. She woke up with a start as they drove into the city limits of Lake Shasta, a small Northern California city.

She was showing signs of confusion and again asked Janet where they were going. After Janet explained that they were going to another clinic, she finally realized that she wasn't still in the hospital. By that time her pain had returned.

"Hang in there, Mom, I'll find us a drugstore and get your medication as soon as I can." She pulled into a small pharmacy-store-gas station combination.

Janet's request to fill her mother's prescription was met with, "I'm sorry, Miss. We don't have anything in stock to fill that prescription. Most of the stuff we have is your commonly used drugs for allergies, colds, antibiotics, insect stings and the like. You'll have to go to Redding, up the road a piece, about an hour's drive, to get a store large enough that carries what you need. Sorry, young lady."

Janet drove eighty to ninety miles an hour and was in Redding in less than forty-five minutes. She pulled into a Long's Drug Store, had the prescription filled, and was out in fifteen minutes. Giving her mother two pills with a cup of water that she had gotten from the pharmacist, she breathed a sigh of relief for the first time that day.

Once her mother had settled down, Janet said, "Tell you what, Mom, there's a Denny's there on the corner and a motel across the street. What do you say we grab a bite to eat, get a good night's sleep, and continue on tomorrow, refreshed?"

"The rest sounds good, honey, but to tell you the truth, the stuff they gave me at the hospital made my stomach upset. I don't think I can keep anything down."

"Well, let's give it a try anyway. Maybe just a little something to keep up your strength. I think a rest will do us both a world of good, too."

Janet ordered a french dip with french fries, a salad, and a Coke. Her mother tried a B.L.T. with a glass of whole milk, but halfway through dinner she excused herself and made for the ladies room as fast as she could. Janet followed close behind.

"Sorry. Told you, my stomach just can't take it."

"That's okay, Mom. Not to worry. I'm not that hungry anyway. Let's go back to the room and rest. Tomorrow we'll get an early start. There's a lot of road to cover before we get to Mexico."

"Mexico?" She said as if it were the first time she had heard the word. Why are we going to Mexico?"

"Mom, I told you, we are going to a clinic to try to get you well. Don't you remember?"

It was obvious that she was not only confused but disoriented. She thought they were still in Oregon and would be going home after dinner. Despite her confusion, she put herself in Janet's care without question.

As for Janet's mental welfare, she felt like her mind was in limbo and her body in transit. Only yesterday she had been on her way to Dave Moore's pad for a little carefree sex, and now the life of her mother hung in the balance by a thread. How things can change so quickly, she thought.

* * * * * *

After three full days of driving, Janet and her mother arrived at WHTC, the Whole Health Therapy Center in Baja California. The building appeared to be more of an apartment or office building than a hospital. The structure itself was a two-story Spanish-style complex with red Spanish tile accented with numerous decorative balconies. The building had been landscaped with large palm trees and bushes surrounded by a deep green, lush grass. It was obvious that a lot of care had been taken in maintaining the property. It gave Janet the impression of a comfortably run establishment where relaxation was the order of the day.

They were met by a kindly looking elderly lady, a Doctor Maria Gonzales, director of the institute, dressed in a white smock. She had soft grey hair. Her skin radiated a blush, as if someone just slapped her on the side of the face and the sting was still apparent by the color in her cheeks. She was the picture of health. "I am so pleased that you have chosen to visit our clinic here in Baja," she said with a slight Spanish accent.

"Steve Daniels called three days ago and said to expect you, and be sure to give you the red carpet treatment." She laughed. "You will find that your choice to come to the Whole Health Therapy Center has been a wise one. Many people come here from your country seeking the truth and healing powers they need, away from those butchers who call themselves 'doctors' pretending to heal while only pushing us further into the grasp of death with their knives and medicines. Here, we seek to train our bodies and minds to heal themselves as only God meant for us to do, without the butchering of flesh and altering minds with the drugs."

Dr. Gonzales held Mrs. Friend's hands in hers, squeezing them for a moment. Looking into her eyes she said, "I'm glad you came, Mrs. Friend. And, in a short time, you will be glad, too." Standing up, she said, "Come with me. Let's get started."

She led them into a large office with a red stone tile floor and pure white, heavily stuccoed walls. Pulling out a new file, she labeled it, then read the medical file that Janet had brought from Dr. Hofmann. She asked questions, filling in any gaps. When she was finished, she closed the file and began what Janet thought must have been the same introduction given to each incoming patient.

"Mrs. Friend, the Whole Health Therapy Center is an intensive, nutrition-based medical treatment facility that works closely with nature to help the sick body rid itself of disease. This is accomplished by a process of simple foods, juices, and non-toxic medications." She explained that her diet would consist of low sodium and high potassium foods with severe fat restriction as well as protein restricted food. This would be supplemented by a high dosage of vitamins and minerals, rich fluids, and high micronutrients. The main diet would consist of three fresh vegetarian meals, prepared from organically grown vegetables, fruits and whole grains. This would be augmented by thirteen glasses of fresh raw juices prepared hourly from organically grown vegetables and fruits as well as green plants and raw calve's liver. "On top of all this, you will receive daily medications of vitamins to strengthen and cleanse your body."

"Wow. That sounds like a real turn-around in my eating habit, considering I love potato chips, pastry, soft drinks, and an occasional Big Mac with french fries."

She laughed. "Your body is going to get a real cleaning. When we get through with you, you'll be embarrassed that you ever let such things touch your lips, let alone get into your system. And when I mean into your system, I mean your liver, blood, heart, bones, everywhere. One of the things we do to assist your body is to give you periodic coffee enemas."

"You've got to be kidding! Coffee enemas? I've heard of approaching the problem from the bottom up, but this takes the cake," she said with a nervous laugh.

"You'll be surprised how soon you'll see results, Mrs. Friend." A nurse dressed in a blue striped uniform entered the room. "Ah, this is nurse Julie. Mrs. Friend, would you go with her now, and she'll give you a complete physical examination. I'll stay here and chat with Janet."

After they had left the room, Miss Gonzales turned to Janet. "I have to tell you candidly, Mrs. Neilson, from what I've read in her medical file, your mother appears to have an advanced case of melanoma. If we could have had her in the earlier stages of her illness, I believe our success rate would have been one hundred percent, but we will have a fight on our hands now." She patted Janet on her hands. "Faith, Mrs. Neilson. Faith."

"What can I do to help?" Janet asked, feeling helpless.

"Our rooms are equipped to house both patient and relative. Most of our patients have a loved one stay right here with them. It helps to keep them from feeling like they've been abandoned. Should you decide to stay with us, we encourage you to change your lifestyle along with your mother."

"How's that?"

"Eat the same foods, drink the same juices, take the same vitamins. In short, rid yourself of the toxic chemicals that are in your system, right along with your mother. The change in eating and living habits could end up saving your life eventually."

"Sounds like you take this eating proper foods business seriously," she said with a nervous laugh.

"The food you eat fuels your body and mind. You won't believe the changes that will take place within your system in a short time. You wouldn't put dirty, greasy water in your car now would you? We don't put it into our bodies either."

* * * * * *

In the proceeding days, Janet and her mother came to know the meaning if that phrase. The first shock came when they were given a glass of green liquid, not dissimilar in appearance to stagnant liquid moss, to drink. It looked alive, like someone had cut flesh from a giant living plant and had stuffed it into a blender. Janet put it to her lips and took a swallow, immediately spitting it up before it even had a chance to clear her gums. The look on her face was that of a person who had just been forced to swallow a hand full of live worms. "Yuck!" She said out loud, wiping her mouth with her sleeve.

The nurse's look was one of disdain, no doubt practiced from the thousands of times she had seen and heard the same response. "Really, Mrs. Neilson! Don't act like a child! You had better get used to it. This is going to be your diet for the rest of your life."

"That's what you think, bitch," she said under her breath.

"What's that, you say?" she challenged.

"I said, this stuff stinks." With that she held her nose and drank the whole glass in one fell swoop. "Yuck!" she said again, sticking out her tongue with a disgusted look.

The coffee enemas were another experience altogether. The motto around the clinic was, "Morning coffee? Bend over, grab your cheeks, and smile, 'cause here it comes, bottoms up! And no cream or sugar, thank you." The coffee enemas were to rid the liver of the bile that had accumulated throughout years of bad eating. Once the system was fed healthy foods, and the toxins had been eliminated from the body, the body still wasn't designed to get rid of the toxins fast enough, thus the reason for the coffee enemas. Somehow they made the bile dissipate in bulk through the liver.

As one can well imagine, this wasn't the usual topic at tea. "Have a big one today, Margaret? How about you, everything come out all right, Julie?"

An equally discouraging, but necessary, side affect of the treatment was the patient's body usually went through periods of denial, which resulted with the insides cramping up, accompanied with a great deal of pain. This was enough reason to give the average patient the feeling that maybe dying was an easier way out after all.

In the final analysis, when the initial treatments were terminated and the home training period completed, patient and family departed for home, armed and trained with the proper way to live and eat. They were usually accompanied by a new juicer to make their own juices—sold to the patient by the clinic at four thousand dollars each.

The first few weeks at home went superbly. Janet's mother felt great. She stayed on the juice, raw fruit, and vegetable diet. Even the raw calve's liver was tolerated.

Janet's mother took short walks in her garden, sat on the porch in the afternoon sun, and reflected on her life. The Bible was her constant companion. One thing Janet noticed was that her mother seemed to have found peace within herself. She no longer feared death or the dreaded disease that lay dormant, waiting for an excuse to unleash itself.

Janet came to visit every day, sitting hours at a time, talking to her mother until she became too tired and went to sleep. Janet would spend that quiet time thinking about the hand that life had dealt her, wondering what the future held. From time to time her mind wandered to her childhood, remembering the good times.

Like most people, childhood was that time of her life most fondly remembered. It had been the introduction of adolescence that made life complicated. Janet's lack of physical development had spawned the seed of insecurity. The trauma of adolescence plunged her into new depths, when she had been told that she had been adopted. This had become the turning point of her life.

Adopted! She began to be obsessed with the fact that some person, or persons, had consciously, willing and knowingly, given her up, like a sack of potatoes. She felt that knot in her stomach again, the one that left her feeling like a helpless waif, left alone to drift at sea on a raft with nothing to hold onto. No past. No history. No genes or relatives or blood lines to look to. Her emotions vacillated from feeling sorry for herself to rage toward her unknown parentage. This led to repressed ill feelings towards her adoptive mother and father, going so far as to blame them for their part in her adoption.

Janet's thoughts were interrupted by a cry from the porch, where her mother had been resting. "Janet. Janet, come quick." She was holding her side with both hands, her face distorted in pain. Perspiration had broken out on her forehead.

Panicked, Janet managed to get her into the car and to the emergency room at the hospital. She called ahead on her car phone, hoping Dr. Hofmann would be there waiting for them when they arrived. Janet looked for the "I told you so" look on his face, but there was none of that as he took her mother into the examination room.

"I'll have to keep her here for tests until tomorrow," he said. "I've given her a sedative and she's resting comfortably. Go home and get some rest, Janet. You look like hell."

"Thanks for the compliment." She drove home, weary, feeling the shock and pain of not knowing what to expect next.

The next day, Janet's worst fears were realized. "Your mother's cancer has spread into her internal organs and there's even an indication that it's gone into the bone marrow. She has to have treatment immediately. I've given her some morphine to keep the pain down, but we have to attack the source."

"Chemotherapy?"

"As soon as possible."

"Right," Janet resigned herself. "Right," she said quietly as she walked away.

During the next three weeks, her mother vacillated between pain and unconsciousness. Janet sat at her bedside by the hour, holding her hand, talking to her in a quiet voice, telling her how much she loved her, how grateful she was to have had her for a mother. The tenth day, as she sat at her bedside, talking to her softly, Janet kissed her mother on the forehead and said that soon she would be in another place. A place without pain and suffering. A place where Janet knew she would be happy. With a slight smile on her lips and a peaceful look on her face, her mother lightly squeezed Janet's hand.

As the sun set in the evening, Mrs. Friend slipped away to the land of the free.

Chapter Sixteen

A light mist fell as Janet stood among her mother's friends as the minister reiterated words that he had said hundreds of times before. As she stood there, she felt abandoned by the one person who had really loved her unconditionally. The ministers words seemed empty, meaningless. She found her mind wandering, elevating to another level, isolating her alone with her thoughts. It's a shame one doesn't fully appreciate a friend or family member until they're gone, especially when that person is your closest friend. Then its's too late, she thought to herself.

Her heart ached with an unrelenting pain. Tears flowed down her cheeks. At that moment, if it were possible, she would have crawled in next to her mother and called it quits on the spot. But she was alive, healthy, and yes, she did have a life with her husband. Brad. He's all I have now. Somehow that thought didn't give her much solace. She would have to work on that…some other time.

Driving home after the funeral, Janet felt depressed, alone, and confused about the direction her life had taken this past year. It was as if everything that had ever had meaning had been brutally ripped from her life, leaving a huge void which unexplainably could not be filled by Brad, her work, or any other facet of her being. Life just didn't seem to hold any interest anymore.

Out of desperation more than anything, she asked Steve Daniels for some time off. "To get myself together. To find myself," she had told him. "I feel like a lost asteroid floating in the nebulousness of space. Burnt out with no purpose and no place to go."

Steve sensed not only the need to get away, but picked up a suicidal overtone that greatly concerned him. "Take all the time you need, kid," he had said. "We'll hold down the fort. You just go and do whatever it is you feel you need to. You've been through a lot lately. Most normal people would have gone off the deep end by this time. Say, why don't you go to the beach! I have a time-share in this little house sitting on a cliff overlooking the ocean at Seaside. It's usually vacant in the winter. You'd have the whole place to yourself. You'll love it there. What do you say?"

It was like a gift from heaven. Just what the doctor ordered. A chateau hideaway. No telephone. No schedules. No demands and, most of all, no company. "Thanks, Steve. You're a life saver. A real doll." She hugged him, and after getting the address, directions and a key, was off to pack.

Needless to say, Brad wasn't at all pleased to hear that she was off on another tangent. He was in the kitchen making himself dinner—a ham, cheese, and tomato sandwich on rye—when Janet advised him of her plans to spend the next week solo at Daniel's time-share at Seaside. He hit the roof, throwing his freshly made sandwich against the cupboard door, leaving it looking like a three dimensional Salvador Dali painting. He paced the kitchen floor, pushing chairs aside, trying to contain his anger.

"I don't understand you, Janet," he exploded. Ever since you've gotten that damn law degree of yours, you've been in another world." His eyes were ablaze and his face flushed with anger.

"First, you have to make your mark in the legal world, which I understand and respect," he said, stopping in front of her, momentarily looking her in the eye before continuing his pacing. "Then, you go out of town on lengthy assignments, which I don't like…but even that I can understand," he said, punctuating the statement with his arm jutting in the air. "Now, you're going someplace to fuckin' "find yourself"? What the hell is this, anyway? Why didn't you try finding yourself before you hooked up with me? Are you so weak and confused? Maybe what you need is a psychiatrist. You may be a great attorney, I don't know. You may even have been a wonderful daughter. I don't really know that either. What I do know is that your role as a wife sucks! On a scale of one to ten, you're barely nosing above zero. I'm beginning to think that what you need isn't a husband. What you need is a puppy that will jump circles at your every whim, be there panting when you come home—whatever the time—and be undyingly grateful for the smallest scrap of time you give him. Just rub his wet nose, pat him on the head, and give him a dog biscuit, and he's in dog heaven. Well, I've got news for you, I'm no woman's puppy and have no intention of becoming one, either."

Brad stormed out of the kitchen, leaving Janet standing there with her mouth open without comment. A few moments later he returned, one hand on his forehead and the other waving in the air, mumbling something under his breath. That was followed with both hands around his head, as if he was trying to squeeze out a solution to the problem, while still pacing the floor.

Stopping in front of Janet, he took a very long look at her, then softly and deliberately said, "Look, I love you, Janet. Nothing is more important to me in this life than you. I'd do anything for you, but goddamn it, we have a contract, you and I, to love, honor, and obey until death do us part, and I'm afraid you're just not living up to your part of the bargain. You keep going the way you are now and we're certainly not going to make it to the "till death do us part" part. You get my drift, swifty?" He looked at Janet long and hard, as if waiting an answer. She met his stare momentarily, then looked down, not wanting to meet his eyes any longer.

Finally, Janet took a deep breath, "I understand what you're saying, Brad, but you have to understand, I've been through a lot lately. I nearly lost my life trying to do my job the best way I know how. Now I've lost the only person who has every loved me unconditionally…and now…I just don't know what's important anymore. I don't know if I want to be an attorney and, frankly, I don't even know if I want to be a wife. I'm as confused as hell and I'm scared too. I have to have some time to myself to figure out who I am and where I'm going."

Grabbing Brad by the shoulders and looking him in the eye, she said, "I feel this tremendous void in my life. A void that was once filled with love and understanding and security and all that bullshit. I need some space, Brad, and you've got to give it to me, like it or not."

Brad hesitated for a moment, then said, "Take a moment and look at it from my perspective. How do you think it feels to be this unnecessary dangling appendage when it comes to your life? Have you ever heard of the concept that marriage is a two way street? You're supposed to share in the duties, the problems, and the pleasures. You…you keep everything to yourself, go places alone, and keep your thoughts to yourself. I not only feel totally unnecessary, but unless to boot. Lately, the only contribution you've made to this relationship of ours is to drive a wedge deeper and deeper between us with these mood swings of yours."

"Come on, try to be a little understanding, Brad."

"A little understanding? Shit, I've spend the greater part of the last year eating breakfast and dinner at McDonald's. When I was single, at least I had someone to cook dinner and talk to. This isn't a marriage. It's a trial by fire. The only one getting their feet burned is yours truly. And I have to tell you kid, I've about had the course. I'm sorry about all your troubles and stuff, but, like I said before, marriage is a two way street. I either want to be in or I'm out, but one way or the other, I want a commitment from you!" Brad walked around in a circle in the kitchen waving his arms in the air as he talked. "You take off without me now, Janet,…I don't know, I may might not be here when you return." He turned to look her in the eye.

Janet stared right back at him. "I'm not fond of ultimatums, Brad. I guess you'll have to do what you have to do and I'll have to do what I have to do. If we don't meet in the middle, well, maybe that's the way it has to be."

"Bullshit! You and your goddamn fatalistic philosophy. 'What will be, will be.' You sound like Doris Day without the freckles."

Janet was in no mood for an argument. She felt like a balloon with the helium all but dissipated, just barely dragging its string on the ground. "I'm going to pack, Brad. If you're here when I return from the beach, maybe we can have a long talk and work through everything, but for now…I'm sorry, but I'm just drained, and frankly, my dear, I just don't give a damn."

* * * * * *

The drive west along the Columbia River to the beach was peaceful. Giant fir and birch trees lined the freeway, casting giant shadows along the road, lending to the scene of tranquility. Weekdays, the road to the ocean was usually void of much traffic save a periodic car or truck now and then. She had her favorite pianist, Jonathan Lee from Carmel playing on the CD. Washing her mind of all thoughts, listening to the tranquil piano music, she leaned the back of her head on the seat's headrest and put herself in a trance-like state, feeling at peace with the world for once. The drive took a little over two hours, but seemed to go by quickly.

Daniels had given her a map of the area, so she had little difficulty finding the cottage. The "cottage" perched fifty feet above the beach overlooking the ocean turned out to be a three bedroom, three bath fully furnished house. The family room had exposed beams with a vaulted ceiling containing a twelve foot tall stone fireplace on the far wall with floor to ceiling windows overlooking the ocean. A black chain link swing, large enough to lie in, was accented with throw pillows, was suspended from the ceilings beams. Janet spun around like a ballerina, her arms extended, squealing with delight. She was alone and in heaven.

Lost Woman

She walked out onto the balcony that ran the perimeter of the two story house. Closing her eyes, she felt the ocean salty mist on her face from the light fog hanging in the air. While she stood there, feeling the immense strength of the sea, a white sea gull landed on the railing a few feet away, looked at Janet then began slowly walking toward her.

"So, you're my greeting party? A more noble one, I could not want. Thanks for coming," she said to the gull, who was pecking at the ring on her outstretched hand.

Anxious to walk on the beach, she ran back into the house and undressed in the middle of the living room floor, where she had previously set her over night bag. After putting on a pair of shorts and a sweatshirt, she skipped out the side door to the stairs leading to the beach. The cool sand felt good squeezing between her toes as she walked to the ocean's edge, kicking sand and dancing in circles like a child as she went.

The tide was on its way out, and in its receding path left little bubbles in the wet sand. Dropping to her knees, she sunk her fingers deep into the sand, pulling out a large handful of wet sand, creating a little pool of water in the cavity that she had just created.

To her amazement, the mound of sand started to move. A thumb-sized sand dab emerged, his beady eyes looking for a place to escape. Janet set him back down on the sand, where he disappeared in a moment, leaving no trace of his departure. "I know how you feel, little fellah. Sometimes I wish I could dig my way out of sight, too."

She continued walking down the beach for a mile or so, then cut across the sand up to the base of the cliff, where a mammoth pile of driftwood had accumulated over the years from previous storms. She loved a good treasure hunt. Sifting through the wooden debris, she found several treasures of knurled pieces of cypress trees worn smooth over a period of time in the water.

The setting sun reflected a beam of light off a smooth surface several feet deep within the driftwood pile. Not one to turn down a challenge, let alone a possible hidden treasure, Janet carefully began removing the several layers of wood covering the object until she reached a round, smooth surface encased in a sort of rope-like latticework.

Her heart quickened as she visually fantasized a hidden treasure left undiscovered over the years, carried by the sea from some distant land.

As she dug to free her find, the object appeared to be larger than first anticipated, mostly submerged in the sand. Grabbing hold of the rope exterior, she tugged at it until the sand gave way. Holding it up to the light, dusting the sand from its surface, she discovered a perfectly-formed, large, deep sea-green Japanese glass fishing float about a foot in diameter.

Pleased with her find, she quickly looked around to see if anyone had noticed her, almost anticipating someone to appear and demand the return of the lost treasure. Satisfied that no one was going to relieve her of her treasure, she gathered up the other driftwood pieces she had found and walked back to the house. As the sun set into the water, she was pleased with her first day at the beach.

Upon returning to the house, she took a long warm bath, after which she put on a terry cloth bathrobe. Sipping a cup of hot cider, she built a fire, put another Jonathan Lee CD on the stereo, Janet fell into a deep sleep that lasted until the following morning.

* * * * * *

The beach had a soft fog hanging just above the water, giving an eerie feeling of surrealism. The light mist that emanated from the fog felt good on Janet's face as she walked at the water's edge, dodging waves as they relentlessly came and retreated, one after another. Between waves, she could see the small rocks and shells left by the previous wave, often picking up a small agate or a shell that caught her eye.

An elderly man stood knee-deep in the surf in his hip boots, fishing. Children ran ahead of their mother, darting between the waves, playing tag with the water. a man tugged at a string in an attempt to make his multi-colored-tiered kite dance. He could make it climb, then swoop down until it almost touched the ground, then, pulling on a set of strings, made it climb to the heavens again. "Grown boys," Janet mused as she watched a Sea gull repeated the time-long ritual of landing on the spot where a wave had just regressed, digging their beaks into the sand looking for sand dabs, then, at the last moment, just before the next wave overcame them, jumped into the air, squawking, repeating the routine again on the next wave. Those seagulls successful in finding a treasure were soon surrounded by those less fortunate, trying to take away their food. Sometimes, they would find something inedible, like a plastic toy, and swallow it, only to regurgitate it a moment later and continue seeking another morsel more fitting to their appetite.

It felt good, not having to worry about punching a time clock, meeting a deadline, having to go to court and fight someone else's battle. Here, time had no relevance. The only thing of significance was the constant ebb and flow of the ocean. Its motion was hypnotic and soothing.

Yet, among all this tranquility, Janet was keenly aware of a gnawing feeling that something was not right in her world. Even though she tried to repress it, the feeling wouldn't let her rest. She didn't know what it was, but nonetheless, there it was, like a infected sliver in her finger, ever present. She would let it lie dormant for the time being, sitting at he edge of consciousness, knowing that when the time was right her brain would somehow sort through the problem. In its own time, it would lay whatever was bothering her out for Janet to see and deal with. She didn't know how this problem solving process had first come about, but surmised it had probably evolved during her years at Lewis and Clark College.

Janet's mother had raised her to be a religious person. Without fail, each Sunday the family went to a small Baptist Church, first Sunday School, then Church. There was never any question about her relationship with The Almighty or the role religion played in her life.

It was when she had applied for and had been accepted into Lewis and Clark College, a small Oregon Presbyterian school, that there, along with her regular curriculum, she had attended chapel each Wednesday and Sunday. Her faith had deepened and grown to the point that it was the one thing that, when all else seemed to crumble, was constant. It was the one stable facet in her life that she knew would never let her down.

Included in the school's curriculum was a required religion course, to be taken during the student's junior year. Unbeknownst to the weary student, however, the other required school curriculum taken during the student's freshman and sophomore years skillfully and methodically tore down and destroyed the "Sunday School beliefs" that most young people had been taught as a child, which had been the foundation of their faith. The school's intent was to start building a more "mature and solid" foundation during the student's junior year when they took the required follow-up religion course.

As the sophomore student began to question their now-shaken faith, small groups of students could be found huddled in dormitory rooms, trying to understand what was happening to them. Janet was no exception. She had found herself floundering and feeling insecure. The one stable facet of her life had always been her faith, and now that too was in question.

She wrestled with the problem of "Does God really exist", and worried about her ultimate existence after death. She finally became so insecure that, by the end of her sophomore year, she'd developed a peptic ulcer.

Lost Woman

Unable to regain her faith, the experience did leave her with one positive aspect: she learned to never get caught in the trap of worrying needlessly about anything over which she had no direct control. Worrying, she would later tell anyone interested enough to listen, was an exercise in futility. Not only does it not produce anything positive, its counter product is that it prohibits the person from solving problems objectively. In short, worrying creates problems, not solve them.

* * * * * *

Janet knew that sooner or later her mind would begin producing thoughts for her to consciously work on. At the moment, however, here she was, walking alone on a beach, happy yet unhappy and confused in what should be the best years of her life.

On the positive side, she was a successful attorney, had come through that terrible experience in San Francisco, and still had her health, and had some wonderful friends.

On the other side of the coin, her marriage to Brad just didn't seem to be working. Not that she didn't love him, for she felt that, down deep, there was a genuine love between them, but that feeling of deep committed love just didn't seem to be there. Now, with the recent death of her mother, she had lost the only real family she had ever known. Somehow this seemed to be the crux of her dilemma. Her success as an attorney or the money she made didn't seem to really matter when the chips were down. It was clear that her life, as she now knew it, wasn't working.

It was getting late, and she was a long way from the house. As she walked back, small groups of kids, families, and couples were gathering driftwood to build fires on the beach, breaking out marshmallows to roast, while someone in another group played a guitar while everyone sang softly. There were groups sitting, talking low, enjoying each others company. The joy and companionship everyone else was having made her feel all the more alone and isolated. She longed to be part of something permanent, for the feeling of that warmth and security that everyone else enjoyed.

      *   *   *   *   *   *

When she finally returned to the house it was stark dark outside. As she climbed the steps leading to the house, she was aware that some of the lights were on. "I don't remember leaving the lights on," she said aloud to herself. Quietly, she tip-toed around the balcony, peering into the family room. Inside, sitting on the hearth, next to the fireplace, was Mary Lee, listening to Janet's Jonathan Lee CD, sipping something hot from a cup.

"What the hell are you doing here?" Janet demanded, bursting into the room. Mary Lee calmly looked up at Janet and smiled. Janet looked a fright. The evening mist had taken all the body out of her hair and it hung limp, resembling a cat emerging from a pond of water.

"What are you grinning about! What's so funny?"

"Sorry, honey, it's just that you look like something the cat dragged in and the dog wouldn't touch. No offense intended." With a smile, she rose and patted Janet on the shoulder. She went to the kitchen and brought back a cup of hot apple cider for her.

"I wanted to come and speak to you alone—about the other day at Dave's—you know."

"What about it?" Janet said in a demanding voice. "There's nothing to apologize for. I don't own him." Her voice softened, taking on a tone of embarrassment. "I had no business going to his place unannounced, anyway. I guess I'm the one who should apologize."

"I just wanted you to know that there isn't anything serious between Dave and myself. I'm sorry you came in when you did, but Dave and I go back a long way. We're sort of…"soul-mates" you might say. In one sense we have a lot in common and enjoy each other's company, yet in another sense, we have very little in common at all. I guess that's why we attract each other."

She smiled at Janet and, putting down her cup, extended her hands to her. "A relationship with all the perks and no commitments. It probably sounds shallow to you, but I really neither want nor need a situation that demands anything more than time at this point in my life, and preferably not much of that. That's why Dave and I fit together like a two piece puzzle. Had I known you had a thing going, I never would have put myself in a spot to get caught like that…we would have gone to *my* place," she said with a laugh.

"Aw, there's nothing to be sorry for. In a way, I'm a lot like you. Dave's been a great comfort to me in the past, too. We also have this `special relationship' with each other. I don't know, I guess it started years ago when I first joined the firm," Janet said, sitting down.

"We hit it off at once. You know how it is when sometimes you meet someone for the first time and, `bam', you both know there's a spark between you. At first we just sort of gravitated towards each other, each not wanting to tell the other how we felt about one another." She paused to take a deep breath, looking at her own reflection in the window.

"Then…one day we went out for lunch together, brown bagging it." She chuckled. "We were sitting in the park on this bench when, all of a sudden, a cloudburst exploded above us and rain came down in buckets. Dave took off his jacket and put it over our heads and there we sat…like two dummies under a pup tent." She looked at Mary Lee for a moment.

"He looked down at me and I looked up at him and our eyes locked in this trance-like stare, you know, like you see in the movies sometimes. The next thing I knew, we were passionately kissing each other as if it was our last day on earth. We must have sat there for over an hour, drenched to the bone, necking on the park bench like a couple teenagers."

"Sounds exciting. I get goosebumps just listening to you tell the story," Mary Lee said with an impish smile.

"I think that hour was one of the most exciting sixty minutes in my life." She looked at Mary Lee, somewhat embarrassed.

She continued, "We've been at it ever since. We've always been careful not to be seen by someone else, 'cause the last thing I want to do is hurt Brad. You see, here's the rub. Believe it or not, I do love him—Brad, that is—but it's different with David. With him, its more of a…a sex game without fear of being hurt or having to make a commitment. Am I making any sense?"

"You're making all the sense in the world. It's as if you just told my story, from a different angle of course, but with the same goal and the same results. It's great, isn't it?"

"For me, he's become sort of a safety valve," Janet said. "But doesn't it bother you that I have the same feelings about him that you do…that I've been sleeping with him too?"

"Not in the slightest. Like I said, there are no bonds between us. You have Brad…and Dave. I have Dave and anyone else I want." Throwing her hands in the air with a laugh, she said, "Who could ask for more?"

Janet went to Mary Lee's outstretched arms and hugged her. "Thanks for being so understanding. I'm sure glad you came. It means a lot to me, especially now. I feel a lot better. You've been a real friend, and I need all the friends I can get. Believe me, I don't have many. On top of it all, you were a great help in that Francisco fiasco, for which I'm eternally grateful. You put it all on the line for me, and I haven't even thanked you." There was a large smile on her face as she hugged Mary Lee, squeezing her hard.

"If you ever need a friend, or just want to talk, I'll be here for you," Mary Lee offered. "I'm glad we had this talk. I just had to come down here and square things away with you." She paused. "Well, I better get out of here," she said, looking at her watch. "It's getting late, and the drive back home is brutal at night."

"You'll do no such thing, young lady," Janet said, putting her arm around her shoulder. "This place is huge and scary, and you're not leaving me here all alone. Stay a day or two, and we'll terrorize the village shops tomorrow. What do you say?"

"Sounds good to me. You got a deal."

Janet felt as if she had just found one of those missing links she had been looking for: a real friend. They sat by the fireplace with their hot apple cider, talking far into the night, sharing stories and life's experiences.

Chapter Seventeen

The beach was shrouded with a heavy fog, which was constantly in motion. For the moment, it appeared to be moving out to sea. A few hearty souls walked the shoreline looking for any treasure the sea may have coughed up the previous night. A man and his son stood hip-deep in the freezing water, protected by rubber hip waders, fishing for perch.

Janet stood looking out the kitchen window at the lazy, picturesque, ocean scene, warming her hands on a coffee mug, when Mary Lee strolled in, raising her arms with a big yawn. "Good morning. It is morning, isn't it?"

Janet threw a small sofa pillow at her and said with a giggle, "Yes, it's still morning, barely."

"Well, I see you're already dressed for a little serious walking. You haven't been out already, have you?" she asked, looking at the kitchen clock. "Holy smoke, it's nearly noon. Wow! I haven't slept this well in years. The beach air must agree with me," she said stretching again. "Well, what's on the agenda for the day?"

"Well, I thought we would walk down to the Shilo Inn for a spot of breakfast, then hit the shops. What do you say, up for for some nourishment?"

"You just said the two magic words that get my attention: 'food and shopping'. One more and you would have had a quinella for the big prize."

"Sex," Janet said, pointing her finger at her.
"Bingo! Give that lady five silver dollars."

* * * * * *

The brisk air felt good as they walked on the sand towards the boardwalk. Janet could feel the remnant of the cold night's fog on the cool sand squashing through her toes. It reminded her of the days of her childhood when she used to like to walk in puddles and feel the mud ooze through her toes, tickling them, making her giggle.

The beach front boardwalk had a few people walking on it, mostly couples strolling towards the shops or back to the beach after eating brunch or window-shopping. The Shilo Inn fronted on the beach with the dining room facing the ocean. The informal breakfast and lunch room was called "The Pelican". Appropriately, a large wood carving of a pelican eating a fish stood next to the front door.

The waiter gave them a window booth which was elevated a few feet above the boardwalk so those walking below couldn't look directly into the diner's face as they were eating. It also gave them an unobstructed, commanding view of the ocean. "Isn't it magnificent?" Janet said, looking out at its vast expanse. "Whenever I come here, I always feel so insignificant."

"How's that?" Mary Lee asked, looking at Janet, puzzled.

"Well, just think about it. For over six billion years, the tide has been coming in and going out relentlessly. It's seen the earth go from the dinosaur age, ice age, jet age, and who knows what, and for the next six billion years, the tide will still be coming in and going out like clockwork. Kind of puts things in perspective, don't you think?" she said, looking at Mary Lee. "I mean, how important can our little problems be, in reality? When you get right down to it, the only thing that's really significant is one's health and the ability to enjoy the life that's been

Howard Losness

given to us…to get through it with the least amount of pain and discomfort as possible." She paused, mesmerized by the ocean before finally looking at Mary Lee. "What's important to you, Mary Lee? I mean really important, above all?"

"Well…you don't mind asking tough questions do you?"

"I'm not talking about clothes, cars, or any of the trappings in life, I mean what's *really* important, *the* most important thing in your life?"

She paused for a moment before saying, "I would have to say my family. My Mom and…my Dad died several years ago, so I guess he's out of the picture…my Mom and my kid, Joseph."

"You have a son! I didn't know that. How old is he? How come you never mentioned him before?"

"Joseph is nineteen. He's from my first marriage, the only good thing that came out of it. I think if it hadn't been for him, I might have cashed in a long time ago," she said with a faraway look. "He's the one thing I live for. I think I know what you're driving at," she said, looking at Janet. "His health and happiness is really the only thing that matters. Men come and go, jobs come and go, the economy is up, its down, but the one stable thing in my life is Joseph." She looked at Janet with a smile, lightly punching her on the shoulder. "Very good, Janet. I've never quite thought about it in those terms, but you're absolutely right, nothing else does matter."

"I envy you. I don't have any children. My relationship with Brad is less than perfect, and since my mother died, I feel like a wounded fish in a shark tank. If I didn't know better, I'd start walking out in the ocean and not stop until it's all over. I think the only reason I don't is that I'm chicken," she said with a laugh.

"Kid, you got a lot of years ahead of you. Don't even think of cashing your chips in yet."

"I really envy you. Tell me, if this is a delicate subject, just hit me alongside the head and I'll understand, but how were you able to bring yourself to jump that sleazebag Francisco's bones just so we could bag him?"

"It really wasn't that bad. I don't want you to get the impression I jump in the sack with anyone, any time of the day."

"I wasn't even thinking along that line. It's just, to me he was so sleazy...yuck." She shivered, making a face.

"You're looking at it from a personal perspective, for what he did to you. Actually, he wasn't a bad-looking guy. He had a nice build and was well mannered; he just wasn't able to hold his liquor and wasn't very couth when it came to making love, which actually made my job a little easier. It's when you get one that likes to fight or gets nasty when he's so oiled that it becomes a problem. And, you have to admit, the money isn't bad, either...ten grand for an evening's work! I enjoy my work and, after all, it was for a good cause." She laughed, putting her hand on Janet's.

"Well, I just want you to know, I really appreciate it. You're a good friend."

"Thanks, I like that. Now let's eat!"

After breakfast, they hit the shops. They laughed at themselves trying on funny beach hats and large sun glasses. Mary Lee bought a large pink hat to keep the sun out of her eyes. Janet bought a sweatshirt with shells all over the front, while Mary Lee bought a couple of muscle shirts for her son.

They were enjoying some pink cotton candy, sitting on the boardwalk bench, when a couple of suntanned, young, hard-bodied guys in their late twenties leaned against the railing next to them with the line, "Hey, ah...don't tell me it's...I just can't bring the name up, wait, it's coming, it's...."

"Nice try, guys, but I'm afraid you're barking up the wrong tree. These two chicks aren't puttin' out today. Good luck next time," Mary Lee said with a smile, waving them on.

"You certainly handled that with diplomacy. I would have just told them to get lost and been done with it, but I like your style a lot more."

"It's not worth going around with a chip on your shoulder, daring someone to knock it off, because, you know what, sooner or later someone will. It takes less energy, and certainly less hassle, to be nice to people and roll with the punches. You'll get a lot further in life."

"See, that's what I mean about you—you seem to have your shit together all the time. You know who you are and where you're going. Anything that comes up, you automatically know how to handle it. Me, I come unglued."

"Aw, come on, you're being too hard on yourself. You're going through some hard times, but you'll come out of it. Just give yourself a little time and cut yourself some slack. Come on, let's hit the beach."

They found a nice clean patch of sand and lay on the rice mats purchased at the beach store. After rubbing cocoa oil on each other, they let the sun wash their bodies with its warm rays.

They enjoyed the quiet solitude with the ocean pounding on the sand and the sea gulls squawking someone broke the tranquility. "Well, what have we here? A couple sun bunnies. You gals care for a little company?"

Janet looked up through the slits in her fingers at the same two guys they had seen earlier They were kneeling beside them in the sand. "Don't you guys ever…." Janet began.

"Hi guys," Mary Lee interrupted, sitting up, putting on her pink hat so the sun wouldn't shine in her eyes. "No luck on the boardwalk?" She winked at Janet, putting her more at ease than she had been a moment earlier. "This all you guys got to do is hassle little gals like us on the beach all day long?" she said with a smile.

"To tell you the truth, me and my friend Hal, here—by the way my name's Mike—we're visiting from back east for a few days, and are just looking for a couple friendly females to pass the time with…nothing serious, you know."

"Well, my name is Mary Lee and this here is Janet. We're sisters on a short vacation from California, just trying to wind down a bit."

"Oh, what do you do?"

"We work for the State of California."

"Social workers?"

"No, we're with the C.H.P."

"C.H.P.?"

"California Highway Patrol. We're police officers. Narcotics division, undercover work, you know." Mary Lee looked at Janet, whose mouth had dropped open.

Visually stunned, the younger one said, "Well, ah, listen, you gals have a great time. We're going to ah, just wander on down the beach and see what's cookin."

"Hey, don't run off," Mary Lee said, leaning back, showing off her full figure. "Stick around, the action might pick up later. You might get lucky," she said with a wink.

"Uh, thanks anyway. Maybe we'll be back later. We're just going to saunter down the beach a piece," he said, almost falling over his feet trying to get going. Within moments, they were a hundred feet away and still going strong.

Mary Lee and Janet laughed so hard their sides hurt. "Where on earth did you pull that one from? You even had me believing it there for a moment."

"I just love playing off guys like that. They come on so macho, trying to take charge, and the slightest little threat sends them off with their tails between their legs. One time I told this guy I was a double black belt karate instructor. You should have seen him turn tail and run. I laughed for days about that one. And there was this time I told this guy I'd go out with him if he'd skydive with me. He took off so fast, I thought he had jets in his pants."

"Oh, you're bad. You are real bad, but I like it. It's so much fun being with you. I really appreciate your staying and spending time with me. It's giving me a whole new perspective on life."

"Why are you so lost, kid? You've got a good education, a law practice—successful, too, so I hear—a husband that adores you, you're healthy. What else is there?"

"I don't know, Mary Lee. Ever since my mother died, I just feel like I'm half a person. I can't concentrate on my work, my family life is the shits, and I just don't seem to care about anything."

"She really meant a lot to you, didn't she?" Mary Lee said, caressing her hair.

Janet nodded, choking back a tear. "It's not just that. I guess Daniels probably told you. I was adopted. I just have this feeling like I've been cheated, like all the kids have parents but me and I'm being punished or something."

"This may sound stupid or simplistic, but why don't you try to find them?"

There was a long silence as Janet looked at Mary Lee with a sort of vacant hypnotic stare, as if she were looking right through her.

"Did I say something that offended you? If so, I'm sorry," she said after a long silence.

"It's simple. It's so friggin' simple that I couldn't see the forest for the trees. What a dummy," she said, hitting herself on the forehead with her hand and a smile on her face.

"Well! I don't remember seeing that smile before."

"You're a genius. God, I love you," she said hugging Mary Lee. "It's so simple. Why didn't I think of it before?" Suddenly, like a bolt of lightning, it became crystal clear. She would find them. No matter how long it took, no matter where she had to go, she would find her parents.

Janet jumped up, pulling Mary Lee up by the hands and danced around in a circle. "Say…wait a minute. Something's fishy here. You didn't come all the way down here just to apologize about that little deal with Dave, did you? I'll bet Danielson sent you here to cheer me up, didn't he?" she said, poking her on the shoulder with her finger, a big smile on her face.

Mary Lee looked at Janet with a smirk. "I don't know what you're talking about. You know I don't do underhanded things like that."

"No, not much," she said grabbing Mary Lee by the shoulders. She hugged her so hard Mary Lee had to say, "Easy girl, easy. I'm not really with the C.H.P." she laughed.

The rest of the day Janet felt as if she was weightless. She couldn't wait to begin the hunt. Deep in her soul, she knew she was destined to find her mother. Her real mother. Who knows what else she might find in the process.

Chapter Eighteen

Janet thought the best way to attack the problem of finding her mother was to treat herself as if she were one of her own clients. The few years she had been in practice had taught her the only way to develop a case was to be able to visually see it graphed out in front of her on paper. She accomplished this by diagramming the case, assigning a name or label to each event, in the order of their appearance or importance. She then arranged them in neat little boxes, in chronological order, as they related to one another. Using this method of plotting out the characters and pertinent events, enabled her to intelligently correlate events and draw conclusions that could be visualized in a glance.

She would start with what she knew for sure. Her mother had said she had been born in a hospital in La Grande, Oregon. La Grande was a small mountain community, so, in all probability, there would be just one hospital.

Next, she would have to interview doctors, especially any that might be practicing who were there at time of her birth. Then she would have to hope that they would cooperate with her by allowing her to look at any records containing parental information that her mother must have given the hospital in order to be admitted.

The next task would be to locate the birth records. These could be found and researched at the hospital or the county where she was born. Satisfied that she had enough direction to begin her quest, Janet went to Steve Daniels' office. "I know this is beginning to be a habit," she said, somewhat sheepishly, "but I need another favor."

"You're beginning to be a real pain in the behind, Neilson," he said with a grin. "What is it this time? Want to move into a full partnership or just start your own firm?"

"Nothing quite so simple as all that, I'm afraid." She told Steve, "I really appreciate your giving me time off at the beach and all," she paused for a moment. "But I still feel like a lost goose in a snowstorm. I don't know who I am, where I'm at, or where I'm going, and I'm not going to be of any use to anyone until I find out. I hope you'll forgive me and indulge this one last whim. I don't know how I'm going to do it, but I have to find out who Janet Neilson really is." She looked at him like a puppy looking at her master.

"I feel, like you, that you have every right to seek your birthright, but you know the laws of this state. You have to understand, if the records are sealed, no court in the land will open them for you. When your birth mother gave you up for adoption, she not only relinquished all rights to raising you but, unfortunately, at the same time, sealed your fate as well. I'm afraid you're facing an impossible task," he said, shrugging his shoulders.

"I have to try, Steve. I'll never be able to look myself in the mirror if I don't."

"What about Brad? I assume he's going with you, too. I thought he was in the middle of that Lakeview Development deal. It's gotta be bad timing for him."

"He's not going," she said flatly.

"I don't know, Janet, you're like the proverbial wandering Jew, traveling from place to place with no permanent spot to park your sandals. I can't imagine he's going to be too happy about this."

"I haven't wanted to mention it, but Brad and I have separated. When I returned home from the beach, I found that he had moved some of his stuff out. He left a note saying it was his turn to find himself and, until further notice, I was to consider myself a free woman, to do as I wish."

"I'm sorry to hear that, Janet. That must have been quite a blow to you. How do you feel about that?"

"It hurts, but I guess I asked for it. Down deep, I feel there is something there for us, but at the moment, a separation is probably best. There's a lot of sorting out to be done. For the first time in my life, I feel like I know what I'm doing. I'm not just going through the motions. I've set a goal for myself, one that will probably alter my life forever. Hopefully, for the best. What do you say boss? Can I take time off…please?" she begged, holding her hands together, in a praying gesture.

"I say, go for it."

"Thanks, I knew I could count on you. You're solid gold. There's none better."

"Get out of here," he said, slapping her on her fanny as they walked to the door. "I've got work to do. And Janet…."

She turned around. "Yes?"

"Don't forget to invite me to the family reunion."

"You're top on the list."

*   *   *   *   *   *

The drive from Portland to La Grande usually took about six hours. The road winds along the Columbia River to eastern Oregon, then veers southeast through wheat country, with the last leg going into the Cascade Mountain Range. Janet left early in the morning, so she would have the advantage of driving during the daylight hours. The sun usually set around five thirty this time of the year, and driving through the mountain pass to La Grande at night was an experience she could have done without.

The last time she had made this trip had been in high school. Coach Rucker had been driving the school bus to a basketball game. It was late in the day, and the setting sun cast long shadows on the road, through the tall pine trees, making driving all the more difficult.

All of a sudden, a buck had jumped out of the forest in front of the bus. The coach had jerked the steering wheel to the side quick enough to miss the large buck, but a moment later, the bus slammed into his mate, a doe weighing no more than a hundred-fifty pounds.

The impact had killed the deer instantly, leaving the front of the bus caved in. Fortunately, no one inside was injured, but the radiator had been ruined, with water and green coolant spilling onto the road.

They had missed the basketball game, waiting over an hour for a tow truck. The experience had left an indelible mark on Janet's memory. After that, she avoided night travel in the mountains whenever possible.

The Columbia Gorge was beautiful this time of the year, with the mountains jutting above the Columbia River like Grecian gods reaching for the sky. The slow-moving river was deep blue. You could tell, just by looking at it, that it was mighty cold.

An unweary traveler, driving the gorge in the early morning hours, negotiating a turn at anything more than forty miles an hour could get the surprise of his life. With temperatures dipping below the freezing level, any moisture left from an evening rain, melted snow, or morning frost left a road cover known affectionately as "black ice", an invisible sheet of ice so slick one could fall on one's kiester at the blink of an eye. Once a moving car starts to slide on black ice, there is little or nothing an unskilled driver can do to avert a possible disaster.

Fortunately, Janet had lived her entire life in this type of weather. Between being taught to drive on winter roads by her dad and having experienced, in some small way, the helplessness of two thousand pounds of metal sliding out of control on fresh fallen show, she had learned how to navigate this type of road condition. Fate has its way of reiterating its lessons, however, when one least expects it.

Coming around the bend at the "Bridge of Gods", right before her eyes, was a little red MGA slowly spinning out of control in the middle of the two-lane freeway, heading straight toward Janet's white BMW. She knew better, but her instincts took over and she did it anyway. She slammed on her brakes. Janet's white BMW and the little red MGA were about to merge.

As much as she knew she had to do it, but felt wrong doing so, Janet turned her wheels into the direction of her slide, heading straight for the river, all the while gently pumping the brakes.

Perspiration formed on her forehead. Her eyes were wide as saucers, but her mind was crisp and clear.

As Janet's car slowly moved toward the edge of the bank, the red MGA spun harmlessly past Janet, its occupant's mouth wide open in a silent scream, knuckles white, grasping the steering wheel with all her might, and, in all probability, her foot jammed as hard as she could on the brake pedal.

As Janet neared the side of the unfenced ledge. She looked at the river fifty feet below. Opening the car door, she had her left foot on the door-casing, ready to abandon ship if necessary. Once on the side of the road, however, the rough gravel gave the front tires something to dig into, and the BMW came to a safe stop.

Janet looked around just in time to see the MGA disappear around the bend. The driver had righted the car and, without missing a beat, had kept on traveling down the road without so much as a wave, a "sorry", or "how do you do". Wide awake and fully alert, Janet proceeded with her pulse and heartbeat drumming twice it's normal speed.

By mid-day she turned off the Columbia Gorge at McNary Dam, heading into wheat country. Although there were miles of nothing but rolling wheat land, she always enjoyed seeking out the "mystery paths" in the wheat fields. Even after the grain had been cut, the path of the old original Oregon Trail could still clearly be seen in the stubble.

Years of wagon trains traveling west had somehow left their permanent historical impression on the land. The wheat always grew darker where the trail had once been constantly traveled during the birth of the West. No amount of plowing, planting, or fertilization had ever covered or altered the visibility of the "Old Oregon Trail" for the past hundred years.

Janet pulled into the La Grande Travel Lodge just as the sun was setting. She would go over her battle plan one more time before retiring for the evening. Her mind was whirling with excitement in anticipation of the following day. At the same time, she was concerned about the possibility of failure that could stop her dead in her tracks.

* * * * * *

The first stop was the hospital. If she had been born here, there would be records, and she hoped to get access to them. As Daniels had so aptly pointed out earlier, however, Oregon law strictly prohibited adopted children from meddling in the affairs of their adoption when the biological mother had requested anonymity. Janet hoped that her knowledge of the law would help sway any argument a simple office girl might have for not assisting her.

The administration office was manned—or in this case, womaned—by a young girl who looked no more than nineteen. Janet put on her legal face, approaching the desk with an air of authority sprinkled with a dash of arrogance.

"Can I help you?" the young girl asked, looking over a pair of half-frame reading glasses.

"Yes, please," she said, setting her brief case on the counter, opening the lid, leafing through several loose papers. "Could you direct me to the hospital archives? I need some information relative to a legal matter that I'm led to believe is stored in that area."

"Archives?" the young speckled girl asked. "What kind of a disease is that?"

Janet knew she had the upper hand. She explained that she was an attorney and that she had traveled all the way from Portland to get evidence for a case she was trying—a very important case. A matter of life and death. She needed a copy of a birth certificate for a client born in this hospital in 1955.

The girl asked Janet to wait, saying she would be right back. Janet's pulse quickened. "This is going to easier than I thought," she said to herself quietly.

The girl returned with a heavy set lady who had the look and gait of an army sergeant. "Joy here tells me you want to get into the archives," she said, challenging and unsmiling, putting a yellow pencil behind her ear.

Janet repeated her spiel to the Sergeant. "Any records older than three years are on micro fiche. You can come this way, and I'll show you the files."

Eagerly, Janet flashed through the years until she came to 1955. She found February twenty-fifth. There had been three babies born on that day. A Baby Jane appeared as the third and final birth of the day. The card read, Baby's Name: Baby Jane. Time of Birth: 22.50 hours. Mother: data not available. Father: data not available. Doctor: Henry Hines, M.D.

"That's gotta be me. There couldn't be more than one 'Baby Jane' born the same day. That's me!" she said under her breath.

"Miss. Could you help me here?" she asked the young girl.

"I'm sorry, I don't know anything about that end of the business. You will have to ask Ms. Joan Marie."

"Great!" she said to herself.

"Yes. What can I do for you?" The tone of impatience was as if Janet had interrupted her morning bowel movement.

"What does the name 'Baby Jane' mean when it appears on a birth certificate?" Janet asked, full well knowing the answer.

"That's the name given any newborn female child put up for adoption if a name isn't given at birth," she said matter-of-factly.

"The record on this micro fiche seems to be incomplete," Janet said, motioning towards the machine with her head. "I need to have more information relative to one of the births on this date," she said holding out a three-by-five card with the date February twenty-fifth, nineteen fifty-five written on it. "I would appreciate it if you could help me here. What I need is...."

The Sergeant interrupted. "What's on the tape is all there is. There ain't no more," she said, slapping the palm of her hand on the desktop for effect.

"But there has to be. You see, the parents of this particular child aren't named in this document! I need to have their names in order to complete my investigation," Janet said, changing her voice from one of authority to one of pleading for help. Her eyebrows furrowed together to accent the plea.

"Let me see," the sergeant said briskly, looking at Janet with a questionable look. Peering at the micro fiche, she said gruffly, "This code here," she said pointing her finger at the index numbers at the right of the micro fiche, "indicates that the names of this particular birth were withheld by request of the parents in conjunction with hospital policy. Either way, the name 'Baby Jane' is all that's recorded. If you need a name beyond that, you'll need a court order."

"This case number at the top of the certificate. How do I get access to that file?"

"You don't. That code number indicates the documents are sealed and not accessible. They are sealed in the hospital achieves below, and no one is allowed access without a judge's signature," she said, glancing at Janet's brief case.

"But I've come all the way from Portland on a very important and official case. I must have access to that file." Janet's voice was beginning to show the strain of frustration.

The Sergeant was clearly enjoying her display of authority. "I'm sorry, miss. I don't care if you came from Portland, Maine. Unless you have a court order, signed by a judge of this county, that file is sealed and stays sealed. Neither you nor anyone else can have access to the file. Now, if you'll excuse me, I'm very busy."

For two cents, Janet would have thrown the micro fiche book at her, but elected to hold her temper for now. She walked away frustrated, but not defeated.

The next stop was the courthouse. It didn't take much research to find that Judge Knowles had been the presiding Judge in 1955, but had since retired and moved to California. The presiding Judge now was Irvin Cross. His picture adorned the wall, behind the long row of judges who had preceded him. His picture was displayed with a stern look, as if to say, "five years at hard labor! Next case."

She knocked on his chamber door.

"Enter."

Janet was surprised to see the judge sitting behind the desk in a polo shirt. Judges in Portland usually wear a suit and tie to work and either put their robe on over the suit or sometimes just over the shirt and tie, weather permitting. This was the first time she had seen one just lounging about in his office in a polo shirt. He appeared to be a little older than Janet. His greying brown hair was parted near the middle of his forehead, giving a youthful appearance. Despite his being a judge, his eyes were kind, and he had a friendly smile which was nowhere as fierce as the picture on the hall appeared to make him.

"Thank you for seeing me, Your Honor," she said, extending him her hand with her business card in it. She decided to level with him, feeling that he, too, was an attorney, and would have compassion for a fellow member of the Bar.

After baring her soul, she looked through tired, pleading eyes, hoping for a favorable decision. "I'm very sorry, Miss Neilson. I appreciate your plight, but, as you well know, Oregon law is quite clear in this matter. If a mother desires to give a child up for adoption and doesn't want her identity divulged, the case is sealed. There can be no access. There are no exceptions. I'm sorry."

No use arguing. That was that. Janet smiled weakly, extended her hand thanking him for his time and consideration, and left.

The last stop was the Recorder's office. It would be blind luck if she found anything different, but she couldn't overlook the possibility that her birth certificate or some corresponding document may have unwittingly been filed, showing the parents' name. She didn't have much hope, but had to explore all alternatives. As suspected, the only document filed was a copy of that found in the hospital.

A dead end.

Not one to be outdone, she returned to the hospital with renewed vigor. This time she went direct to Personnel. The attendant was a kindly looking elderly lady with a disarming smile. "I drove all the way from Portland yesterday," Janet began, "and I need to find a doctor that was working here at the hospital back in 1955. A doctor Henry Hines. It's very important that I find him. It's a matter of life and death, you might say," Janet said, hoping to play on the woman's sympathy. "So far, I've run into a dead end. Can you help me?"

"Well, let's see, dearie. The name doesn't ring a bell. Have you tried the doctor's directory?"

"That's the first place I looked," Janet said. "No luck. He's probably retired. I thought, because he was on the hospital staff, the records here might indicate where he retired to."

"Let me look into the historical personnel file. Take a seat if you like. It'll take a moment."

"Take all the time you want. I appreciate any help you can give me."

A few minutes later, the lady returned. "I'm sorry, miss. According to the records, Doctor Hines died of a heart attack at the age of eight-six back in 1984."

Janet stood silently with her eyes lowered for a few minutes. "Could you tell me where the hospital archives are, she asked timidly?"

"Why, yes. They're located in the basement. Down next to the equipment room. But you can't get in there, dearie. The room is locked, and only the hospital administrative staff has access to that area."

"Thanks," she said, and departed.

Janet located the stairs to the basement around the corner from the admittance desk, at the end of the hallway, near a waiting room. Looking around to see if anyone was paying any attention to her, she cautiously approached the door. It was a windowless, solid oak door with a metal casing. It didn't surprise her to find it locked. It was probably one that permanently locked from either side when closed.

Looking around to see if anyone had taken note of her presence, she entered the waiting room, then sat against the far wall, where she could see out of the large, screened window into the hallway.

There were two elderly ladies sitting on the adjacent wall. Apparently they had been there for quite some time, as brown sandwich bags containing empty soft drink cans, pieces of uneaten food, and orange peels lay on the floor beneath the couches. One of the women was sleeping while the other quietly watched television, not even acknowledging Janet's presence.

Vending machines stood in an alcove of the waiting room containing soft drinks, candy, and hot soup. Janet put three quarters in the machine and pushed the Pepsi button. A loud rolling clank announced the arrival of her drink as the elderly sleeping lady stirred.

Janet returned to her seat. Taking a refreshing sip from the can, she closed her eyes for a moment, then opened her briefcase and removed several business cards. She methodically folded each one in half the long way, periodically looking up through the glass door.

No more than a half hour had gone by when her senses perked up to the sound of a metal bucket clanging against the hall wall. Soon, an elderly black man dressed in drab green pants and shirt shuffled by towards the end of the hall.

Janet quietly rose from her seat, almost tip-toeing across the carpet, until she reached the door. She looked around the corner just in time to see the heavy door slowly swing itself shut, then hesitate for a moment before the automatic closer brought the door catch home.

She looked down, smiling as she pointed her finger at the mop and bucket left standing next to the door. "Gotcha."

Pushing her briefcase under the lamp table, Janet walked down the hall, positioning herself just behind the basement door. Soon the door opened again, almost hitting Janet in the face. The janitor picked up his pail and mop and shuffled down the hallway again.

As the door swung to close, Janet grabbed the side of it, halting its closure. Looking around and seeing no one, she stuck several business cards folded in half between the latch portion of the door jamb, and the door. There was a muffled sound as the door latch hit the door jamb but no final "click" sounded. The door was shut, but not locked!

She held her breath as a bead of perspiration ran down the side of her face as she watched the janitor shuffle around the corner at the end of the hall.

Janet quietly pulled the heavy door open, letting the folded cards fall inside the door. Picking them up, she folded them into a small, tight square and forced them into the latch receptacle, thus preventing the door latch from locking. The door closed.

The wide stairwell was well lit. After taking off her shoes, Janet quietly made her way down to the basement, pausing at the bottom to listen for any sound that would indicate there were other people there.

All was quiet.

She found the equipment room easily enough. The grey metal door was plainly labeled "Equipment Room". Below the sign was a small square window with wire mesh between the glass panes. Janet peered in. The room was large, and brightly lit, filled with tanks, tools, air conditioning and heating equipment, furnaces, generators, and such. The floor was painted grey, with red-lined paths winding through the machinery. No one appeared to be in the room.

At the end of the short hall Janet found a door with a red light over it. The sign said "Private. No entry. Keep Out." Janet tried the heavy silver doorknob to no avail. It was locked.

She had seen movies where a burglar would jam his credit card into the space between the door and the latch and the door would magically open. After removing one of her plastic credit cards, she pushed it hard between the small space between the door and the door latch.

Finding resistance, she moved it back and forth, pushing even harder. The card snapped in her hand, stinging her fingers. "Shit!," she said, "that was my only gas card, too."

Setting her shoes on the floor next to the door, he returned to the equipment room. Peering through the small glass window, she saw no one there. Quietly she turned the doorknob. It was unlocked! She stuck her head around the corner without actually going into the room. The room was filled with the high-pitched hum of machinery.

On the wall opposite of the boiler was a work bench with tools hanging on the wall. Each tool had been outlined in red. Janet quickly, but quietly, tip-toed across the room, eyes still searching for workers, her heart beating like a drum.

Looking over the display of tools, she reached for a two foot pipe wrench. She didn't realize how heavy it was, catching it with both hands before it fell to the bench. Retreating as quickly and quietly as she had come, she closed the door behind her. She ran in her stocking feet back to the file room door.

After opening the wrench to the size of the doorknob, she placed the open wrenches' steel teeth on the knob. Putting all her weight on the wrench, she tried to twist the doorknob.

Nothing!

Time was precious. Maybe this wasn't such a good idea. She looked around again.

"Got to try again. I have to get in!"

She bounced on the end of the handle, once, twice. Suddenly, the wrench fell to the floor with a clang, the doorknob in its jaws.

Janet stood like a statue, holding her breath.

Listening.

Looking.

No one had heard her. Beads of perspiration stood out on her forehead. Her hands shook.

Inside the door, where the doorknob once had stood, she could see the latching mechanism. She pulled the t-shaped appendage back with the broken credit card, releasing the door latch.

The door opened!

Picking up her shoes, the broken doorknob and pipe wrench, Janet stepped into the dark cold, room, searching the side wall for a light switch. She found it right where it should be.

The room proved to be filled with stacks of cardboard file cabinets. Each cabinet was marked at the upper top corner with the year and contents in red.

1988—operational expenses. 1988—patients. Now all she had to do was find 1955. Suddenly, the silence of the room was filled with the sound of a metal door banging shut. Someone was coming!

She darted towards the door, hitting the light switch with the palm of her hand. The room became dark again as she quietly sank to the floor by the door, not daring to breathe, her heart pounding so hard she was sure it's echo could be heard throughout the basement.

The sound of shuffling feet became louder, until Janet was sure the door would open at any moment and she would be exposed for the criminal she was.

Instead, she heard the sound as the equipment room door opened, then close, leaving a void of any sound in the basement, only to be opened and closed again a few moments later. The shuffle of feet ascended the stairs, followed by the clanging of the metal door at the top of the stairs.

It seemed an eternity before Janet allowed herself to breathe again. Her blouse wet with perspiration, hands trembling, she slowly lifted the light switch, startling herself with an audible "ahh" as the room lit up again.

Hands trembling, heart trying to beat its way out of her chest, eyes wide open, she scampered between the tiers of boxes like a wild woman until she found 1955. She was petrified that someone would find her here. She had broken and entered an area clearly meant to be secure. She could lose her license to practice law, and would probably go to jail. She would have no defense.

Brushing the thought from her mind, she continued.

1955—patients! She seemed to have no control over her fingers. They stumbled over the files—January, February! February twenty-fifth, 1955. The folders were alphabetically filed. The name on the blue label of the first file read "Baby Jane—Friend, Janet Caroline".

Janet held the file with trembling hands, momentarily stunned. Without opening the file, she picked up her shoes, the pipe, wrench and tip-toed out the door, slipping the doorknob back onto the broken receptacle, being careful to wipe both sides of the knob with her skirt. It wouldn't do to have her fingerprints circulating around the police department, looking for a match somewhere.

Returning to the equipment room, Janet replaced the wrench on the painted space after first wiping it clean of any fingerprints too. Fairly flying up the stairs in stocking feet, she gently pushed her weight against the steel door.

It opened! She breathed a sigh of relief as she retrieved the folded cards from the latch receptacle.

Peering around the corner to see if anyone was in the hallway, Janet slipped out, quietly shutting the door behind her. After replacing her shoes, she walked out the side exit as quickly as possible, without drawing attention to herself. Once outside, she removed her shoes and raced to her car, jubilant as a kid in a candy store.

Janet drove the distance from the hospital to her motel in record time, eyes glued to the rearview mirror. Even when she had arrived to the motel, she half expected to be met by the sheriff.

Fairly flying up the stairs to her room, she locked the door behind her, standing in the darkness with her back to the door for several minutes… breathing…listening….

Only after several minutes of standing panicked in the darkness did she remove the file from under her overcoat and sit it down on the gaming table, turning on the overhead hanging lamp.

It was then that it suddenly hit her. Her briefcase! She had left her briefcase in the waiting room of the hospital. What if they discovered the break in? They'd eventually find her briefcase with her business cards and identification.

"I have to go back."

She picked up the hospital file. Looked around the room, then, going to the bed, lifted one side of the mattress, depositing the file under the mattress.

"Tacky. Any fool will look there."

She retrieved the file from the bed again. Going to the corner of the room, Janet dropped to her knees and tore up the corner of the carpet, breaking a fingernail in the process.

"Damn. I hate it when I do that," she said, sticking the finger in her mouth.

Replacing the carpet after depositing the file, satisfied that no one would think of looking there, she drove back to the hospital as fast as she could, yet obeying the speed limit. "No use getting caught at this stage of the game."

She found that all of a sudden she had become calm, knowing that now fate was in her hands as long as she didn't screw up.

Her briefcase was exactly where she had left it, as were the two old women. Clutching it like a child, Janet quickly retreated.

Back in the motel, having retrieved the file from under the carpet, she sat in the chair, looking at the unopened folder. Finally, with trembling hands, Janet unsealed it.

Stapled to the inside flap was the original birth certificate, the same one she had seen on the hospital micro fiche and at the courthouse. There were two birth certificates, one stapled to the other, back to back. The first one had the child's name as, "Baby Jane". The second one said Baby Johnson. Johnson!

The other side of the jacket contained the hospital health file. There was a formal document entitled "Hospital Consent and Release Agreement", a document filled out in the event of a live birth wherein the mother elected to relinquish custody of the child.

The form was signed, dated and notarized.

Doctor: Henry Hines, M.D.

Mother: Lillian Agnes Johnson.
Father: Unknown.
She paused, mouthing the name…"Lillian Agnes Johnson". Then, "Father…unknown". That caused her concern.
Father—unknown.
She closed her eyes, sitting back in the chair for several minutes before continuing through the file.
She flipped to the admission page.
Patient: Lillian Agnes Johnson.
Age: 17.
Reason for Admission: Pregnancy.
Father: Not Available.
Address: 1438 Oak Street, Springfield, Oregon.
There were other documents in the file… health certificate, blood type, a daily log of the time spent in the hospital.
The last entry was a document of release to a Mr. & Mrs. Ralph Emerson Friend.
Janet sank back in the chair, her heart pounding in her chest. She had wanted to know. Now that she had a name to attach to the faceless figure, it scared her. She felt a tinge of uneasiness. What if her real mother was dead? What if she can't find her? What if she found her and she didn't want to see her? Maybe she didn't even remember having her! A cold shiver ran through her body. Doubt soon passed, however, and was replaced by a feeling of ecstasy.
She had done it!
She would not be denied.

Chapter Nineteen

She picked up the telephone and dialed information. "What city, please?"

"Springfield. Lillian Agnes Johnson at 1438 Oak Street." The chance of her still being at that address and unmarried was remote, but it was worth a try.

"Sorry, no listing for that name."

Janet decided to drive to Springfield the following morning. The day's events had left her mentally, and physically drained. A good night's sleep would be a welcomed relief right now. She took a hot shower and, without even eating dinner, slipped into a fitful slumber, the likes of which she had not had for a long time.

The next day, she drove straight to the Springfield main post office. Once there, she told the postmaster she was searching for a long lost cousin and gave him her last known address from back in 1962. It took several minutes before he returned with a yellow three-by-five inch card.

It said, "Lillian Agnes Miller Current Address: 1438 Oak Street, Springfield, Oregon. New Address: 234 Sea Side Drive, Santa Cruz, California 95061. Date: June 24, 1964. Signed Lillian A. Miller"

"Miller," she said aloud. "She has a nice signature," she thought as she idylly ran her finger over the card Apparently, she had married and moved to California in '64, Janet surmised. With any luck, she'd still living there. She graciously thanked the postmaster, skipping out of the post office like a schoolgirl.

Janet was so nervous, she could hardly dial the telephone. "Operator."

"Could you give me Santa Cruz, California information please?"
"Dial 408-555-1212."

Janet dialed. When the operator answered she asked for the phone number of Lillian Agnes Miller. A moment later a recorded voice gave her the telephone number.

She hung up the phone. Her hands were trembling now. "I've come this far…there's no turning back."

She dialed the number. It rang. Once. Twice. Then, a pleasant woman's voice said, "Miller residence."

A pause.

"Hello…is anyone there?"

A pause, then a dial tone.

Slowly, Janet replaced the receiver. She wasn't prepared to speak. "What would I say? Who do I say I am? Why am I calling after all this time? What if she doesn't want to see me? Oh God, what if she doesn't? What if she really doesn't want to see me?"

She sat in her car for a long time, just sitting, sort of in a trance. Finally, she snapped out of it and turned on the ignition. "I'm going to California. Santa Cruz, here I come."

"Wait a minute! Wait just a darn minute. I don't have any clothes. I have a job. Shit, I even have a husband somewhere. I can't just pick up and go to California on a minute's notice!" She sat in her car for few minutes, thinking before picking up her car phone.

"Molly, this is Janet Neilson. Fine, thank you. Molly, would you give Steve a message for me? Tell him everything is working out so far. Tell him I have to go to California! Oh, and Molly, tell him I hope to have that invitation we talked about printed soon. He'll understand."

Eight hours later, Janet's white BMW pulled into Howard Johnson's Motel in Redding, California. She was so tired, she lay on the bed and fell fast asleep, clothes on and all. When she awoke, it was ten o'clock in the morning. She showered, brushed her teeth, combed her hair, then paused to look at herself in the mirror. "Gad, what a fright." She hadn't changed her clothes since leaving Portland, and it was beginning to show. Her slacks were wrinkled and the blouse and sweater she wore were a little worse for wear. She could even detect a body odor on them. "You look like something the cat dragged in and the dog wouldn't touch," she said aloud. "Aw, what the hell. I'm not going to a beauty contest. I can shop in Santa Cruz. Buy myself a souvenir, if nothing else." She drove through a Jack in The Box, ordered a Breakfast Jack and two orange juices, and was on her way.

Nine hours later, she pulled into the sleepy town of Santa Cruz. The sun was just setting as she drove onto the pier that jetties out into the ocean from the Boardwalk. "So, this is Santa Cruz."

The lights from the stores, eating establishments, and the boardwalk rides reflected off the waves slapping at the beach. She could hear the kids scream as the roller-coaster car dove down the track and the clack-clack-clack as it climbed back up again. Couples were walking on the beach hand in hand. An old man scanned the sand with a metal detector searching for lost valuables, and a few fishermen had their poles in the water at the end of the pier.

"This is the kind of atmosphere I could call home," she mused, leaning on the rail, watching a sea otter dive for fish beneath the pier. In the distance the constant "ark, ark, ark" of the sea lion and the "kee, kee" from the sea gulls supplied background music. She walked the pier, looking into the shops. She bought herself a white sweater with "Santa Cruz" printed in pink lettering across the chest. She found pair of matching shorts, a pair of white, low-cut tennis shoes, and a cute culotte set accented with sea shells sewn to the blouse.

Looking at the houses on the cliff overlooking the beach, she wondered if her mother lived in one of them. She was starting to get that panicky feeling again, with butterflies in her stomach. She had come all this way and was so close. She couldn't help but wonder what the next day would bring. One way or another, she knew her life would never be the same once she met her mother.

She was up and dressed in her new clothes by eight o'clock the next morning. She had breakfast at a restaurant on the beach. The weather was delightful. A soft breeze kissed her cheek as she sat on the veranda sipping a large glass of orange juice. The table where she sat table overlooked the beach, where she could watch the activity below. The same old man was scanning the beach for lost treasures with his metal detector, periodically digging into the sand, only to find a small toy or coin. Once in a while he would shove something into his pocket, unearthed from beneath the sand. Several joggers were running on the beach, getting their morning exercise. A young man threw a Frisbee for his small dog, who displayed great exuberance catching and returning the small plastic disk to its owner for another turn. A group of young people were stretching a volleyball net in the sand, marking their territory for the day's activities.

"Today, is going to be a red letter day," she said softly to herself, raising her glass to the morning sun.

After breakfast, she bought a pair of sunglasses and a city map. The city of Santa Cruz wasn't very large. The whole city map took less space than the size of the palm of her hand. She quickly located Sea Side Drive, a rather short street running into a road fronting on the ocean.

Somehow it didn't surprise her to find the street located just off the beach. She had always had a strong attraction to water…water of any kind—lakes, streams, or the ocean. "I'm sure we share the same interests," she thought, wondering what other traits they might have in common. "I wonder if we look alike", she thought aloud.

She was holding the map, sort of in a trance, thinking about her mother. Focusing on the map again, she stared at it, as if trying to project herself onto the street to see what the house where her mother lived in looked like.

She checked her watch…only eight-thirty. "Think I'll go for a walk on this beach of yours," she mused, as if talking to her mother. "Maybe I'll move here some day. Wouldn't that surprise everyone."

An amazing calm had overtaken her since her arrival last night. She knew that, no matter what the outcome, the large void that had existed her whole adult life was about to be satisfied, one way or another.

It was ten o'clock when she pulled in front of the house on Sea Side Drive. It was a moderate, wood-sided house, painted grey with blue trim, and blue shutters, located just a hundred feet or so off the beach. There were flowers and plants hanging in wooden baskets from the rafters and potted plants sitting on the porch. The front yard had large lava rocks strewn around with ice plants and jade bushes planted in between. On one side of the porch a swing hung from the ceiling.

"The person who lives in this house obviously has a green thumb," Janet mused. She closed her eyes as she smelled the salt from the ocean in the air.

Janet sat looking at the house for a long time, half expecting its occupant to come out and greet her and half scared to death to knock on the door.

"Well, this is it!" Janet slowly climbed the stairs to the porch. The door contained a large stained glass window depicting a hummingbird sucking nectar from a flowered bush.

She lightly rapped on the stained glass window portion of the door. Her heart nearly jumped out of her chest when the door opened. Standing in front of her was a slender lady, about Janet's height, in her early fifties, Janet guessed. She wore white tennis shoes with a matched aqua-colored jogging suit accented with white racing strips down the sleeves and pants. Her hair was short and neatly combed. She was tanned and wore little makeup. At first glance, it was apparent that she took good care of herself.

The woman said nothing, but looked at Janet, waiting for her to speak. "Mrs. Miller. Lillian Agnes Miller?"

"Yes," the lady said. "What can I do for you?"

"Ah, h...hello. You don't know me, but my name is Janet. Janet Neilson." Pausing again for a moment, studying the woman's face as if looking for some recognition, she finally said, "I'm your daughter." Stunned that she had actually said the words, Janet just stood waiting for a response.

There was a short pause, then, "I beg your pardon."

"I'm your daughter," Janet repeated. "You gave birth to me February twenty-fifth, 1955, in La Grande, Oregon," she said so quickly the words almost ran into one another. "I know I should have called first or something, but...well, here I am," she said with outstretched arms, as if presenting herself.

Mrs. Miller looked at Janet for the longest time, then said, "Please come in." Her voice wasn't one of rejection, nor of acceptance, not of excitement, nor disappointment...more a tone of resignation. "I've often wondered if you would ever show up on my doorstep," she said, without much expression. "I was just making myself a cup of herbal tea. Care to join me?"

"Yes...thank you. That would be nice." Janet was taken back her casual, unemotional attitude. She had anticipated, or at least hoped, for a warmer welcome, maybe even a feeling that her mother would be happy to see her.

While she waited for the tea to arrive, she looked around. The room was generally plain, with soft yellow walls set off by a white ceiling. Several landscape paintings decorated the wall with the name "Miller" painted in small letters on the lower right hand corner. A large, handmade, woven, circular rug lay in front of an early-American couch. There was a small piano against the far wall, with a photo of a family sitting on top of a doily. The picture was of the woman and what must be her husband and three children—two girls and a boy—ages ranging, she guessed, from nineteen to twenty-five or so. She was studying the photo when her mother returned with a wooden tray filled with a ceramic teapot, two cups, spoons, and a sugar bowl.

"Your family?" Janet asked.

Smiling with obvious pride, she said, "Yes," as she set down the tray. "This is my husband, Tom. He works as a consultant for the Ford Aero-Space company. Travels a lot. This is Tim, the oldest. He's finishing his doctor's degree in clinical psychology at Stanford. He loves children. Wants to start his own clinic someday for the homeless and abused children. He has a heart of gold, that one. He'd give you the shirt off his back and then ask if you needed a pair of shoes, too. He's doing intern work at Children's Hospital in Palo Alto," she said with obvious pride.

"He looks very nice, and intelligent too. I can see you in his eyes."

"Thank you. These are the twins, Nancy and Jennie. They're roommates at the University of Santa Clara. They look a lot alike. They're not identical in appearance, as you can see, and have personalities as different as day and night. Nancy here takes after her brother. She's full of love and affection. Never an ill word passes her lips. She could find some good in Charlie Manson, if there is any to be found. Jennie, on the other hand, is smart as a whip. When she graduates from college, she wants to go into corporate business. Nothing gets by her. It's like she has a third eye that sees the unseen."

It was obvious from the tender way she looked at her family and how she spoke of them how much she loved them.

"That's quite a handful you've raised there," Janet said, studying their faces intently, looking for any resemblance to herself. Suddenly aware that her mother was looking carefully at her, Janet blushed. "I guess I owe you an apology, dropping a time bomb on you like this. I'm really sorry. I'll bet the last thing you ever expected, or wanted to see, was me," she said with a light laugh, searching her mother's eyes for some degree of acceptance, but finding none.

"How did you find me? Even though I always thought that someday you would, I'm truly amazed that you were able to find out not only who I am, but where. I know the records of your birth were sealed and put away, or so I was told," she said, twisting her hair at the side of her face.

Janet couldn't help but smile to herself. That was the same mannerism she had when she felt insecure or frightened. Not wanting to interrupt her mother with this similarity, but obviously pleased that they shared the same trait, Janet continued listening.

"Both my parents have since died, so that end of the trail was gone," she continued. "On top of that, obviously I'm married, and of course I've moved since you were born. I don't think that even I could find myself by backtracking after all these years, and I know who I am and where I've been," she said with a forced smile.

"I guess being an attorney, I have a nose for detail and research. It's a trait that helps get to the bottom of things and factoring out the truth. It's no secret that it took a certain amount of luck and other things that I won't go into at this point, and, of course, perseverance. When I put my mind to a task, nothing can deter me, come hell or high water. One way or another, I get the job done."

"Sounds familiar," she said, catching herself before she said any more.

Janet caught her meaning. She told of her life with her mother and father, explaining briefly that her had father died a number of years ago and just recently she had lost her mother to cancer, which had been very traumatic for her.

"I'm genuinely sorry to hear that you have had such a rough time of it," she said, patting Janet on the hand like a child, showing the first sign of affection since she had arrived. "Believe it or not, I've thought of you a million times if I thought of you once. I often wondered who raised you. Tell me about your adopted parents. I'm sorry I never got to meet them or even know who they were, but the rules of isolation held for me as well, you know."

"I have to admit that once my mother died—my adopted mother," she said somewhat apologetically.

"I understand."

"Well, when I lost my mother, I realized that somewhere out there, my biological mother, you, hopefully were alive and well. I loved my mom as if she were my own, but from the day I found out I was adopted, I felt like a leaf in a windstorm. There were always so many unanswered questions. I have a family tree I've never known. I vowed to find out about my past, who my parents were, why I was put up for adoption, what kind of genes I was made of, or what sort of heritage I came from. In short, there is a whole part of my life that has a ton of questions…but no answers. Do you know what I mean?" she said, looking at her mother with a tear rolling down her cheek.

"I think I understand," she said, turning her head so Janet wouldn't see the pain written on her face. "You have to understand that I, too, harbor deep feelings. Feelings that have been pushed so far into my subconscious that they've been out of reach all these years. For my own protection, my own sanity, my own piece of mind…I had to try to forget that you ever existed, because…for me…you don't. As far as I'm concerned, you're a mistake in my past that…that I've had to convince myself never really happened. As a result, I have feelings that you can't begin to understand."

"I understand that you had some sort of an intimate relationship that resulted in your getting pregnant with someone who's my father, despite of what you might think or have thought of him. I understand that you carried me in your body for nine months. Your body nurtured and cared for me. You must have cared for me, otherwise you would have had an abortion. I further understand that, when I was born…you gave me away, walked out of my life forever, leaving me to…who knows what. How could you have done that to me!"

Tears were rolling down Janet's cheeks. She was letting a lifetime of anger and frustration pour out all at once. Pausing to compose herself, she tried to look her mother in the eye to see if her words had any impact, but instead her mother turned her head, refusing to look at her.

Emotionally frustrated and physically spent, Janet sat on the couch, head down, sobbing quietly. After several minutes, she composed herself, wiped her eyes, gave a big sigh, and said, "I'm sorry. Maybe I should leave now. I've unloaded a hell of a burden on you all at once, and you probably need time to think about it, maybe even talk to your family. Why don't I leave and give you some time to yourself?" she said, looking at her mother, who still had her head turned away, wiping her eyes with a Kleenex.

Janet rose to go to the door, pausing next to her mother, whose head was now bowed and still turned away. Without saying another word, she put her hand on top of her mother's head, pausing for a moment, she bent down and gently kissed the top of her head, then walked out of the house, closing the door quietly behind her.

She left her car parked across the street from her mother's house and walked to the beach. By this time, the sun was full in the sky, wrapping its warm rays around Janet as she slowly walked down the beach toward the yacht harbor. She hadn't expected her first meeting to go like this. The surge of years of emotions trapped inside her seemed to jump out of her mouth by themselves. She wished she could rewind and retract what she had said and how she had acted, but what was done was done. The words had been unleased as if they'd had a mind of their own.

After walking on the beach for an hour or more, she found herself back at the yacht harbor. Finding an empty table facing the ocean, she ordered lunch. She ate a sandwich, oblivious to the sailboats coming and going and the people playing on the beach.

She sat for a long time after she was had finished eating, fixed in a trance-like state. It was only when the waitress, a young college gal, tapped her lightly on the shoulder with a concerned look in her eye, asking if she was all right, that she snapped out of it.

"Yes. Thank you for asking." Taking a deep breath, she walked to the outdoor telephone and dialed her mother. "Miller residence."

"Hi," she said sheepishly, "This is Janet." She paused. There was silence at the other end of the telephone. "I want to apologize for my outburst earlier today. I guess I just had so much anger and confusion built up, coupled with so many unanswered questions, my mouth took over before the brain was in gear." She chuckled nervously. "I was wondering if maybe I could come over and we could have a long talk."

"I'll tell you what," the voice said somewhat softly but, with a definite distant tone to it, "my husband will be home shortly, and he doesn't know anything about my past or about you." There was a pause. "I think maybe we should just leave it that way. It was nice meeting you. I just think it's better to leave things as they are." Janet could detect that her voice was faltering. There was a pause, then a dial tone from the other end.

Janet stood for a long time with the phone held to her ear, as if waiting for her to come back on the line again. Slowly, she hung up the receiver. Wiping a tear that had trickled down her cheek, she slowly walked back to her car.

A blue El Dorado sat in the driveway that hadn't been there before. Dejected, she slowly drove back to the hotel without being aware of anything aside from the empty feeling in the pit of her stomach.

At the motel, Janet took out a legal pad, the only paper she had, and began writing a letter to her mother. When she had finished, there were tear stains on the paper obliterating some of the words. She folded it anyway, and put it into the envelope. She mailed it at the post office, registered mail so her mother would have to sign for it. No use having the letter fall into the wrong hands, she thought.

It was going to be a long, agonizing ride home.

Chapter Twenty

"Hey, Mom, we're home!" Nancy hollered as she walked in the front door.

Mrs. Miller stuck her head around the corner from the kitchen. "Hey, glad to see you guys."

"You're stuck with us for the weekend. College is closed Monday for teacher in-service training or something, so Jennie and I decided to harass you for a few days."

"You're welcome anytime, you know that. I just made some chocolate cookies. Care for a couple with a glass of milk?"

"Boy, would I. All we get at school is our terrible cooking. Spaghetti and baked potatoes one day, soup the next and T.V. dinners or pot pies the next. The only time we get a decent meal is when we come home to mooch off you and Dad. Speaking of Dad, where is he?"

"Oh, he had new grips put on his golf clubs. The pro shop called to say they were ready, so he went down to get them before we played today."

"You guys playing golf on a Saturday? With the rest of the mob? I thought you only played on weekdays, so you don't have to fight the touristas."

"Your dad was fighting a little cold this past week, so he laid off. He was feeling better yesterday, though, so he made a tee time for us today at eleven-fifteen. You guys can fend for yourselves for a few hours, can't you?"

"I think we can manage. Maybe we'll get a small keg and have a beer party while you're gone," she said teasingly. "We could use the coins."

"You do that, and see how much tuition money you get from the old folks," she retorted. "By the way, is Tim off this weekend, too? It would be nice to have the whole family together for a Sunday dinner. I could cook a nice pot roast, mashed potatoes, gravy...."

"Aw, Mom, come on, cut it out. My stomach is already aching. Don't do that to me. Can you imagine when the last time was that we had a dinner like that? Wow."

Her mother laughed. "Oh, here's Dad now. Quick, hide behind the door and surprise him."

"Where are those rascals?" their father said as he came in the house, looking around.

"How did you know we were here?" the twins said in unison, disappointed.

"Do you think I'm blind as well as senile? Your car's parked in the driveway"! The girls ran over and gave him a big hug and a kiss. Although it had never been said aloud, their father was their favorite parent. Their mother always seemed to be a bit distant or detached, while, in many ways, their father was like a big brother. They shared a relationship with him as close as any parent could have with their offspring. It was always a mutually gratifying experience when they got together. Although their mother never said anything about the obviously close relationship, secretly, she resented her husband for that special closeness. Nonetheless, it caused no real conflict in the family.

"Hey, Dad, Mom says she's going to have roast for dinner Sunday. How about tonight you cooking some of those Norwegian meatballs you're so famous for?"

"Yeah, Dad, that would be great. Jennie is such a terrible cook, she even burns water."

"You ought to complain. How about your burning spaghetti last week?"

"Hey, I had a hot phone call. You don't think I'm going to interrupt what could be the love of my life for a bowl of spaghetti, do you?"

"See what I have to put up with, Dad?"

"I thought we would all go out for pizza tonight," he said. "Give mom a break from the kitchen. I'll cook meatballs later on in the week. All we need now is to have your brother come home and the zoo will be complete. There's never a dull moment when all you house-apes are home."

"Speak of the devil, look who just drove up in a yellow bug!"

"When do you suppose he's ever going to get rid of that beat-up old Volkswagen?" Nancy chimed in. "It's an embarrassment to the family."

"That's his status symbol," Jennie retorted. "You know all psych majors have to wear pain and poverty on their sleeves, even if they don't have any."

"Or drive around in it," Nancy laughed.

Tim walked in wearing a pair of faded blue jeans and a tweed jacket with leather patches on the elbows. He had a pipe clenched between his teeth. His wavy brown hair was combed to the side, falling in his eyes as it always seemed to do. Nancy and Jennie looked at each other at the same time and laughed.

"Hey, what's so funny?" Tim said, looking at the three of them standing there, looking at him.

"Well, Doc, I thought the jacket with patches on the sleeve and driving a broken down yellow bug was enough of a status symbol, but I see now you've taken to smoking a pipe, too." They all laughed, except Tim.

"Don't you know you can get lip cancer from those things?" Nancy asked.

"Hey, there's nothing in the bowl. See." He turned the pipe upside-down, hitting it on his hand. He chuckled out loud. "I think I look pretty sophisticated, don't you think?" he said, striking a sophisticated profile for the group.

The girls giggled.

Dad said, "Sure son, sure."

"Hey, Mom, if we're going to tee off at eleven-fifteen you better get out of here," Jennie said, pointing to her Mickey Mouse wrist watch.

She walked into the room wearing a peach-colored golf skirt with matching top and a white sweater. Tim whistled. "I don't know, Dad. I don't think I would let her walk around looking like that. She's going to get looks. There's a lot of bachelors playing golf these days, looking for a little action."

"Get out of here," his mother said with a laugh as she hugged him. "Home for the weekend, Tim?"

"Yeah, thought I would take a break and get a little home cookin' in the process. Brought my laundry, too. Hope you don't mind."

"Yeah, Mom, we brought a few things home, too," Nancy chimed in.

"Kids! Let's get out of here Tom, before they ask us for money."

"Hey, thanks for reminding us," Jennie said, joking, holding out her hand. "A few extra coins would be acceptable."

Her father gave her a "high five". "That's the only handout you're going to get."

After they left, the three of them turned on some music, sat on the couches, and exchanged stories, each telling the other what was happening in school.

"Is it my imagination, or did mom seem to look a little worn out," Jennie said.

"I notice that too," Tom agreed. "Maybe she's been playing too much golf," he said light-heartidly. "She walks the whole eighteen holes. That would certainly wear me out, dragging a bag of clubs and all. She's not a young chicken any more, you know." They dismissed it at that and talked about school.

Tom's life seemed to be filled with writing his doctoral dissertation. Apparently, he had invented a test called the O.R.T. The "Object Relation Test," he told Jennie when she asked what that was.

"Sounds interesting. Tell me about it."

"Well, I have these ten eight-and-a-half by eleven inch cards, each with a figure or figures on it in shadow form. Somewhat like the T.A.T."

"T.A.T?"

"Thematic Apperception Test. I have the patient tell a story about the various shadowy forms on the card. Then, I analyze the story and correlate that with the Rorschach, Stanford Benet, and others to help formulate the personality pattern."

"Sounds fascinating," Nancy said.

"Sounds like plagiarism to me," Jennie said. "Isn't that what the T.A.T. does?"

"The difference is, the figures in my test aren't clearly delineated like the T.A.T., allowing the patient the latitude of adapting his personality to the picture more accurately. In addition, I have three different sets of the same picture. The first set of pictures is in the dark reds, the second in deep blues and the third set is yellow. This way, I can retest the patient in subsequent sessions and see what effect color has on his responses."

"How will color help determine the patient's personality?" Nancy asked, impressed with her brother's test.

"Well, take the picture where the images are standing in sort of a circle, bending and bowing slightly. A patient seeing the images in a deep blue setting might view this as a tragedy and relate it to an important event in their life such as a funeral, someone that was sick, etc. On the other hand, looking at the same card in a yellow setting, the story might change from one of tragedy to one of a happy event, such as a birthday party or some festive family gathering."

"So what is all this proving?" Nancy asked.

"That's the whole point of the study…to see how color can alter a person's perception of something when looking at virtually the same picture. I'm getting fabulous results."

"What will you do with the study if it's successful?"

"I've already applied for a patent on the test. I think I'm onto something that will affect people's clothes, working environment, the color of houses, cars, everything! You've heard of people that keep on buying the same-colored car over and over again or won't wear a certain color because it makes them nervous. Take me for instance. I never wear green. I just don't feel good wearing it, and I don't think I look good in it. I'm more of a Autumn-colored person."

"You look white to me, "Nancy said, giving him a hug.

"Doorbell!"

"Answer the door, will you sis?" Tim asked Nancy.

"Hey, its `Marvelous Marvin', America's answer to the Mail Man. How you doing' Marv? What ya got there? Hope its a check from Ed McMahon. I keep sending those Reader's Digest forms in, just like clockwork. I figure I'm about due."

"You and half the rest of the world," Jennie quipped from behind, joining Nancy at the door.

"How you doin', Marvin?" she said.

"Well, if it isn't Santa Cruz's answer to the Marx Brothers. How you doing, girls? Your mom home? I got a registered letter here for her."

"She's golfin', Nancy said. "Here, I'll sign for it."

"Sorry, this has to be signed by her, or she'll have to pick it up at the post office downtown."

"Come on, Marv, you mean she has to come all the way down to the post office and sign her name just to pick up the letter when you're already here?"

"Yup. `Fraid so."

"Hey, I hear mom coming in the back door now," Nancy said, grabbing the letter from Marvin's hand. "Back in a flash!"

Nancy went to the dining room table and signed Lillian Miller, and dated the receipt. "Here you go, Marv. She said she looked a fright. Didn't want to embarrass you...you know how women are."

Marvin looked at Nancy with his eyebrow raised. "If I didn't know you kids, I'd kick your britches." He smiled.

"Hey, get off my porch before I sic my cat on you," Jennie said, patting Marvin on the seat of his pants. "Nice ass for a mail man."

"Keep out of trouble now, you hear?" he said, walking down the steps with a wide grin.

"Keep out of trouble? Want us to be bored with life, do you?" they said in unison.

"What was that all about?" Tim asked as they closed the door behind themselves.

"A registered letter for Mom."

"Here, let me see," said Tim.

"Gee, I wonder if it's something important. Who would send Mom something registered? The last time Dad got a registered letter someone was suing him."

"Yeah, I remember that. He hit someone with a golf ball while playing Pebble Beach. The guy probably thought Dad was loaded."

"Maybe we should open it. It could be important."

"I don't think so," said Tim. "It's not addressed to us. It's not our place to open someone else's mail. Privacy, you know."

"I don't know, either," said Nancy. "It is addressed to Mom. It might be secret or personal."

"Oh, sure!" Jennie said. "Her boyfriend is sending registered love letters through the mail. Here, let me have it. If it was sent registered, that means there's a sense of urgency about whatever is inside. Look, it was sent from right here in Santa Cruz!" Tearing off the end of the envelope, she said, "I vote we check it out. If it were any of us, and we were out playing golf for the day, and an urgent letter came for one of us, we would want to know if it was an emergency or not. Right?" She looked at her brother and sister with a question in her eyes. They looked back with a vacant look.

She began to read aloud:

Dear Mother (Mrs. Miller),

There are several things I need to say, not having had the chance to do so at our brief meeting today. I'm taking this opportunity to say them now.

I feel that I must apologize for my abrupt intrusion into what must be a very comfortable and satisfying life for you. It's important for you to realize that I meant no harm or discomfort by wanting to meet you. After all, it's not everyday that a person gets to meet her "real" mother for the first time. Additionally, I want you to know that I will try not to embarrass you in the future by bouncing into your life unannounced.

I can't promise, however, that I will never see you again. I can't just forget you never existed. You are my one and only mother.

In the event I do call or write in the future, I will do so discreetly, until such time that I have your approval to do otherwise. There is nothing worse, in my mind's eye, than wanting to be with someone, even your own family, when they don't want to be with you. I've had enough of that to last a lifetime.

I would dearly have loved to have met your family, my half sisters and half brother and your husband. I can only assume that he isn't my father. It's very hard for me to know that I have a family out there somewhere, then to find that family, only to discover you prefer I have nothing to do with you and not be a part of your life.

I don't mean to be maudlin, and I apologize if I sound like I am. I guess I'm just feeling sorry for myself.

Perhaps, in another time and another place, things would have been different.

The one thing that neither time or place can change is the fact that you are my mother and I am your daughter.

I am grateful for the opportunity to have at least seen and met you.

Always Yours,
Janet Nelson

P.S. Should you want to write to me, my Address is: Janet Neilson
212 Oakwood Circle,
Gresham, Oregon; 97030

There was a long silence. Jennie looked at the tear-stained pages for a long time, then slowly folded the letter and put it back into the envelope. They all looked at one another. "What have we done?" Nancy asked.

"We haven't done anything," Tim said. The question is, what has our mother done? Do you realize what has just happened?" he said, looking first at Jennie and then Nancy, who were looking as if they had just broken their favorite doll. "We just found out that we have a sister—half sister," he corrected himself, "that's been around our entire lifetime and before. And our dear mother has never told us about her. She's kept this a secret all these years. Why?"

"Do you think Dad knows?"

"I don't know. I just don't know. Maybe that's the key."

"I kinda don't think so," Jennie said. "The letter only referred to Mother, not Dad."

"I would surmise that our mother had this girl before she and Dad were married, probably even before they knew each other, and when she was born, mom gave her up for adoption. That's the only explanation I can think of for her to say she never knew her real mother."

"Jesus, our mother?"

"I can't believe it!"

"It's just like a storybook. Actually, it's exciting. Just think, we have a sister we've never met."

"I wonder what she looks like?"

"I feel like I've been cheated," Nancy said with a frown. "What are we going to do?" They both looked at Tim. He was the oldest and wisest and they always trusted his judgement.

After a long pause, Tim said "I think, before we say anything to upset Mom, we should talk to Dad. At least we'll have another piece of the puzzle. Maybe he's the father and doesn't know it."

"Maybe he isn't the father. Then what? Either way, Mom's in a pickle."

The three of them sat in a tight huddle, talking in hushed tones until they heard a car pull up in the driveway.

"They're here."

They quickly decided that Tim should take their father out of the house and show him the letter. That way, if he hits the roof, Tim would have some time to calm him down so he wouldn't do anything rash, like hit their mother or stalk out of the house and vow never to come back again or, even worse, throw her out of the house, not that he would do such a thing.

"How did the game go, Dad?" Tim asked as they came in.

"Fair. I shot a thirty-seven on the front nine and a thirty-nine on the back. The course was packed. I get pooped out with all that waiting. Hit the ball and wait, hit and wait. Playing on the weekend is for the birds. Remind me never to do that again."

"How did you do, Mom?" Nancy and Jennie asked in unison. There was an audible tension in their voice, but neither parent detected it.

"Like your Dad said, never again on Saturday. I'm dog-tired. I even got so tired that I hit myself on the leg with my own club," she said pointing to a dark-blue spot on her leg. "Seems like my arms had rocks tied to them. I think I'm getting too old for this game. If you guys will excuse me, I think I'll take a little nap."

"That looks like an ugly bruise, Mom, Jennie said. "Better put some ice on it."

"I'll be alright. I just need a rest." She shuffled off to her bedroom with Jennie looking concerned.

"Say, Dad, I could use a beer, Tim said. "Care to join me for a tip down at the Rusty Scupper? I'll even buy."

"Wow! Did you hear that, Mom?" he called after her. "Tim's going to buy. I can't turn this down. I thought you didn't like the stuff, Tim. You always said it was like drinking cow pee."

"Well, I think I need one now. I need to have a little…er, man to man talk. What do you say?"

"Man to man, eh? We haven't had one of those since the time I told you about the birds and the bees," he said with a deep laugh. "Even then, you didn't pay any attention. I think you knew more about that subject than I did. Well…we'll be back in a bit, Mom," he said, winking to his wife.

Tim and his father walked out the door, father's arm around his son. He could be heard joking to Tim, "You haven't gone and gotten a little gal in trouble now, have you?"

Chapter Twenty-One

Tom Miller sat in front of his untouched beer, staring at the letter. There was no visible expression on his face to indicate what he was thinking. Tim searched his father's eyes for a clue as to what must be going on in his brain. Unable to restrain himself any longer, he asked in a quiet voice, "Were you aware of this Janet Neilson person, Dad?"

His father slowly shook his head without comment.

"Would you like to be left alone for a while?" he asked in an almost inaudible voice. "I know this must be quite a shock to your system."

Without responding to the question, he asked, "What did you and your sisters think when you read the letter?"

"To be utterly frank, we were shocked at first. We even thought it might be a practical joke. May still be, for that matter, but as to your question, in general I think we felt cheated and…embarrassed. Assuming everything is as represented, we have a half-sister out there somewhere that's looking for her family. A family that, in her eyes, doesn't want anything to do with her. If, in fact, she really is our half-sister, she's our flesh and blood…a person we could have known…and enjoyed the totality of our life, and now—who knows?" he hung his head, as if in shame or disbelief.

"When you think about it, it's really sad and embarrassing. Here is a person that was born and apparently had been given up for adoption by a mother who didn't want her, for whatever the reason. Taking this all into account—and add the fact that sometime in her life she was told that she was adopted—you can imagine what must have gone through her mind. She has feelings like the rest of us, Dad. She probably felt like all adopted people when they find out they're been adopted, that she was an unwanted child. That concept in and of itself is overwhelming. Considering the laws protecting adopted children from their parents, she must have gone through hell to find her maternal mother, only to be rebuffed after all these years."

Tom was silent for a while, sipping his beer. "How old do you think she is?" He asked off-handedly.

"Well, I'm twenty-three. You knew mother a few years before you married her, so she must be at least thirty. What are you thinking?"

"Well, as you know, I've always tried to help those less fortunate than ourselves. I firmly believe that those who have should share, and those who seek, should be helped. And here, it appears, is our own flesh and blood asking for love and acceptance, and what do we do but turn her away?"

"Dad?"

"No, son, she's not mine. But, in a way, I could be the father she never had. We are the family she's searching for."

"What do you think should be done?"

"I think we should give her a chance."

"I knew I picked the right man when I picked you for a father. I'm proud of you," he said, hugging him.

"Tell you what, Tim, I need a little time alone. Do you mind having a brew by yourself while I walk around outside a bit? There's a few things I need to think through and straighten out in my own mind before going home. Do you understand what I'm saying?"

"You take all the time you want, Dad. I'll be right here, waiting for you," he said, smiling with pride.

When his father returned, his face had a look of peace and contentment. He put his arm around Tim and said, "Lets go talk to your mother." This was the first time Tim had had such a feeling of deep respect for his father. He admired him, and was indeed proud to be his son.

* * * * * *

"Well, here's father and son—or is it counselor and counselee? The question is, which is which?" Tim's mother said as they walked in the door. "Did you two solve the problems of the world?"

Nancy and Jennie looked for a clue in Tim's face, but found none. "Sit down, Mom", her husband said. "I've got something I want you to read." He handed the envelope to her with the Registered Mail tag still attached, addressed to her. Looking confused, she looked at the front of the letter. With a concerned look, she took out the handwritten contents.

All eyes were upon her as the read the letter. The blood visibly drained from her face, first registering shock, then anger. When she finished reading, she threw the letter and the envelope at Tom, who was sitting next to her, anger clearly registering on her face.

"How dare you read my mail! How dare all of you gang up on me this way! How dare you!" She stood up, burst into tears and ran from the room, slamming the bedroom door behind her. Everyone looked at each other, gesturing with their eyes or their shoulders, as if to say, "Now what?". It was clearly an embarrassing, uneasy time for the family, but the ball was in motion and the cat had been let out of the bag. There was no turning back. They were all involved, like it or not.

No one spoke for a long time, each sitting and trying to deal with their own emotions and thoughts. More than an hour passed before Mrs. Miller came out of her room. It was evident that she had been crying. She looked even more tired than she had been when she returned from golfing earlier in the day. No one rose, moved, or said a word as she came into the room. All eyes were upon her.

She sat down in the corner overstuffed chair by herself, folding her hands in her lap, looked at each person momentarily, then began. "It all happened when I was just seventeen years of age, in Springfield," she said quietly.

Everyone leaned a little closer, as her voice was barely audible. "I was going steady with this boy Paul, in high school. We had known each other since grade school, but had only been dating since summer. We were both very active in school projects; he was in sports and I was on the school paper and chaired various committees. Anyway,...the Senior Ball was coming up. In our school, the Senior Ball was the dance of the year, especially for the seniors, as it would be the last big dance that they would all be together. He had invited me, and naturally I accepted." She paused, taking a deep breath before continuing.

"Take your time, Mom," Tim said.

Ignoring him, she continued, "The night of the dance, he picked me up at my house in his new Chevy. I was excited, as most girls are going to their Senior Ball, and was determined to make it the most memorable occasion of our year. We danced a lot and, in the process, I guess drank a little too much punch. To liven up the party the boys had been pouring vodka and Southern Comfort in the punch bowl, I suppose just like all seniors have done in the past." She paused with a sigh, her eyes still looking down at her hands.

"It was near the middle of the evening when Paul and I sneaked out while his parents were chaperoning the dance. Paul drove to their house, knowing that no one would be home for hours. He knew where the key to his father's liquor cabinet had been hidden. I guess we got a little carried away. After a while, we decided to go for a dip in the pool. By that time, the fact that we didn't have bathing suits didn't seem to make any difference. One thing led to another, and...well, you can imagine the rest." Tears were streaming down her cheeks, but she was determined to continue.

"Anyway, by the time we graduated, I knew I was pregnant. I was so scared I didn't dare tell my parents, but it wasn't long before I began to get sick in the mornings. Pretty soon, I began to show." She wiped her eyes and took a deep breath.

"When my father finally found out, he was outraged. He went to Paul's father, told him the situation, and demanded that Paul "do the right thing". He was a rich and influential man in Springfield, owned the town newspaper, had lots of real estate, and that sort of stuff. Anyway, he said that his son wasn't going to marry some gold diggin' teenager and ruin his life. He offered to pay for an abortion, which just added insult to injury as far as my father was concerned. By that time, I was too far along to even consider aborting the baby anyway, even if I wanted to." She took a deep breath and paused, looking at Tom.

"Dad sent me to visit uncle Joseph in La Grande until I was due. The day the baby was born, I signed a paper, putting her up for adoption, giving up all my rights to the baby, stating that I wouldn't try to get her back. I never saw her again, until yesterday, when she knocked on my door."

"What did you tell her when she came to talk to you?" Tom asked. "From the tone of the letter, it seems that things didn't go well."

"Well, she introduced herself. I invited her in, and we had a short chat. Things kinda got out of hand after that. It soon became obvious that she harbored a lot of angry, frustrated feelings. To be perfectly frank, it scared me. It got a little tense for a few minutes, then Janet—that's her name—said she was going for a walk to cool down. After a while she called back and said she wanted to talk. I told her I didn't think it was a good idea. I guess I gave her the impression that I didn't want anything to do with her." She paused, with her eyes downcast.

"I didn't want any of you to know what happened to me when I was young. I thought, if you knew that I had a child before I had met you, Tom, you would think I was spoiled goods and wouldn't want me anymore," she said, tears welling up in her eyes. "I didn't want any of you to think I was a woman without morals. What happened to me happened a long time ago and was an unfortunate accident. I've been paying for it every day of my life since that day I gave her up. It was so long ago," she said, pleading with her hands. "You can't imagine how difficult it's been to carry that burden inside me all this time, always scared that sometime, when you least expect it, something would surface and expose me. Now, it's happened, and you all know." Wiping her eyes, she looked up. "How can you forgive me—especially you, Tom?"

Tom moved over to sit on the couch next to his wife. "If you don't know the depth of my love for you by now, woman, you never will. We've all made mistakes at one time or another in our life, some more serious than others. What happened to you happened before I came along. Even if I had known about it before I married you, I doubt it would have made any difference. I love you for what you are, not for what you think you should be."

He took her chin in the cup of his hand and, looking her in the eyes, said, "Listen, woman. I love you. Since the day I met you, I've loved you, and always will. Nothing is going to change that, especially something that happened years and years ago. Okay? If anything, this experience has made me realize how much I love you. I think you're a wonderful person, an outstanding mother, and a good friend. Above all, I'm proud to have you as a wife."

She laid her head on his shoulder. "I love you, Tom Miller. Thank you for understanding. I don't know how I could be blessed with such a man. God knows, I don't deserve you."

There was a long silence as everyone in the room wiped the tears from their eyes. It was an emotional time for the whole family. The tears helped wash away the pain they felt for their mother.

"Well, now that that's behind us, let's discuss the matter at hand," Tom said, bringing the atmosphere back to focus on the letter. "We have a golden opportunity here, all of us, to put a wrong, right. Not that anything you did was wrong, honey, but we have a rare opportunity, a second chance so to speak, to make a broken life whole again. How do you guys feel about it?" he asked, looking at the twins and Tim, who had been silent all this time.

"I think whatever makes Mom happy, makes me happy" Tim said. "We have a wonderful, happy family, and there's sure enough love to go around for one more person, especially a family member," he said, looking at his mother. "Personally, I'd welcome an older, saner female to the group," he quipped with a chuckle, trying to add a little lightness to the topic, looking at his sisters, "One... more mature, if you get my drift."

"I'm with you," Nancy said. I think it would be fun to have a grown sister to talk to. It's exciting. Just think, all these years, we've had a big sister, and didn't even know it. We don't know if she's married, has a family, or anything about her, do we, Mom?"

Mrs. Miller looked at Nancy without comment. After a short pause, she said, "You all make this sound as if we're bringing a puppy into the family or something. I don't think you understand. This is my life we're talking about here. I'm not ready to bare feelings that have been buried deep in my soul all these years just to improve your social life. Do you think I can just open my arms and welcome someone I haven't seen for nearly thirty years, someone I have dreaded walking into my life after all this time?" Her eyes were ablaze with anger. "It's my decision to decide what's to be done with this business, and my decision is I don't want her in this house or my life, now or ever. Furthermore, I don't want anyone speaking of the matter again...ever! Case closed. Understand?" She rose from the chair, faltering for a moment, then gaining her composure, grabbed her wind breaker from the hall closet and stormed out the front door, heading for the beach.

Everyone was silent for a while. Finally, Tom quietly said, with a note of disappointment, "I certainly didn't expect this sort of a reaction."

"You have to understand that she's had quite a shock to her system, Dad," Tim said. "She's repressed the guilt feelings she has about this person—her own child—all these years, and all of a sudden they're unearthed by, first, Janet showing up unannounced, then, secondly, we all of a sudden decide to bring her into the family, automatically assuming that it's okay with Mom."

"Well, to be perfectly honest, I'm a little upset at Mom for keeping this from us all this time," Jennie said. "I mean, here we are, a nice, tight-knit little family, all secure and snug in each other's living patterns, and, "bam" we get this bomb dropped on us. I really don't feel it's fair! I don't think I want to meet this Janet person, either. I don't think I want her to be a part of our family. Why doesn't she just stay where she is? We got along just fine without her so far, thank you. We were a family before she showed up, and I want to keep it that way!" She hurriedly walked out of the room with her head down, clutching a small couch pillow to her stomach.

"Apparently Jenny is also feeling threatened right now," Tim said. "She's obviously feeling a little insecure, as if her position in the family is being challenged."

"Why is that, Tim?" Nancy asked. "We all love her just the same. No one is going to come between us. Not even a brand new, older sister."

"I know, but you have to understand that, for twenty years, you and Jennie have been the only girls in the family. Now there's an older sister, older even than me. I think that both Jennie and Mom, each for different reasons, are feeling very vulnerable right about now. Perhaps they're feeling that we might take some of the affection we have for them and give it to Janet."

"That's ridiculous. You can't out portion love like a cook, mixing a batter of cookies."

"You and I know that, but they're having trouble with that concept right now. Give 'em some time. Let 'em think about it. They'll come

Lost Woman

around. The person I'm most concerned about right now is Mom. She has all those feelings, not the least of which is the guilt, repressed all those years, suddenly brought to the surface, almost by force. She's going to need our love and support," Tim said. "Especially yours, Dad," he said, as he put his arm around his father's shoulder.

"You're the psychologist in the family, Tim," his father said, "This situation is much more complex that I first thought. We're all going to have to pull together on this one."

"Count me in," Nancy said.

"Me too," chimed Tim. "If it's one thing this family has been famous for all these years, its propinquity."

Nancy and her father looked at each other. "Propinquity?" they both said in unison.

"Propinquity. Togetherness. We've always been a closely knit family. There's no reason to change now, is there?"

The rest of the weekend went by rather slowly. Each family member knew that the issue foremost on the mind of the others was Janet Neilson. She occupied the majority of the waking hours of each one of them.

Monday, Tom went off to work, kissing the girls goodbye, shaking Tom's hand, and, with a wink, patted him on the shoulder. Later that day, Tim, Jenny, and Nancy loaded their cars and were off to school again.

"The house is always so quiet and lonely when the children leave," Lillian thought. She sat in her easy chair with a cup of tea, a tearstained, yellow handwritten letter on her lap. She felt old and tired. She closed her eyes and dreamt of a small child taken from her years ago, feeling the constant yearning to have her return to her breast once more. It was a dream that frequently haunted her sleep, leaving a noticeable but unspeakable pain in her life.

- 216 -

Chapter Twenty-Two

Nancy and Jennie didn't talk a whole lot on the way back to their apartment in Santa Clara. It was obvious that Jennie was still upset, while Nancy was chomping at the bit to talk about their new sister. Each time she brought up the topic of Janet, Jennie responded with a comment, like, "She's not my sister, so stop referring to her as if she is," or, "You sound like a morning soap opera. Why don't you just knock it off?"

Nancy wasn't about to be put off, however. As soon as she had unpacked her clothes, she sat down at her desk and began composing a letter.

Dear Janet Neilson,

You don't know me, but, believe it or not, we're sisters…Well, actually, half sisters. I'm really sorry I didn't get a chance to meet you this last weekend when you were in Santa Cruz, visiting my Mom. Boy, you really caught her by surprise! She's still reeling from the shock that you found her after all these years, but hey, Dad, Tim and I are tickled pink about it.

You'll have to forgive Mom, though. You have to understand that this has been a real shock to the system, seeing you and all. She'll come around, you'll see. The rest of us will work on her.

You'll love our family. My older brother Tim is studying to be a psychologist at Stanford. He's the brains in the family. Don't get me wrong, he's not stuffy or anything like that. He's a real regular guy. Guess he would be your 'little' brother, even though he's six-foot-two inches tall.

Jennie, my twin sister, and I are roomies here at the University of Santa Clara. We'll graduate this year, then probably go to graduate school, just like Tim. She's all right, a bit of a pain sometimes—but, in general, I wouldn't trade her for anything. Well, maybe a handsome, blond, hunk, ha ha.

I know it's going to be a little while before we can work things out with the family, but, for the time being, maybe we can be pen pals or something.

I've enclosed a picture of myself and Jennie for you. I'm the one with the long blond hair. Jennie's hair is shorter and a little darker. If you have a picture of yourself, I would really like to have one. If you have a family or a boyfriend or something, I would like that, too.

Well, its getting late, and I have an early class. Write when you have time. I would love to hear from you.

Maybe we can meet sometime in the near future. I would like that.

Sincerely,
Your "new" sister,
Nancy Miller

*   *   *   *   *   *

"You're going to be late for work, Thomas Miller," Lillian told her husband. "Get a move on, or they'll fire you. Then where will I be? I'll have to put up with you roaming around the house, getting in the way all day long. Come on, be gone with thee."

"Not today, woman. I took the day off. Ever since Janet Neilson came into this house, you haven't been the same. I give you an "E" for effort, but I can see the pain you're trying to hide. You're tired from worry. I can see that in your eyes. That bruise you got golfing Saturday doesn't seem to be getting any better either," he said bending down to touch it.

"Ouch!" she said as he lightly touched it.

"Better have Doc. Trygve look at that. That's an ugly one."

"I'm okay. It's just a bruise. Now what were you saying in defense to your not going to work," she challenged with a smile.

"I was saying that I realize that after all these years the introduction of Janet in your life has been a revelation. You've obviously been doing a lot of soul searching, but, whether you know it or not, it's affecting our relationship as well as our marriage, and I simply can't allow that. I love you too much," he said, hugging her.

"So, what are you going to do about it? It's my problem. I'm the one that has to live with it, not you."

"Come on, Lil. Lighten up. This is your husband, remember. Before she came into this house, it was your problem, but only because no one else knew about it. The moment that woman walked through that door, announcing who she was, it was no longer 'your' problem. It became 'our' problem: yours, mine, and the kids!"

"So, what do you propose we do about it?"

"I propose the one thing we don't do is sweep it under the carpet, like you're trying to do. It's not going to go away. It's always going to be there, rearing its ugly head when you least expect it, until you deal with it."

"I'm listening."

"Okay. Hear me out—without interruptions. Okay?"

"You have the floor."

"I want you to call her, or write to her if that's easier for you, and invite her to spend a weekend with us."

"Now, hold on, Tex!"

"I thought you said you wouldn't interrupt me."

"Proceed."

"Let's step back from the scene for a moment and look at what we have to deal with. The brief time she was here, you had a short, pleasant conversation that eventually erupted with each of you, each in your own way, venting your feelings: Janet, giving you the business for giving her up at birth, and you, for her dropping in uninvited and unannounced. No one can blame either one of you. She certainly has the right to her feelings. Any one of us would feel the same way if our parents dumped us on some hospital's doorstep, to be picked up and raised by someone other than our parents. We would want to know who our real parents were, too, what sort of family background we came from. It's her God-given right." He paused, allowing time for her to reflect on his thoughts.

"Think, Lillian, think how Jenny, Nancy, or Tim would feel if we adopted them and then, one day, right out of the blue, told them they were adopted. Wouldn't they want to know who their real parents were? On the other hand, you're entitled to your feelings, too. You've been living with this secret all these years. You may have even have forgotten about her from time to time, then, all of a sudden, bam, there she was, on your doorstep. Sort of like an IRS audit. It catches you off balance and makes you mad at the same time."

Putting his arms around her, he continued, "You have a chance to see and get acquainted with the child you never knew. It's like a surprise package that's been waiting to be opened all these years, and now you have the chance to see what's inside."

Holding her by the shoulder, looking her in the eyes, he said, "Invite her over. Let her get acquainted with the family. Then, if either you or she wants to discontinue the relationship, at least you'll have the satisfaction of knowing you gave each other the opportunity to know one another. That's not too much to ask, is it?"

Lillian sat down, thinking about what Tom had said before answering. "You may be right, but right now, I'm not ready to face my past. I have too many other things on my mind. It's true, I have carried this iron medallion called guilt around all these years, and yes, I always did wonder what kind of a person she turned out to be, what kind of a child she was, and who raised her—if she had a happy life." Looking up at Tom, she said, "I'm sorry Tom, I'm just not ready to run headlong into a thirty-year old nightmare. Now, if you don't mind, I'm tired and want to rest."

Tom looked at his wife. She did look tired. Too tired. He was concerned about all the stress that the sudden introduction of Janet into her life that was affecting her. The last thing he wanted was for her to get sick. Nothing was worth loosing his wife…Janet or no Janet.

As she slowly walked to her back bedroom, Tom dialed Dr. Trygve's phone number.

Chapter Twenty-Three

During the long drive home from Santa Cruz, Janet's mind played and replayed the scene at her mother's house, chastising herself each time, wishing she could have the time to redo that day. Shrugging her shoulders, she said aloud, "Only a playwright has that privilege".

By the time she pulled up to her house, it was four A.M. She didn't even bother unpacking the car. After locking the car in the driveway, she went straight to her room without bothering to see the condition of the house, her mail, whether she had any phone messages, or even taking a shower. She took off her shoes, and, without bothering to undress, fell on her bed, mentally and physically exhausted.

It wasn't until ten-thirty the next morning that she awoke. It took a moment or two to realize where she was. She hadn't moved an inch from the spot where she had crashed the previous night—or morning, as the case may be. The six-and-one-half-hours sleep hadn't revived her. Still physically and mentally drained, she managed to drag herself to the shower, brush her teeth, comb her hair, and make a cup of decaf for herself. Only then did she began to feel like a person again.

She noticed that Brad had apparently been home during her absence. There were dirty dishes in the sink, a bath towel lay on the guest bed—still damp—and a pair of shorts and socks on the floor next to the bed. "The guy can't pick up anything. Leaves a trail everywhere he goes. I'll bet he was a snail in his previous life."

Without much enthusiasm, Janet decided it was time she pulled what was left of her life together and get on with it. She still hadn't sorted out what to do about her mother. She really blew that one. It would just have to evolve itself with the passage of time, she concluded. Maybe something would come of it, and maybe she was pushing a large rock uphill.

Her mind had been so preoccupied with the episode with her mother, that she hadn't taken the effort to even think about Brad. He was, after all, the only family she had at this point, and the way things were going, their future wasn't too bright. Maybe there was a way to salvage her marriage, and maybe she should just cut the cord and get on with it. She was still too exhausted to deal with it. She'd had enough disappointment this past week to last a lifetime. Time would just have to take its course.

Last, and probably least, she had given no thought whatsoever to her job. Nothing had been further from her mind, but now it was time to pay the piper and start straightening herself out. "Enough of this wallowing in self pity," she told herself. "If it's alone I stand, then so be it. It appears that life has destined me to be my own nucleus. Depend on no one and share with no one. Keep everyone at a distance, that's going to be my motto from now on. To hell with everyone. Who needs 'em, anyway?"

Even though it was Saturday, Janet needed a distraction. Checking into the office seemed to be the logical thing to do. Armed with her briefcase, she headed towards town. She had worked herself into an attitude, and it probably was a bad time to be driving, when the man in the car behind her honked his horn, reminding her that the light had turned green and she could go. With clenched teeth, she slammed the gear shift into reverse and squealed into the car's bumper. Giving him the one finger salute, she drove off, fuming.

The following Monday, Nancy's letter arrived. She read and reread its contents with great care. The letter brought more than a ray of hope, lightening Janet's burden immensely. She immediately sat down and wrote a letter back, expressing the gratitude she felt in hearing from her.

Lost Woman

She wrote that she knew her visit had been untimely and perhaps not well thought-out, but, given her emotional status at the time, if she had the chance, she would probably do it all over again. The only thing she would do differently would be to attempt to vary the results of her first meeting with their mother by being more tactful.

She wrote that she would love to meet Nancy. She would even fly down to San Jose and spend the weekend if Nancy's schedule allowed the time. She was careful to stress that she didn't want her to compromise her family status, however.

A few days later, Nancy called back, arranging a meeting between the girls the following weekend. Janet would fly Alaskan Air into San Jose, as agreed. The girls would meet her at the airport. They decided a restaurant would be an appropriate place to meet.

* * * * * *

Janet was dressed smartly in a pin-striped suit with a white blouse accented with ruffles. She looked more like a lawyer going to trial than a gal meeting her sister for the first time. She was more nervous than she had been on her first court case with Howard Chase. Nancy, on the other hand, wore blue jeans, white tennis shoes, and a white sweatshirt with "Santa Clara University" painted across the front. She looked as fresh as a peach blossom and just as calm.

They recognized each other immediately, stopping an arm's length from one another for a few moments, looking at each other as if looking for a family resemblance. They each saw characteristics of themselves in each other. Nancy spoke, stiffly at first, "Janet?"

"Nancy!"

The next several moments were memorialized in the longest hug in airport history. They finally broke, holding each other at arm's length. Janet had tears rolling down her cheeks, while Nancy had a smile so radiant it lit up her whole face. More hugs were in order. Finally, they walked out of the airport, arm in arm, like long-lost sisters.

Nancy drove Janet to the Red Lion Hotel, where they had lunch and spent the next several hours asking each other questions about their families and respective lives. Their conversations were periodically punctuated with hugs, laughter, and hand holding. Janet couldn't remember ever having such a glorious time with any other human being in her entire life.

They talked all day and far into the night. Totally exhausted, they agreed to meet for breakfast the following day and begin afresh. Before Janet retired to her hotel room and Nancy returned to her apartment, Janet had two requests: First, to bring as many pictures of the family as Nancy could find, and, secondly, if it was at all possible, to bring Jennie, even if she felt uncomfortable meeting Janet for the first time.

Nancy agreed.

The following morning, Janet was dressed in casual attire, wearing navy blue slacks with shoes to match, a blouse designed to look like a sailor's top, bib and all, accented with a red tie around her neck. She looked very smart, and much younger than she did in her, "I'm going to court and sue your ass", pin stripe suit.

Nancy, intimidated by Janet's attire the previous day, dressed in black slacks and a white sweater, which accentuated her tall, trim build. Walking next to her was Jennie, obviously nervous and uneasy. She wore a plaid skirt and white sweater. Both girl's hair was combed to perfection. It was apparent that they had been raised to take care of themselves. Janet noticed that most of the businessmen milling around the lobby stopped whatever it was they were doing at the moment, taking time to appreciate the girls as they walked though the hotel.

Nancy hugged Janet the moment they met. "This is my ugly sister, Jennie. You can tell there's no family resemblance between the two of us." She chuckled.

LOST WOMAN

Jennie held out her hand to Janet, who took it warmly in both of her hands. With a big smile, she said, "I'm so glad to meet you, Jennie. I've been waiting for this moment longer than you can imagine." They held hands for a moment, their eyes meeting, passing messages between themselves, then Janet gently pulled Jennie into her arms. They hugged each other, Janet more warmly than Jennie, but there was definitely sibling electricity passing between them. Jennie smiled at Janet for the first time, a smile that emitted a warmth that let Janet know she had made it past first base.

"I thought we'd spend the day at the park," Nancy said. I've packed some chicken, cheese, and crackers, and, of course, a bottle of California's best."

"Sounds wonderful to me," Janet said enthusiastically.

They spent the day at Alum Rock Park, walking trails that wound through the trees and hills. They sat at the edge of a stream, watching trout jump at insects for their lunch. Kids rode on their bikes and couples were walking hand in hand exploring trails.

"I want both of you to know that nothing is further from my mind than creating a problem between you or with your mother or any member of the family," Janet said when they had settled down. "I only want a chance to get to know you. I've never had a sister, let alone two sisters. Oh, I know that we're not full sisters, but…we are sisters. I had a mother and father who raised me, and, believe me, I loved them both every much, as you love your mother and father, but when I discovered they weren't my real parents, there was a void left in my life big enough to drive a Mack truck through. I don't know if you can understand that, your having parents and all."

"I have a rough idea what you went through and how you must have felt. I know, when someone lies or deceives me, how I feel about it. And that's just a little thing in comparison to the feeling you must have felt, thinking your parents were your real parents, then suddenly—wrong! Wow, that has to be heavy," Jennie said.

"After my mother died, there was a period when I felt so lost. I took some time to myself, walking the beach, just thinking about the past…my life. It was then that I decided that no matter what, I was going to find my heritage. Everyone knows their lineage, where they came from, who their ancestors were, who's in the family tree, good or bad. Me, I didn't even have leaves, let alone a tree. I was just a stump with no identification. It was a terrible feeling.

"You can't believe the hoops I went through to find your mother. I lied—actually broke the law by breaking into a security area. I even stole sealed documents to discover my true identity, and I would have even gone further than that if need be. That's how important you are to me."

Her eyes were moist. She tried to fight back the tears, but the emotion was too overwhelming. Both Nancy and Jennie, one on each side, put their arms around Janet's shoulders with their heads against hers. The three of them sat hugging one another. A permanent bond had been formed that nothing could destroy.

It was hard for the three of them to say goodbye, as Janet's plane was ready to leave. They each promised to write and call regularly. Most important, both Nancy and Jennie vowed they would have Janet invited to their house, with their mother's approval, within the next month, a time period no one expected to keep, yet all pledged to.

Janet's mind transcended the hour and forty-five minutes it took for the plane to travel from San Jose to Portland. She was conscious only of the abundance of love she had discovered these past two days. She now knew that, she would at least become a part of the family she had been searching for for so long.

Chapter Twenty-Four

As she rounded the corner on the street leading to their house, Janet saw Brad's truck in the driveway. She touched the hood as she walked by it. "Stone cold. My guess is he's been here most of the day," she mused to herself.

Brad was sitting in front of the blank television screen as she walked in. "I've got a flash for you," she said in a light, bouncy tone.

"What's that?"

"You have to turn it on to get a picture." She chuckled.

"You seem to be in a decent mood today. You get laid or something?"

"Come on, Brad. Drop the tough-guy act. I don't think either one of us is doing the other a favor by constantly cutting each other down. What you say we call a truce?"

"Okay…truce." He made a writing motion with his right index finger over the palm of his left hand. Sign here."

They had first started "signing truces" when they were in college. It had become their way of burying the hatchet without any hard feelings. No one won and, more important, no one lost.

Janet made a signing motion on his hand with the nail of her right forefinger. "There. We both signed the truce." She smiled. "Now, isn't that better?"

Brad smiled back. They stood facing each other awkwardly for a moment, as if meeting for the first time, neither knowing what to say or do. "I apologize…." Brad started out.

"I'm sorry for being such a…." Janet started to say at the same time.

They both laughed. It was the first time they had laughed for a long time. "You know, we used to do that all the time."

"What's that?" Brad asked.

"Laugh. We used to laugh all the time, remember?"

"Yeah, that was the second most likeable thing about you when we were dating."

"Second? What was the first?"

"This," he said, taking her in his arms, then kissing her lightly on the lips.

"Um, that was great. Don't stop now."

Brad kissed her again, long and hard. One kiss led to another and another, leaving only a moment to breathe between kisses.

Janet was beginning to have feelings she hadn't felt for a long, long time. She let her mind float like a bird on a breeze, soaring wherever Brad led her. The feeling was one of euphoria, like being high on a drug, yet clear-headed and eager to forge ahead.

They spent the remainder of the day and the whole of the night loving and making love, slipping into slumberland and out to ecstasy. Not since their earlier dating days had a day and night passed with such passion.

Janet woke up in Brad's arms and found him gently stroking her hair. "By the way, what did you say your name was?" she asked.

"Shh, no names. It's best you don't know. I'm working undercover for a secret country. Knowing my true identity could compromise your safety," he said with an accent. "I'd hate to have to kill you."

Reaching under the covers, she grabbed him. "I'll say you're working undercover. She tickled him, and they both laughed and wrestled. It was a morning to remember.

"You know something?" Brad said. "This is the first day of the rest of our lives. Considering the past twenty-four hours, I'd say it's a great way to start."

"I couldn't agree more." She had been enjoying her renewed, new-found love so much she almost forgot to mention her new-found family. This isn't the time to bring that up, she thought to herself. Later will be plenty of time. No sense spoiling a good thing, now that something is going right for once. She closed her eyes and fell back into slumberland.

Chapter Twenty-Five

"Dr. Trygve will see you now, Mrs. Miller. You can come, too, if you like, Mr. Miller, the nurse said with a warm smile, extending her left arm, pointing the way to the doctor's office.

Dr. Trygve had not only been the family physician for the past twenty years, he was a close family friend as well. He and his wife Agnes had played golf with the Millers every Tuesday afternoon, schedule allowing, of course, for years. After golf, they usually retired to one house or another for a barbecue, then an evening of bridge or whist.

The walls of his office had been warmly decorated with a peach-colored wall covering, accented by dark-brown venetian blinds. Autumn-toned paintings hung around the room, including one with Tom Miller's name on the lower right-hand corner. It had been given to him several years previous as a memento to their friendship. One wall, the dark walnut paneled one behind his cherry-wood desk, had been reserved for certificates and degrees that delineated his years of education, achievement, and practice. There was even a letter from President Ford among his mementos. While playing golf at Pebble Beach he had had a chest pain. Dr. Trygve, a spectator in the gallery at the time, had come forward and treated him right there on the tenth putting green. It had turned out to be just a slight case of food indigestion. Nonetheless, President Ford had been grateful.

"To what do I owe the pleasure of this visit?" Dr. Hans Trygve said, shutting his office door, extending his hand to Tom and giving Lillian a kiss on the cheek and a hug.

He was a tall man, measuring six-foot-two with gray hair receding slightly at the temples. He was slight of build, yet obviously athletic, with a quick smile and a sharp wit to match.

"Hate to bother you like this, Hans, but Lillian's been feeling awfully tired lately and…."

"Oh, posh," she interrupted. "He thinks every time I sneeze, I'm getting pneumonia," she said apologetically.

Hans looked at Tom for verification.

"She's got this ugly bruise on her leg, Hans. She hit herself playing golf last week, and it seems to be getting worse. I just thought you should have a look. She hasn't been up to par lately—no pun intended."

"Well, it never hurts to be safe. Let me see what you have there, Lil," he said, looking at her leg. How in the world did you end up hitting yourself with a club?" he inquired, rubbing the bruise with his forefinger.

"Ouch. That's tender," she said, grimacing. "I don't know, lately it seems that my arms feel like they have lead weights tied to them. I guess I swung my club and, for some unknown reason, halfway through the swing, got lazy. Instead of hitting through the ball, my arms seemed to lose power and…I hit myself." She fought back a tear.

"Tell you what, Lil, let's have you go down to the lab and let's get a blood work-up. That'll tell us what direction to go. Go down the hall to the sign sticking out that says 'lab'. Josie will take good care of you."

Mrs. Miller started down the hall. Dr. Trygve held Tom's arm, nodding his head back towards his office. Once inside, Tom couldn't but help notice the concerned look on his face. "Tell me more about Lillian, Tom. What have you noticed lately, aside from the bruise and tiredness, that is?"

"That's mostly it. Lately, she does seem to bruise easily, as you can see by the looks of her leg. When she does get a bruise, it seems to take forever to heal. I don't know, maybe it's just old age setting in, but I don't remember her being so tired. To tell you the truth, it worries me."

"You did the right thing bringing her in." He patted Tom on the shoulder. "We'll know a lot more after the blood test. In the meantime, keep her quiet. Don't let her exert herself any more than necessary. As soon as the tests are complete, I'll let you know."

After the tests, Tom brought Lillian home to rest. She slept all that day and into the next, arising only to eat a portion of the food Tom brought to her bedside and to go to the bathroom. Ten o'clock the next morning, the telephone rang.

"Tom? Hans here. We've got the results from the blood test back from the lab, but I need to run a few more tests to be conclusive. I want you to bring Lillian to the hospital as soon as possible." There was a sense of urgency to his voice.

"I'll have her there in an hour, Hans. What is it? What have you found?"

"Meet me at the admissions desk, Tom. I'll be there to make arrangements before you get there. I'll explain everything to you at that time." He hung up the phone without further comment.

It took a little longer than expected to get Lillian up and dressed. She said her body was like a bag of stones. She was groggy and lethargic, with no concept of what was happening or where she was going. Tom brought her a cup of black coffee, thinking that would give her some stimulation. The coffee plus a cold wash-rag on her face seemed to bring her around.

"Where am I?" she stammered. "What day is it?"

"You've been asleep for a day and a half, honey," Tom said softly. The results of your blood tests are in and Hans wants to meet us at the hospital to go over them with us."

"The hospital? Why the hospital?" She was becoming more alert.

"I don't know. He'll tell us when we get there. Hurry now, or we'll be late."

They drove to the hospital in silence, each with their own thoughts. As promised, Hans met them at the admissions desk. "There's a private office we can use down the hall," he said with tension showing on his face. "Step over here, and we can go through the lab tests." His attitude towards them was very official, an attitude unfamiliar to either Tom or Lillian.

Closing the door quietly, as if not wanting to disturb anyone, he motioned them to the couch. He picked an office chair for himself which he turned to face the couch.

"Your lab tests are in, Lillian," he said, his voice taking on an air of distant authority. He paused to look at his hands before continuing. When he looked up at Lillian, his eyes were moist. "The lab tests show you have leukemia." He paused again, letting the words sink in. "I'm so sorry."

"Leukemia!" She held her hand over her mouth in shock, tears immediately welling up in her eyes. "How can I have leukemia? What did I do? How did I get it?"

"We don't think you necessarily did anything. Leukemia has a tendency to just happen when you least expect it. Let's try not to worry too much until we know more about what we're dealing with."

Lillian sat with her head bowed, in a daze. Tom had his arm around her, his head next to hers. Hans was leaning forward in his chair, holding her hands. The horrible word "leukemia" had just shattered their lives.

"What's the next step?" Tom asked quietly.

"Leukemia is a cancer," Hans Said.

Lillian gasped. "Cancer. The one word I've always dreaded. Cancer." She held both hands over her mouth, choking back deep sobs that escaped through her fingers.

"We need to run further tests to determine the type of leukemia she has, then we'll begin treatment immediately. We can't begin the treatment, however, until we know precisely what we're dealing with."

"How do we find out? What tests do we have to do?" Her mind visualized people cutting her open, sticking probes into her body, extracting specimens to see what horrible disease she had.

"We'll do a bone marrow biopsy today. Once we have that, we'll know what treatment to initiate."

Lillian Miller was led to a small room with a single bed with stainless-steel metal cabinets lining the wall. A tray with surgical tools encased in clear, sterile containers sat next to the bed.

"If you don't mind, Mr. Miller," the nurse said, "you can wait across the hall. This won't take long."

Tom kissed Lillian before leaving. He could see the fear in her eyes, not wanting him to leave. He had to be strong for her, so he winked and forced a smile on his face as he departed. "Whatever it is, gal, we're going to beat it. We'll beat it together."

* * * * * *

Tom and Lillian sat in the waiting room as Hans came over to them. "Well, the good news is that we now know the type of leukemia you have. The bad news is, we've identified it as a disease called acute biphenotypic leukemia. Sometime, somewhere in the makeup of your bone marrow, your genetic makeup caused a cell to change. When that happened, the cell began to multiply and sort of went crazy, making other mutant cells. The mutant cells became leukemic, multiplied, and began to crowd out the normal cells. Once that process begins the mutant cells are very hard to kill."

"When do we start treatment?" Tom asked.

"I want to put Lillian on a chemotherapy regimen starting tomorrow morning. This disease needs to be taken very seriously. By and large, you're in good physical condition, Lillian, and that's in our favor. In all probability, we can bring this disease to full remission."

Lost Woman

The next morning, Lillian started chemotherapy. She thought that she would be given a pill or maybe even a shot. She was totally unprepared for the procedure that followed.

The first thing they did was completely numb that portion of the skin in her lower back. They then inserted a long needle into her spine. As the chemicals entered her bloodstream, she felt like throwing up. What followed was even worse, as she began to feel like the top of her head was coming off. The nurse labeled the sensation a "spinal headache", a pain that was almost unbearable for Lillian.

After the treatment, Tom was allowed to come into the room. Seeing his wife in such pain, a helpless victim of the dreaded disease, he tried in vain to hide the tears streaming down his face. "If I could take your disease and pain from you and keep it myself, I would do it in a minute," he whispered in her ear, laying his head next to hers. "Be strong, my love. I'm right here beside you."

Tom was drained when he finally arrived home. He dreaded telling Tim and the girls about their mother's condition, but knew that, even though it would be emotionally traumatic for them and would undoubtedly disturb their school schedule, they deserved to know.

Jennie, Nancy, Tim, and their father were at Lillian Miller's bedside the next morning. Cautioned by their father that she would appear tired and drained of all energy, they were to portray the picture of cheer and optimism. Her burden was heavy enough—no need to add feelings of the children's grief on top of everything.

Tim had always been the tower of strength in the family. He acted as though he had just awakened his mother from a long nap—being as cheerful and supportive.

Nancy, also strong-willed by nature, was able to maintain a strong front, even joking with her mother. "I swear, Mom, you'll do anything to get out of housework. If you think we're going to give you a few extra strokes off your golf game because of a little illness, you've got another think comin'."

Jennie, however, hung back in the pack, unable to hold back the tears that were streaming from her eyes. She had taken the news of her mother's illness harder than the rest of the family -at least she showed the emotional strain more. Her mother immediately sensed her pain and held out her arms for her. Jennie fell to the floor on her knees, hugging her mother, sobbing uncontrollably. Her mother stroked her hair, talking softly to her, giving her loving support.

The rest of the family, who had done their best to hold back their emotions, especially Tom, was now unable to stem the flow of tears that flowed down his cheeks.

After they'd visited for forty-five minutes, the nurse came in, saying that Mrs. Miller needed her rest, and that her morning chemotherapy treatment session was about to commence.

"Is she going to die, Daddy?" Jennie sobbed as they left the room.

"How long has she had this disease, Dad? How come we didn't catch it earlier? She's too old to have leukemia." Tim fired a barrage of questions at his father. There was a slight accusatory pitch to his voice, as if his father should have foreseen her condition and somehow acted to prevent the disease.

Only Nancy had no comment. She walked behind everyone else, her arms wrapped close around herself, her head bowed. There was an angry look on her face. She was beginning to feel betrayed. If her mother died, who would be there for them? This wasn't fair!

Tom felt the greatest burden of all. He felt so helpless, so inadequate. What would he do if he lost his wife? Suddenly, he realized what an important part of his life she had been. His life would be unbearable if she died. All these years, he had taken her for granted, as if she was always going to be here. He always knew that he would be the first one to go. That's just the way it is. Men go first.

His heart felt so heavy, he wanted to fall into a heap and cry, but he was a man. The father. The husband. The bread winner of the family. He had to be strong for the rest of them.

The kids stayed the week and through the following weekend. On Monday, reluctant, but knowing that they could be of no further use, they went back to school.

Weeks turned into months, and Lillian's condition continued to weaken. Each day when Tom came to visit, he would sit by his wife's side, reading to her, holding her hand, talking softly, remembering the good times they'd had and the good times they would have when she got out of the hospital. They both knew her time was limited, as she grew weaker by the day, sicker with each dreaded treatment.

She had lost half her weight. Sores formed in her mouth from the treatment. As Tom brushed her hair each day, he tried to hide the brush full of hair that gathered with each brushing. Soon it was too obvious to ignore, however. Large bald spots began to appear, obvious even to Lillian.

The girls visited their mother at the hospital at semester break. They shrunk back in fright at the sight of their emaciated mother wearing a subdued blue-colored bandanna over her bald head. She was but a mere image of her former self. her eyes sunk deeply into her skull, her face simultaneously showing pain and age.

Jennie, the ever-thoughtful one, rushed out to buy a shortie-curly wig, matching her mother's hair as closely as she could. Lillian's eyes sparkled for the first time in days when she opened the box containing the gift. "Oh, thank you, Jennie. You can't imagine how much I wanted one of these. Now I can at least seem presentable," she said with a smile. "I won't have to look like a bald gypsy with this bandanna any more."

They knew they shouldn't stay long. Not only did they not want to fatigue their mother, but the mere sight of her in this condition made their hearts ache beyond words. Once out of the room, the girls sobbed controllably, each leaning on their father's shoulder as they left the hospital. Tim walked with his arm around his father.

Chapter Twenty-Six

Janet arrived home at seven o'clock, dog-tired, as usual. Brad was making a salad as he took the hot baked potatoes out of the oven. He was just waiting for Janet to come home before putting the steaks on the barbecue. He had set the table with red, heart-shaped place mats with white polka-dots. Two oversized crystal wine glasses were placed on the table next to the ice bucket, cooling a bottle of Janet's favorite wine.

"I see you've been busy," she said, brushing his cheek with a kiss as she whisked into the kitchen. "How did your day go? Did you get that lot tied up in Lake Oswego that you want to build a shopping center on so badly?"

"As a matter of fact, I did. If you'll notice, we're celebrating tonight, steak and wine."

"All right! Have I ever told you that I love you, Brad Neilson?"

"Not lately, but you can show me after dinner."

"Ummm, we may have to put dinner off," she said, putting her arms around him, kissing him tenderly.

"Oh, I almost forgot. You got a registered letter today. Who's Nancy Miller?" he asked, picking up a pink envelope, looking at the return address.

Janet's face turned white. "A registered letter?" she said, the color draining from her face. "From Nancy Miller?"

"Yup. Arrived by special messenger after I got home. Had to sign for it," he said, holding it up to the light. "One of your clients suing you?" he said lightheartedly.

"Here, let me have it," she said, reaching for it.

"It'll cost you," he said, playfully holding it out of her reach.

"Come on, Brad. This could be serious."

He could tell by the expression on her face that it was indeed serious. Without asking any more questions, he handed the letter to her. She looked the envelope over thoroughly before slowly opening it, as if she was unsure whether it was a letter or letter-bomb.

Brad watched the expression on her face go from one of casual interest to one of a serious shock.

"What is it?" he asked cautiously. "Bad news?"

After a moment of silence, she said "It's a letter from my sister."

"I beg your pardon?" he said with raised eyebrows.

"My sister. Well, actually, my half-sister," she said quietly. Suddenly realizing that Brad didn't have a clue what she was talking about. Janet started from the beginning, when she had first decided to look for her mother after getting the idea while at the beach with Mary Lee. "My life was upside down, Brad. I went through that ugly incident in San Francisco, then my mother died. I was depressed. Then, to make matters worse, you and I split. Everything was coming apart at the seams. If we were ever to have a life together, a complete life, I knew I had to satisfy myself by trying to find myself…my real self. I needed to know who I really was—where I came from, who my real parents were. I needed to know why I was given up for adoption. Questions, questions, and more questions."

"And this Nancy Miller is your half-sister, and her mother is your biological mother?" he asked, sitting down.

"Yes! I have two sisters and even a brother," she explained with mixed emotions. She described her meeting with Nancy and subsequent meeting with Jennie and Nancy.

"And now?"

"And now…." Janet broke into tears, unable to continue. Brad held her for a few moments, letting her emotion run its course. Janet wiped her eyes and continued. "They say she's dying of leukemia, Brad." She began crying again.

"Oh, Brad. I'll never get to know her now. I was so close. If only I hadn't been so brash. If I would have only been a little more patient. I've got to go see her, Brad. I've got to see her before she's gone—to tell her how much I love her."

From what you've told me, she probably doesn't want to see you, and if she's as sick as they say she is, maybe even on her death bed—the mere sight of you could be enough to cause enough stress to—maybe even kill her. You don't want to take that chance, do you?"

With her head bowed, she shook her head, no.

She would write Nancy, asking her guidance, telling her how much she loved her mother and her half-brother and sisters. She would explain that if her mother was so ill, she would like to visit her before she passed away. She would say she was in a quandary, however, not wanting to shock her mother by her presence. She didn't know what to do. She would ask Nancy's advice.

Nancy didn't write back.

Chapter Twenty-Seven

By Christmas, the Miller family received the gift they had all been praying for. Their mother's health began to improve. The drugs had done their job. The leukemia cells began to dissipate. She was on the mend. She was going to live! The color came back to her cheeks and that twinkle they all loved came back to her eyes, along with her sense of humor.

"Let's have a party!" she said when Dr. Trygve finally told her that her leukemia was in remission.

"Don't get too jubilant," he cautioned. Just because it's in remission doesn't mean we can forget it. It's true, your white-cell count has edged toward normality, and your energy level is returning, but you still have to take care of yourself."

They thanked and hugged Dr. Trygve as Mrs. Miller checked out of the hospital. The fight back to health had been too great not to enjoy its defeat. Hans couldn't help but smile as he saw his good friend and his family pack themselves in their old Chrysler station wagon. He waved as they drove away.

Christmas had never been so joyful as it was this year. It had been a tough year and, more out of economical reasons than anything else, they had agreed to exchange names and buy a gift just for that person whose name they drew. As expected, no one obeyed the rules, and everyone bought something for everyone else.

Tim and the girls cooked a fifteen-pound turkey and made the entire meal themselves, not wanting to drain any more energy from their mother than necessary. After dinner, when the dishwasher was loaded

Lost Woman

and the kitchen cleaned up, they sat around the tree, taking turns opening their gifts. Each gift was met with ooh's and ah's.

After each gift had been opened and the paper neatly folded in one box and the ribbons tucked away in another, Tim sat down to the piano and played Christmas carols in the light of their tree. Mrs. Miller lay her head on Tom's shoulder, happy to be alive and thankful for the family God had given her.

Nancy tip-toed to the back bedroom, quietly closing the door. She picked up the telephone on her mother's dresser and, hesitating for a moment, dialed long distance.

"Hello?" the soft voice came from the other end.

"Janet?"

"Yes."

"Janet. It's me. Nancy. I'm not calling too late, am I?" She said as she checked her watch.

"No. No, not at all. To tell you the truth, Brad and I were just sitting on the floor in front of the fireplace, having a hot brandy. It's very nice to hear from you. Merry Christmas." She was afraid to ask the question that was on the tip of her tongue.

"Merry Christmas, Janet. I can only talk for a moment, but I wanted to call and tell you the good news. Mom's going to be all right. Her leukemia is in remission and she's home."

"Oh, Nancy. That's the best Christmas present anyone could have given me. That's wonderful. How's everyone else?"

"Oh, they're just fine. I'm sorry I haven't gotten back in touch with you before this, but its been so hard...you understand."

"You have nothing to apologize for, Nancy. I'm just delighted you called."

"Well, I've got to run now. Talk to you later. Merry Christmas."

"Merry Christmas, Nancy. Thanks for thinking of me."

"Love you."

"Love you, too…and everyone."

Nancy quietly replaced the receiver, wiping a tear from her eye. Returning to the rest of the family, she sat next to Tim, giving his arm a squeeze.

"Is she all right?" he asked quietly.

"Who?" Nancy asked, innocently.

"Janet."

Nancy looked up into his eyes and nodded her head with a smile, dabbing her eye with a handkerchief again.

Chapter Twenty-Eight

Winter went as California winters go—delightful—and spring was introduced by new buds forming on the trees and bushes. The young people returned to the beaches, dressed warmly, but eager to enjoy the water and the sand and feel the tranquility of the ocean as the clean salty ocean air filled their lungs.

Mrs. Miller sat on the porch swing, exhausted. "I must be getting old," she told Tom. I've just been working in the yard for a little over twenty minutes and already I'm beat. Could you be a dear and get me a glass of water and an aspirin?"

Tom willingly obliged, but did so with a concerned look on his face. Lillian hated taking medication—of any kind—even an aspirin. He knew she must not be feeling well to request medication of any kind.

The next day, he took her to Dr. Trygve for her monthly checkup that had been scheduled for her since her releasee. They were just a precaution, to keep a close watch on her health. If there was any change, Dr. Trygve wanted to catch it as soon as possible.

"If you keep taking blood from me like a vampire, I'll soon run out," she chided the nurse as she drew two vials from her arm.

During the checkup, she tried to mask her recent fatigue, but Tom wouldn't let her get away without telling Hans the truth. "We'll get a good look at your blood and see if maybe you need a vitamin B shot or something," he offered.

"Why don't you come by for dinner tonight?" Tom said. "I'll treat you to a barbecued steak."

"Hey, that sounds great. Tell you what, I'll stop by the lab and bring you the results of the test. We can kill two birds with one stone. Can't have my favorite patient worrying needlessly, now can I?"

Later that afternoon, Hans came by earlier than expected. They could tell by the concerned look on his face that there was something urgent on his mind.

"I'm afraid I've got some unpleasant news," he said, shrugging his shoulders in despair. "Your white-cell blood count has begun to dissipate again." His eyes contained all the pain that Lillian herself felt.

"What does that mean in terms of my future?" she said, fearing the worst, still hoping against hope that this was nothing serious.

Her wish was not to be granted.

"I'm afraid the chemotherapy didn't kill off all the mutant leukemic cells. What's happened is that those, for want of a better word, renegade cell's, have become immune to the chemotherapy treatments."

"Does that mean that there's nothing we can do to stop their reproduction?" she asked with a look of horror in her eyes. "Does that mean that I'm…I'm going to die?"

"I don't want to sugarcoat this for you, Lillian. That wouldn't be fair to you or your family. We have a fight on our hands. The fight of your life, but it doesn't mean that we're going to lose. What it does mean is that we have to attack this disease with every resource available to us."

"What is there besides that damn chemotherapy treatment?" she inquired. "I'll do anything, Hans. Anything, even take chemotherapy, as much as I hate it. I don't want to die. Not now. Not at this time of my life. I haven't even seen my grandchildren yet. You've got to do something, Hans. Help me." She was nearing hysteria.

Tom had to hold her tight while he looked to Hans for answers.

"It's not just what you or I can do, Lillian. Obviously, we'll do everything and use everything we have in our medical arsenal, but you have to help too, by being strong and having a positive attitude. An optimistic patient has a far greater chance of survival than one that shrugs her shoulders, buries her head in the pillow, and waits to die."

"When do we begin?"

"Tomorrow, first thing. I want you to check into the hospital tonight so we can run further tests and, God willing and the tide don't rise, first thing in the morning we go to battle again."

Tom walked Hans to his car. "I want you to be up-front with me, Hans. Tell me, what are her chances, really?"

"It doesn't look good, Tom. We may have to resort to a bone marrow transplant."

"You mean take someone else's bones and give them to Lillian?"

"No. A bone marrow transplant is taking bone marrow, which is in liquid form, from a donor, and injecting it into Lillian's body. The body thinks the new cells are her own healthy cells. They then take over reproduction of normal, healthy white blood cells, bringing the body back into balance."

"Well, hell, Hans, why didn't we do that before? I'll donate some of my marrow. What's involved? Is it painful?"

"I appreciate your enthusiasm, Tom old boy, but I'm afraid it's not all that easy. First of all, we have to find an exact genetic match for Lillian. We're talking about the odds of one person in the entire town of Santa Cruz maybe matching Lillian's cells. The most logical persons to match cells identically to hers are her immediate family—her mother and father, then brothers and sisters."

"Well, we both know that part of the equation is out. Both of her folks are dead and she has no brothers nor sisters."

"Our next option, then, is her son and daughters. You, unfortunately, don't count. If we're lucky enough to find a match, we merely take a couple cups of marrow—a fairly simple and painless procedure—and insert it into Lillian's system, then sit back and wait for nature to take its course. A small prayer never hurts, of course."

"What if there's no match in the kids?"

"Well, we cross our fingers and hit the computer banks, hoping to find a match there."

"And if we don't find one?"

"Then we have our work cut out for us, big guy. Either we find an exact match, or we go down in a blaze. Let's try to think positive, Tom. First things first. Go back in there and give Lillian all the love and support you've got. She's going to need it."

Starting chemotherapy treatments again seemed to take a deeper toll on her body than before. After each treatment, she took longer to recover. Because of her age, she was limited in the dosage her body would tolerate. Even though she knew the higher the dosage she took, the greater the chance she had of knocking leukemia in the jaw, the pain and exhaustion of the drug was just too much for her system. Each time she had a spinal injection, her head felt like an explosion had taken place within her skull. She came to dread the injections so much, each time the nurse entered her room she whimpered like a puppy about to be whipped.

The lab periodically sent the "vampire", as she came to be known, to draw blood to check to see if her white cell count had improved. Each time the answer was the same—no improvement.

Finally, six months after her admission to the hospital, Hans called Tom into his office. "The latest blood tests from Lillian are in. I have to be frank with you, Tom. There's no use continuing the chemotherapy therapy. It's not working, and we're just putting her through mental and physical hell. Considering her age and physical condition, I've ordered the treatment to stop." His voice almost broke. He had been the family physician for nearly twenty years now, and Tom and Lillian were like his brother and sister. It was hard to be objective.

"What else is there to do? I can't just sit and do nothing." Tom was frustrated and angry. He was also scared.

"I don't know, Tom. After the kid's genetic type didn't match, we've searched all the data banks looking for a match, but so far we've struck out. We've come close a time or two, but if we use someone's marrow that's close but not an exact genetic match and the body rejects it, there will be a mutant revolution within her body that will have no equal. I just can't take that chance."

Tom looked as if he was about to lose his best friend—and he was. Time was running out. "I'm going to call Tim and the girls. Maybe with their connections they can get some sort of help from the student body at college or something."

"Anything is better than what we're doing now. It just takes a few moments to get the two tablespoons of blood from a potential donor we need to analyze—less time than it takes to thumb through a magazine."

The next day Tom had the kids home to implement a plan to test as many people as possible, in hopes of finding someone with a perfect match. The plan was for the kids to go to the school's medical facility and try to talk them into starting a school bone marrow match program. If successful, it would be the first of its kind instituted on campus.

Once the concept was presented, the thought of getting students involved excited both the campus student body president—who Nancy had dated several times—as well as the medical staff. The drive could not only help save Lillian Miller's life, but add data to the National Marrow Donor Program, doubling as a lesson in civic duty for the students of the college.

College kids, in general, are great sources of energy for new ideas, especially if they feel their participation can make a marked difference in humanity. In this case, it could mean saving a life. Not just Lillian Miller's life, but perhaps some child who needed to have a bone marrow transplant to save their life. The thought of any one of them making that difference excited them. Their enthusiasm spread through the campus like wildfire.

Dormitories contested against each other for the highest amount of donors. Fraternities pitted themselves against fraternities, sororities against sororities, to see who could be the first to find a match, any match.

The enthusiasm of the students caught the attention of the local newspaper, and soon members of the community were lining up to give samples of blood to save another human being.

Blood samples poured in by the hundreds, more than the local medical team could handle. A member of the National Marrow Donor Program was sent in from Stanford Hospital to lend his assistance.

In the meantime, Lillian contracted pneumonia. "We've got to get her on antibiotics immediately," Dr. Trygve said. "This isn't life threatening, but we can't take any chances. Her resistance is at an all-time low. Frankly, I'm worried."

Three weeks after the marrow donor program was instituted, they still hadn't found a perfect match. Dr. Trygve called a family conference. "We now have several samples where the potential donor's antigens and sub-antigens match Lillian's, but they're not exact."

"I don't understand how some antigens or sub-antigens can match but the other's don't," Jennie complained. "How will they be able to tell which one matches Mom's?"

"The blood sample is fed into the computer and analyzed, filling in two areas of a graph," Dr. Trygve explained. "The computer printout tells us of the 'AB' matches, codes for the first set of antigens that must be checked before any others can be checked for compatibility with your mother. The second stage of testing is called 'DR' antigens. If there is a perfect match, we have a winner. If there is anything less than a perfect match, we would be taking a chance that the body won't accept the bone marrow and...well, you know the rest of the story."

"So what are you suggesting?" Tom asked soberly.

"I don't think we can wait any longer. Lillian's body is showing signs that her line of resistance is low. She has pneumonia, the sores in her

Lost Woman

mouth are healing slowly now that I've taken her off chemotherapy...I just don't see another alternative."

"Who makes the final decision?" Tim asked.

"I think that Lillian should have the final word. It's her body, her life. She's rational enough to decide her own fate. She and you—the family—need to talk about it." Dr. Trygve looked at the four grim faces, none of which wanted to face the task ahead.

"I checked in on her just before you arrived. She's awake. I think you should discuss it with her now."

"Now? Can't we think about it first?" Nancy asked, a tear rolling down her cheek.

"There's no use putting off the inevitable," Tom said stoically. "We've tried every angle, bought as much time as we could, and failed. It's time we take a chance if we're going to beat the demon." He looked at Hans, who affirmed his agreement with a nod.

Lillian was sitting up, facing the window, when they came in. As was their usual practice, they tried to be upbeat and jubilant in greeting her. There was a calm look on her face, one they hadn't seen before, as if she knew her time was near. They all sensed it.

"Lil," Tom started, "we've been talking to Hans, and he thinks that, because we haven't been able to find a perfect match, we should try using a donor who's most compatible to your blood, even though it's not an exact match. We've tried everything we can to find an exact match, but so far we've failed. Hans thinks it's a decision that you should make, but we feel that we should make it as a family. What do you think?"

"I agree." She was silent for a moment, looking at each face, studying it before moving on to the next, ending with Tom, which is where she began. "I want you to promise me something, Tom."

"Yes?"

"If the transplant fails and…I don't want to be hooked up to a life-support system just to be kept alive. I want you to promise me that you won't allow that."

Tom lowered his head. The words were labored. "I promise."

"And, Nancy?"

"Yes, Mom?" she asked, tears flowing.

Wiping her face, her mother said, "I want you to get in touch with Janet. I want to make my peace with her before I go. Could you arrange that?"

"Janet? Yes, of course, Mom. I'll get in touch with her right away and…Janet!" She said aloud with such a burst of energy, it startled everyone. "Janet! We haven't tested Janet, your first born."

"How could we have been so stupid?" Tom said, hitting himself on his forehead with the palm of his hand. "I don't think we should get too optimistic here, but it's more than a fifty-fifty chance."

The girls ran out of the room, leaving Tim and Tom by her side. Smiling, knowingly, Tim left his father and mother alone, closing the door quietly behind himself.

Chapter Twenty-Nine

Janet listened intently, her mind focused on every word her sister has saying. When Nancy had finished her story, leading up to this morning's revelation, Janet said, "I'll be on the first plane to Monterey. I'll call you as soon as I know when the first flight arrives. Thanks for calling, Nancy. I hope and pray that I'm the chosen one."

She immediately called Brad at the Lake Oswego shopping center construction site, explaining the situation. "I have to leave right away, Brad. Come with me. Oh, come with me and meet my family. I'm so proud of them, and I'm proud of you. Please say you'll come."

"Honey, wild horses couldn't keep me away."

Brad knew that time was of the essence, so he hired a private jet to fly them to Monterey.

* * * * * *

Tom Miller met them at the airport, along with Nancy. Although Janet had never met him, she recognized him immediately from the picture her mother had showed her. His eyes were sad and tired from the stress he had undergone since his wife's illness, but despite that, he looked even kinder and more handsome in person.

Nancy ran to hug Janet as soon as they had cleared the deplaning area. Tom followed close behind. "I've never met you before, but it seems, from what the women have been telling me, you're a remarkable gal," he said. "I'm sorry to meet you under such stressful conditions. It's still a real pleasure meeting you. You too, Brad," he said, shaking his hand while patting him on the shoulder with the other hand.

"The rest of the kids thought they would wait for you at the hospital, seeing how this old car will only hold four at a time without feeling like you're in a sardine can," Tom said.

Brad walked on one side of Janet and Tom on the other, each with their arm around hers. Tom gave her shoulder a squeeze and kissed her on the forehead. "I'm glad you could come, Janet. I'm sure it will mean a great deal to Mom."

Before going to the lab, Janet was led to her mother's room, where she lay with her bed tilted up. Her eyes were closed as they entered the room.

"Mom," Tom said, softly. "We've brought a guest."

Lillian slowly opened her eyes, letting them focus on the group, then on Janet. A warm smile formed on her lips as she held out her arms to Janet.

Janet went to her bed, falling into her mother's arms for the first time. Both women wept. Tom motioned to the others with his head to leave. They closed the door behind them. "Let's let them have some time to themselves."

Janet emerged a short time later, wiping her eyes with the back of her hand, apologizing for herself. "No apology is necessary," Tom said. I'd be worried if you were any different."

"You should have stayed, Brad, so I could introduce you," she said, hugging his arm.

"There will be plenty time for that later. This was your time. I didn't want anything to diminish that special moment."

"Thanks for being so understanding. I appreciate that."

"Well, we should get to the task at hand," Tom said, pointing the way to Janet, down the hall to the lab.

"Janet, I want you to meet the best darn doctor-friend a man could ask for. This is Doctor Hans Trygve. Hans, meet Lillian's first daughter."

"It's a real pleasure. I'm going to have to have a talk with that mother of yours, for hiding you from us all these years," he said with a smile. "Let's get business out of the way first, however."

The process of taking the necessary blood sample took only a few minutes. Hans personally took the specimen to the computer room on the second floor of the hospital and waited for the results.

* * * * * *

He entered Lillian's room, where they were all awaiting. The look on Hans's face was stoic, showing no emotion. The girls looked at each other, horror registering in their eyes.

"The results are in," he began, "and all eight of Janet's antigens and all of the sub-antigens match Lillian's to a T," he said with a huge smile.

"Hurrah!" they shouted. Everyone hugged Janet, patting her on the back.

Janet looked down at her mother. "You gave me my life, now it's time I returned the favor." They all hugged for a long time.

"I'm a little tired now," Lillian said. "If you don't mind, maybe I should get some rest. My body has a big fight on its hands and I want to be up for it."

One by one, everyone hugged and kissed her, including Brad, who had been introduced while Janet was giving the lab her blood sample. Lillian closed her eyes. She fell asleep with a smile on her face. Her mind drifted back to a small child, long ago and far away, once lost, but now found.

Chapter Thirty

The dinning room table was decorated with colorful napkins and full of homemade cookies, date bread, brownies, cake, and pies. Twisted red, white, and blue crepe paper hung from the archway and over the dining table. Colored helium-filled balloons floating around the entrance, the dinning room, and hallway saying, "I Love You," "Welcome Home," and "You're The Best."

Tom brought Lillian back to the house she had left so many months previous. She went entered the hospital, fearing she would never return again.

Waiting to greet her first was Jennie, Nancy, and Tim, all with grateful smiles. Their mother had her arms outstretched in a welcomed greeting, hugging each one for a long time.

When her eyes saw Janet, she ran to her, tears streaming down her face, laying her head on her shoulder, hugging her. "Can you ever forgive me?" she whispered softly.

"There's nothing to forgive," Janet said. "You're my mother and I'm your daughter. I love you."

"And I love you."

Soon, everyone was hugging everyone else. Then they all stood in one big circle, hugging each other, their heads touching one another. There wasn't a dry eye in the house.

When Janet had finally composed herself, she stood with her arms around both her mother and Brad. "I've been looking forward to this

Lost Woman

day all my life. Thank you both. Thanks to everyone," she said, raising her arms to all.

Later that day, after everyone had had a chance to talk themselves out, Lillian came over to Janet, putting an arm around her arm, saying, "Why don't you and I go for a little walk on the beach?"

Once outside, they strode arm in arm in silence for a while, until Lillian said, "You know, Janet, when you left last time, I thought my heart was going to break in two. On the one hand, I was so ashamed of myself for what I said, how I acted. On the other hand, I was scared stiff that my family would think I was a tramp for what I did as a child if they found out."

She stopped to face her daughter. "I do hope you can find it in your heart to forgive me. I never want to be apart from you again. Without you all these years, I've felt like a lost soul. You can't imagine how much I hurt inside—the pain I carried all those years. Now, I feel like I'm whole again."

"Mom, you'll have to beat me with a mallet to get rid of me again. Now that I've found you, I'll never let you go. You, too, were the missing link in my life. I thank God I've found you. And, look, two sisters and a brother and father to boot. I'm lonesome already." She laughed. "What do you say we get back to the party?"